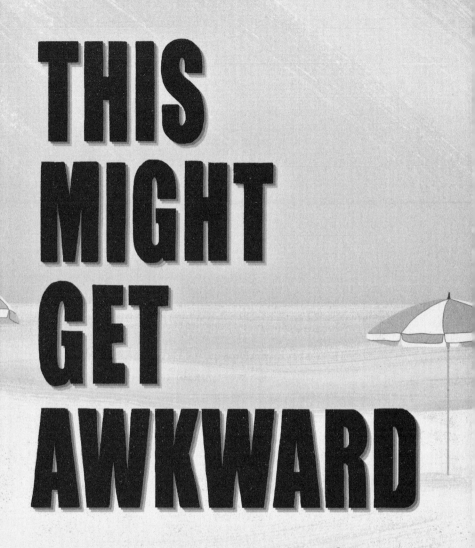

THIS MIGHT GET AWKWARD

Kara McDowell

SCHOLASTIC PRESS
NEW YORK

Library of Congress Cataloging-in-Publication Data available

ISBN: 978-1-338-74623-5

1 2021

Printed in the U.S.A. 23

First edition, March 2022

Book design by Yaffa Jaskoll

To my dad—
thanks for the blueberry muffins

Chapter 1

My favorite kind of beach is an empty one.

Luckily, empty beaches are easy enough to find around here, especially in the off-season. This stretch of pale, powdery sand will be crowded with campers and bonfires by next weekend, but today, it's just mine.

I slip off my flip-flops and sit, digging my toes into the warm sand and leaning back on my palms. The water is glassy down here on the south end of the lake, perfectly reflecting the large sandstone formations across the water. I put my earbuds in, turn the music up loud, and close my eyes. I relax into myself, my muscles loosening for the first time in months. I've been in a state of tightly wound anxiety since school started last August, but now that finals are over, I can breathe a sigh of relief.

The worst thing about school is all the people: the eyes on me during a class presentation, the pressure of not knowing where to sit during lunch, the endless opportunities for me to say or do something embarrassing. Social situations have always been awful, and I'm relieved to have a break from them.

My wiggling toes unearth an unbroken quagga mussel shell, and I pocket it to save for Nina before remembering that she's gone for the summer. My good mood plummets. I've got an endless string of beach days and boat days and anything-I-want days in my future, and I should feel happier. But I can't. Not when I'm here alone and Nina is in the Valley, playing camp counselor to hundreds of mini geniuses at a STEM camp for girls. As my one and only friend, Nina is the exception to my "empty beach" rule, and I kind of wish she were here right now.

I love an empty beach, but I don't want an empty *life*.

"Heads up!" A muffled voice cuts through my music.

I pull my right earphone out and whip my head around to see Ian Radnor leaning out the driver's window of a massive pickup truck. There's a boat trailer attached to the back, and from the look of things, he's attempting to back up right over me and into the lake. I glance around helplessly, wondering why he needs this stretch of sand, and am horrified by the caravan of vehicles descending on all sides. I've heard whispers of beach parties happening here, but I've never had the misfortune of attending one.

I gather my flip-flops and dash out of the way, standing stock-still as a flurry of activity materializes around me. Loud country rap blares from an unseen speaker. A group of jocks from school unload a keg from the back of a shiny SUV. More cars pull up and my classmates spill out of them, laying towels on the sand, unfolding beach chairs, and nestling coolers under open tailgates. Each addition kicks my heart rate up another notch, like my body is preparing for battle. Music? *Threat.* Fun? *Double threat.* People? *Triple threat.* I can't dance, I don't know how to have fun, and I'm mostly incapable of being around people. In a matter of minutes, Lone Rock Beach has transformed into my literal worst nightmare. I feel like I've stepped into a *Riverdale* set piece, only no one gave me my lines.

Or my costume. I'm wearing a baggy T-shirt with a smiling fish on the front. It used to be Dad's and it hangs well past the ends of my cutoff jean shorts. *Cool.* This is perfect. This is exactly how I wanted to be seen by my classmates.

If school hallways are bad, this is much, *much* worse. At school, my body knows what to do. I have years and years of training to fall back on. Keep my head down, do as I'm told, and don't attract attention to myself. But this is a party—something I haven't experienced since my classmates decided bounce houses aren't cool.

My shoulders inch upward as the muscles tighten on instinct. My heart beats double time. *I've got to get out of here.* I'm turning to leave when a voice stops me.

"Is this a good place to build a fire?" volleyball player Marissa Shock asks, her high ponytail swinging from side to side. She drops an armful of firewood at her feet. "I don't know where to start."

I wince. So much for escaping unnoticed. I take a breath, encouraged by the fact that I *do* know how to build a bonfire. If I can prove that I'm useful, maybe it'll distract from the weirdness of showing up to a party uninvited, even if it was an accident. I'll help with the fire, and then I'll escape. "Did you bring a shovel? We should start by digging a circle a couple of feet deep. Then we—"

"I know what I'm doing," Jazmine Clark says. That's when I notice Marissa's teammate standing by her side, a shovel in her right hand. They're wearing matching expressions of confusion and pity, and I realize Marissa was never talking to me at all.

Acid floods my stomach. "Right. Yeah. Sorry." I scramble out of the way and up the beach, weaving around cars, looking for my dad's red pickup truck, Sunday. I find her blocked in on all sides, the worst offender being a giant white Suburban. *Fabulous.* There's no exit, not without hunting down the driver and begging them to move. Talk about awkward.

It's official. I, Gemma Wells, am stuck at a high school party.

I slump against Sunday's warm metal door, stress and anxiety building in my chest. How will I survive hours of this panicky, suffocating feeling? I'm a complete mess in social situations. If there were a prize for most socially awkward human, I'd win. Hands down, every time. Mail my prize to the oldest houseboat in the marina, please; I won't be attending the award ceremony.

My eye catches on the bumper sticker on the back of the white Chevy Suburban next to me. BUY BOOKER BROTHERS' PIZZA. WE KNEAD YOUR DOUGH.

Every sense in my body goes on high alert as I push myself into a standing position. *Beau is here.* Beau Booker, heir to the Booker Brothers' Pizza dynasty, is here at this party. I shouldn't be surprised by this, considering that Beau Booker is the most popular person at Page High. He's also the captain of the swim team and the hottest person I've seen in real life, it's worth mentioning. *Of course* he'd be at the end-of-the-year party.

I scan the beach, searching for his chestnut curls. I quickly find him standing at the edge of the water, his back to me. He's shirtless, wearing the teal swim shorts with the ripped back pocket and the frayed hems that he must have inherited after his older brother left town last summer. (There's a picture on Beau's Instagram of the two of them on the beach, Griff in those same teal shorts, Beau in red ones, and I'm a creep who's looked at it a hundred times. Just like I'm the creep staring at him now.) My stomach swoops low and twisty, the way it always does when I see him, and *just like that*, I want to stay.

SOS, I text Nina. **I came to the beach to be alone, but a party LITERALLY formed around me. Sunday is now blocked in by none other than the Booker Suburban.**

OMG. It's fate! This is your chance to finally talk to him.

I've talked to him! I respond. And I *have*. Freshman year I sat behind Beau in Señorita Bustamante's Spanish class. Once he spent the whole class period doodling song lyrics on his shoes while *I* spent the whole class period watching the way his curls brushed against the collar of his T-shirt, imagining what it would be like to be his girlfriend.

I'm aware it'll never happen. I'm awkward, not delusional. But I can't help but be taken by the fact that Beau is everything I'm not: confident and popular and *shiny*, always the brightest light in the room. So when he ran out of drawing space on those shoes and he asked if he could do mine, the force of his laser-bright attention landing on me for the first time, I nodded yes.

"What's your favorite band?" he asked. My mind blanked so thoroughly that I stared at him slack-jawed until he turned back around. That night, I woke up in a cold sweat, the perfect response on my tongue. *Twenty One Pilots*. An answer that would (hopefully) make me seem cool, but not like I was trying too hard. I planned to tell him the next day, but he never turned around again.

Now, Beau collapses into a beach chair, stretching his long legs out in the sand. He says something I can't hear, and Sofía Lopez rocks with laughter as she smacks his arm. Sofía is Latina; she's short and curvy and gorgeous, with brown skin, nail polish that's never chipped, and perfect eyebrows. I didn't know perfect eyebrows were a thing until I saw hers. Once we sat next to each other at an assembly and she told me about the math test she'd just bombed, and all I could think about was how much I hated my eyebrows. It kept me from adding anything to the one-sided conversation.

A small group forms, magnets pulled in not only by Beau's energy but by Sofía's too. Helpless against the tug, even *I* take a few steps forward. I'd give anything to be sitting around that campfire, to be laughing or flirting or drinking or whatever it is the normal kids do. Instead, I'm stuck here in the sand, a stretch of endless lonely days unfurling in front of me. The weight of it is too much. I swallow the lump in my throat as I watch.

Theoretically, I could walk down the beach right now, barge into their circle, and ask Beau to move his car so I can leave. He'd say yes, and I'd be free. Or maybe the impossible would happen, and he'd convince me to stay. Either option is better than standing here alone, but I can't make my feet move, can't make my mouth form the words.

If I'm a little bit in love with him, why can't I talk to him?

Better yet, why can't I talk to anyone? Why does standing on this crowded beach make my pulse race, triggering a flight-or-fight-or-freeze instinct that I can't seem to shake?

Beau's face falls as he looks at his phone. He glances up and down the beach, and for a beat, we make eye contact. I'm caught. All alone and gawking like a creeper. My skin burns hot and I turn and yank open Sunday's door. Safe inside the cab, I pick up my phone to text Nina, but hers arrives first. **Heading to orientation. Talk later!**

I want to believe that we'll talk later, but I'm worried that her busy schedule will make that impossible. I'm even more worried about what happens if she realizes she doesn't miss me. I'd love to have faith that these next few months won't be the loneliest of my whole life, but I've never been that good at lying to myself.

A knock on the window startles me. I look up, shocked to see Beau standing on the other side. Heart in my throat, I crank the window down (Sunday is ancient), feeling ridiculous.

"Am I blocking you in?" he asks, pointing to his family's Suburban.

"Kinda," I say.

"Are you leaving already? The party just started!" He smiles, his white teeth bracketed by two dimples that are so deep they probably collect water when it rains.

I shrug, sinking deeper into my seat as my cheeks heat.

"You've got somewhere more exciting to be?" He cocks an eyebrow.

I snort-laugh. Mortified, my hands fly to my mouth. That one sound alone will keep me awake for the next three nights.

"I take that as a no?"

"Yeah, no. Nowhere else to be. Not today, and not this whole summer." *Why did I say that?*

Beau runs a hand through his curls as he considers my pathetic admission. He leans a forearm against the open window and tilts his head toward me. "Jenna, right?" he asks, and I want to die. I want to drive straight into the water and never come back up.

"Um, it's Gemma, actually."

"Gemma! Right, I knew that," he says. I doubt he did, though. People don't remember me. Silence stretches between us. Panicked by the lack of words coming out of my mouth, I smile. *Yikes.* That feels too big. I rein it in.

"Gemma's a cool name," he tries again.

If I were a different sort of person, I'd tell him that my mom gave birth to me on a houseboat on the lake between mile markers nineteen and twenty, under a clear sun that showered the surface of the water with sparkling gemstones. It's why she named me Gemma. Something from that time must have seeped into my blood, because I can't remember a day of my life that I've felt as comfortable on land as I do out here, wedged between layers of rock formed more than three hundred million years ago. My soul is filled with ancient sandstone walls and winding canyon paths. My heart belongs to the water.

But I'm not different. I'm the same or worse than I was a year ago when I googled *why can't I talk to people?*, read dozens of articles and forum posts on social anxiety disorder, deleted the history from my phone, and never spoke of it to anyone.

Beau watches me now and my mind goes a particular shade of blank. The kind where I have everything in the world to say, but I can't remember any of it. I turn my attention to my phone, frantic for him to leave, desperate for him to stay.

"I heard you live on a boat," he finally says.

I force myself to make eye contact, but it feels too strange, like he'll know what I'm thinking. I tear my gaze away. "Sometimes." I take off my faded ball cap, the one I stole from my dad, and twist it between my fingers.

"Sounds fun," Beau says.

"It is." I cringe internally, wishing I'd said something better, cooler, funnier. I'm the conversational equivalent of a sea cucumber.

"Booker!" Ian Radnor calls from above an open cooler, a giant energy drink in his hand. His shaggy white-blond hair hangs in his eyes. "We're gonna go tubing. Are you coming, or are you waiting for someone else?" His eyebrows bounce up and down, full of incomprehensible meaning.

Beau rubs his hands over his face, exhaling slowly. But when he drops them, his signature game-for-anything smile is firmly in place. "I'm in. Prepare for a smackdown," he calls over his shoulder.

"We've got room for one more," Ian says, scanning the beach. I can't tell if he's looking for someone specific, or just someone who wants to go. For one wild second I consider volunteering myself. I look away, worried that someone will see, that someone will laugh for thinking I could be one of them.

"No, we don't." Beau reaches through the open window, unlocks the truck, then swings the door open. "Gemma's coming with us."

"Who?" Ian asks as all the muscles in my body tense.

Beau looks down at me, his eyes serious. "Do me a favor?"

Behind him, Ian shrugs and ambles out to the boat, which is currently anchored near the shore.

"What?" I ask Beau.

"Pretend that we're close. That you like me."

"I—" I hesitate, the words at the tip of my tongue. *I do like you.* Instead, I try another version of the truth. "I won't be good at that."

"It's easier than you'd think," he says. "Wanna see?"

I shrug, more confused by this social interaction than any other in my life. Beau motions for me to get out of the driver's seat, and I do. Then he pivots so he's standing next to me. I tense, anticipating contact that doesn't come. He turns his camera to selfie mode and leans in close as he snaps a picture. He tilts the screen so I can see the result; his easy grin and sparkling eyes light up the screen, making me look stiff and frozen by comparison. My eyes don't sparkle. Nope, they're turned up to him in wide disbelief. But even still, it's not the worst picture I've ever taken. If I were mindlessly scrolling, I'd think we look . . . friendly. Almost like *friends*.

"Pretending is easy," he explains as he taps away on his phone. "People will believe anything if you show them the receipts."

"I don't get it. Believe what?" My insides writhe in embarrassment. This is my first real conversation with Beau Booker, and I've never been so lost.

"You two coming or not?" Ian yells as the propeller kicks to life.

"Let's go," Beau urges. "It'll be fun, and we can talk later."

I clench my hat between my fingers as I glance over his

shoulder, unable to hold eye contact. The bow of the boat is sitting too low in the water, something that happens when the engine cap is left open and the engine compartment starts taking on water. It turns out Ian Radnor doesn't know a thing about operating his daddy's boat; it's a few minutes away from sinking.

"I, um . . ." I falter as Beau takes the hat out of my hands and places it on my head. His fingers brush a strand of hair out of my eyes, and I'm frozen.

What in the ever-loving daydream did I just stumble into?

"There's not going to be a boat to ride on if you don't tell Ian to close the drain plug," I finally manage. "He's flooding the engine compartment."

Beau spins, sees how low the boat is sitting, and laughs loudly. "Hey, moron! Check the drain plug!" Beau calls as he jogs toward the boat. Ian kills the engine and scrambles to figure out what he did wrong.

Forgotten, I sag against the truck. My muscles go slack as my self-loathing skyrockets. Gemma Wells: good at boats; bad at conversation, having fun, being normal, flirting with boys, et al. Put it on my tombstone, please. I at least deserve credit for the boat thing.

After Beau leaves, I watch. I watch as Ian lets out a long string of expletives, and I watch while he backs his pickup truck with the attached boat trailer down the beach. His mistake won't do long-term damage, but he'll have to let the engine dry out. I watch as the trailer is backed into the water and Beau pushes the boat securely up onto it. I watch as Beau climbs inside the boat and stands on the back deck, chest and arms sparkling wet in the glowing sunset.

I watch a Frisbee land in front of the truck. Ian hits the brake, and Beau wobbles. *Be careful.* I think it, but I don't say it. I watch and I watch and I watch, until Ian steps on the gas and Beau startles, slipping in the puddle at his feet. Finally, I watch as he stumbles backward, his head connecting with the propeller with a sickening thud as he falls into the water.

Chapter 2

I've spent my whole life watching.

Watching other girls pass notes in school, wondering what it would take to get a paper triangle sent my way. Seeing pictures and videos posted online as my classmates have fun without me. The fact is, I'm good at watching, at staying on the periphery. It's the only place I feel comfortable. So when Beau Booker falls into the water, I gasp. My hands fly to my mouth as I swallow a scream. And then I watch and wait for someone to save him.

Except no one does.

Because no one saw.

"Help!" I choke out the word without moving my eyes from the spot where Beau fell. He hasn't surfaced yet.

How long has it been? He's drowning.

That realization kicks my body into gear. You don't grow up on a lake without knowing how fast a person can drown. Forty seconds for adults. Twenty for kids. My feet move even as my brain struggles to keep up and I fall, my hands and knees sinking into soft sand. "Help!" I scream, pointing a trembling finger to the water. A flash of skin appears beneath a small wave, but no one seems to notice it. They're all staring at me: the uninvited freak ruining the party.

"What is she doing?" a voice asks as I push up onto my feet. I sprint through groups of people, pushing my way to the water's edge. The attention makes my skin crawl, but this time, my fight instinct is winning. Another few seconds and Beau could be gone.

Who am I kidding? He could already be gone.

I splash into the cold water, searching for a glimpse of teal or tan or chestnut. Nothing. My lungs squeeze tight in my chest. *Nothing.*

I dive under and open my eyes. It's useless. Too many people have been out here, kicking up sand and muddying the water. Swirly brown clouds keep me from seeing my own hands. I push off my toes and break the surface, gasping. It's so cold my lungs feel frozen in my chest. Breathing *hurts*. Every inch of my body shakes.

But then I see him. His body is floating ten feet from mine, his head facing downward, under the surface. I swim to him and grab his torso as my feet search for purchase on the ground. But we're too far out, and I can no longer touch the sandy bottom. I stick my nose up to the sky and struggle to flip his body as I kick us both toward the shore.

"Listen up, Beau Booker. You do not get to die before you have the chance to fall in love with me," I mutter before water closes over my mouth and nose. I pull us up again, but he's heavier than I expected. I'm about to panic when my toes scrape against scratchy underwater bushes. A few more feet, and they touch ground.

Ian meets me near the shore and helps me drag Beau's body out of the water and onto the wet sand. People swarm us, the shouting and crying rising to a suffocating pitch.

"His head is bleeding," Sofía says to the 9-1-1 operator. Beau has a gash above his ear. A red trail of blood trickles down his neck, pooling in the hollow spot near his clavicle. My heart stops.

"He's alive," Ian says, fingers on Beau's neck to feel his pulse. "Do you know CPR?"

I drop to my knees next to Beau and start chest compressions, praying he opens his eyes before I have to attempt rescue breathing. I only partially remember what I was taught in freshman Safety Ed, an odd mixture of driving classes and CPR, with a side of STD pictures to scare us away from ever having sex. A snapshot of syphilitic genitals flashes in my mind, and oh my gosh, this is *not* the time. On the plus side, the disturbing mental image keeps me from dwelling on the fact that Beau might be . . . He spasms, vomiting up a bunch of lake water all over me. My muscles go rubbery with relief.

Beau's eyes flutter open. I stare at him through a haze of tears, desperately wanting to say something. The right thing.

You're alive.

You scared me.

I love you.

What I actually say is "You puked on me."

His eyes flutter closed again, and he's gone.

Dad's truck is still blocked in, so when Ian offers me a ride to the hospital, I take it. My legs bounce the whole way, my hands fidgeting nonstop. After the fourth time I've readjusted the AC vent, I sit on them, just to make myself stop.

Ian parks in silence and we burst through the ER doors and run up to the desk. "We're looking for Beau Booker. He was brought here by helicopter," Ian says.

Images of Beau being taken away by medevac come rushing back, bringing a fresh wave of nausea to my stomach. I don't try to block them out; seeing Beau's body limp and helpless was one of the scariest moments of my life, and I already know those memories will haunt me long after my footprints have washed away from the scene.

A short white woman with a severe ponytail points to a corner of the waiting room where a crowd of kids from the beach have already assembled. "Wait over there with everyone else."

"I have to see him," I blurt. Despite pulling him from the water and administering CPR, I still don't know if I did enough to save him. I want to know if he's okay.

"Family only," she says.

"She saved his life!" Ian protests, and the crowd gathering behind us agrees.

Through the glass doors to our right, a stretcher surrounded by doctors is wheeled in. I catch a glimpse of Beau's teal shorts and run. I can't help myself. His eyes are closed. He's wearing an oxygen mask, and there are tubes and wires everywhere. By the time I reach the doors, though, he's gone again: rushed down the hall and away from me.

"You can't go through there," a voice behind me calls.

I lean my head against the door, tears sliding down my cheeks. Except for the few seconds Beau opened his eyes on the beach, he hasn't been conscious since I pulled him out of the water. I'm terrified he's got some horrible brain injury, either from the fall or from almost drowning, and won't ever wake up again.

The fantasy of Beau and me has been keeping me company for too many years to count. When I'm lonely at school or feel like crying myself to sleep at night, I weave elaborate daydreams about what will happen when he finally notices me: how he'll ask me to be his prom date and make me pizza at his family's restaurant and take me to see fireworks on the Fourth of July. Without those dreams, without *him* . . . my throat constricts painfully and my hand presses against the door, pushing it slightly ajar.

"Miss, you can't go back there." A nurse appears at my elbow, her expression sympathetic.

I turn away, embarrassed by my tears. "But I love him," I whisper to myself. "He was going to take me to see fireworks. We would be the perfect couple."

A hand lands on my shoulder. I turn, surprised to see Sofía's long braided hair. She nods back to the waiting room, leading the way.

The wait is excruciating, and it's made better and worse by the fact that Beau's usual crew has stuck by my side all night. To say I'm grateful and anxious would be a gross understatement. I'm scared to be with people, but I hate to be alone. It takes all my focus to keep myself in check: *Don't cry too much, don't say anything strange, don't make them regret sitting by you.* It requires enough of my concentration that I don't have time to obsessively worry about all the *other* people in the waiting room, the ones who were on the beach tonight and are fascinated by the drama of the situation.

Their eyes dart away from me every time I glance their way.

Good. Eye contact just the way I like it: nonexistent.

The hours tick by. Eventually, Nina calls. "What happened?" she whispers. She's not allowed to be making phone calls this late, but social media blew up with posts for Beau and she couldn't wait. I fill her in on the story, starting with Beau and me by the truck, ending with CPR and an air ambulance. "I can't believe you saved his life," she says, her voice full of awe.

I pause, attempting to let that sink in.

Nope, still feels fake.

"I told him he puked on me." It's the one thing about the evening that feels remotely real. Like this whole night has been an elaborate game of two truths and a lie, and my awkward comment was the obvious truth.

"When?" Nina asks.

"On the beach. He spit up a bunch of water and briefly woke up, so naturally I looked deep into his dark brown eyes and said, 'You puked on me.'" I groan and put my hands over my face, mortified by the sheer memory. "Those are probably the last words he heard."

"Weird flex, but okay," Nina jokes. When I don't laugh, she sighs. "This is gonna become a *thing*, isn't it? Like the Spanish class story?"

Oh, it's definitely a thing. A thing I'll obsess over for the rest of human history.

We hang up, and I rejoin Ian and Sofía, although I sit with an empty chair between us in case they've changed their minds or remembered that I'm not one of them. But when the nurse from earlier stops in front of the group and points to me, every back straightens. "Follow me," she says. She has brown skin, dark curly hair pulled up in a bun, and a name badge that says ANDI hanging from a lanyard around her neck. I stand on numb legs and tingling feet. All my extremities have fallen asleep. I follow the nurse through the forbidden doors and down a dimly lit corridor. "His family wants to see you," she says, opening a door to a room and motioning for me to go through.

Terrified and stupidly hopeful, I stumble over the threshold. Five pairs of eyes rise to meet mine: Mr. and Mrs. Booker, both of whom I recognize from the small restaurant they own in town, and Beau's three younger siblings, who are huddled in the corner of the room with swollen eyes, snotty noses, and tearstained cheeks. The only person not openly staring at me is Beau, and that's because his eyes are closed. I step toward his bed, my eyes swarming with tears at the sight of the breathing tube stuck down his throat. He's connected to dozens of wires and monitors. Numbers flash on the screen next to his bed, all of them incomprehensible except for his heart rate and his blood pressure. And even then, I don't know what stats are normal. But the heart rate monitor has a steady beat and—intubation aside—Beau still looks like himself. He's still stomach-churningly beautiful, with a perfect chestnut curl fallen across his pale forehead. My hand physically burns with the need to brush it out of his eyes. I shake out my fingers, swallow the lump in my throat, and furiously blink away the oncoming tears. I *really* don't want to cry in front of his family.

"Who're you?" asks the older boy, whose face I recognize from too many years spent stalking Beau on social media. I'd guess he's seven, maybe eight. His older sister puts an arm around his shoulders and brings him protectively to her side.

"I . . . um . . ." I clear my throat. "I'm—"

Mrs. Booker throws her arms around me and squeezes through big shuddering breaths. I stiffen, unable to remember the last time I was hugged.

"You saved his life," she says, and it sounds like she's crying now. "I'll never be able to thank you. You saved him."

"He's okay?" I ask, glancing again at Beau. There's a worrying-looking bundle of tubes next to his head.

She hugs tighter. "Because of you." Seconds pass. I'm not sure what to do with my hands. The hug doesn't feel wrong, exactly, but it's not a gesture I'm used to. Nina's not a hugger, not like those girls at school who cling together between classes. She snidely refers to them as octopus girls. And my dad and I have said "hello" and "goodbye" and "I love you" with a fist bump since I was twelve years old.

"You're strangling the poor girl," Mr. Booker says quietly. He touches his wife on the shoulder. She releases me but keeps her hands on my arms.

"Yeah, Mom. Don't strangle her! Then we'll have to get another room for her too," the older boy says practically. In any other circumstance, I'd probably laugh.

"What happened to him?" I ask.

"The doctors performed a procedure to relieve the pressure on his brain and control the swelling. Now he's sedated and they're monitoring him with that machine." She points to a screen near his head. "What did they call it? ICP?" She looks to her husband, who nods.

"Intracranial pressure monitoring," he says stiffly.

"What does that mean?" I ask. My vision swims. *I should have been faster, gotten to him sooner.*

"Beau's sedated. He's in a medically induced coma to protect his brain until the swelling goes down."

"For how long?" My tears finally spill over. I feel like I'm going to puke.

"Honey, no. Don't cry. He's stable now. You *saved* him. They don't know how long it'll take, but they're optimistic about his recovery." She smiles encouragingly and gives me another squeeze. I'm so relieved my bones almost give out. Beau's mom is still propping me up, though, keeping me from turning into an invertebrate on the hospital floor.

"What is your name, dear?" she asks, smoothing a wild chunk of hair out of my eyes.

"Gemma."

"And your last name? Does your family live in town?"

"Wells. My dad fixes boats at the marina repair shop and runs boat tours during the summer."

The door opens and the same nurse bustles in, stopping to squirt hand sanitizer into her palms from a dispenser on the wall.

Mrs. Booker turns back to her husband. "Do you know Mr. Wells?"

"I don't think so," he says.

"I'm surprised y'all haven't met yet," Nurse Andi says brightly. "Gemma is Beau's girlfriend!"

Chapter 3

Nurse Andi claps her hands together, a wistful smile on her face. "Saved by his girlfriend. It's so romantic."

Huh.

I open my mouth, but nothing comes out.

Well.

Mrs. Booker hugs me again, the tears running freely down her cheeks. Someone should get this woman a drink of water before she dehydrates.

"Since when does Beau have a new girlfriend?" Beau's little sister appraises me with narrowed eyes.

I'm saved from having to answer by Beau's mom. "I knew he was seeing someone! I was worried it was—well, that's not important. He's seemed a bit off lately—" She must see the alarm on my face, but she mistakes it as a reaction to her words. "Oh, no, not in a bad way. I can just tell he's distracted. But now that I know about you, it makes sense. All those late nights and Saturday afternoons out he's been with you! Isn't that a relief, Justin? Especially now that—again, it's not important." She shakes her head and hugs me again. "We're not exactly sure what Beau's recovery will look like, and I'm so happy you'll be there to keep his spirits up."

"Um. I, um . . ." I awkwardly shrug out of Mrs. Booker's

embrace. Nurse Andi slides behind me and slips out the door. "I'm so sorry about Beau. Excuse me," I say to his family as I turn to leave.

"Wait!" Mrs. Booker grabs her purse off the couch and rummages inside. She withdraws a business card for the restaurant. "Please come see us, anytime. The meal is on us. I'd love to sit and get to know you, or at least feed you some garlic knots." She presses the card into my hand.

In the hall, I flag down Andi, who is sitting behind a desk at the nurse's station. "Why did you tell them I'm Beau's girlfriend?" I whisper, a hint of panic in my voice.

She frowns. "Aren't you?"

"No!"

"In the waiting room you said that he was taking you to the Fourth of July party. You said the two of you were a couple."

"No!" I shoot back, my pulse racing. A man at the next desk turns our way. I lower my voice, desperate to avoid attention, but my cheeks are hot and I'm dizzy on my feet. "I said we *would* be the perfect couple." *In some imaginary, parallel universe where he knows that my name isn't Jenna.* Heat rises in my cheeks and my heart is pounding in my ears. This is a nightmare. As if everyone staring at me and talking about me wasn't bad enough, now they're all going to think I lied about being his girlfriend.

"Oh," she says. And then, "Ohhhhh," as understanding finally dawns on her. I hover in front of her, wringing my hands as I shift my weight from foot to foot. "But I heard the whispers in the waiting room. It's everywhere: the story of how Beau's girlfriend saved his life."

"It's not like that—" I shake my head.

It's so hot in here, and the lights are too bright. And the people. Fewer people would be good.

"Are you okay?" Andi stands, walking around the desk to get a better look at me. "Do you need to sit down?"

"No." I step away from her, mortified. Heat claws up my chest and neck, setting my cheeks on fire. "No, I'm fine. Sorry to bother you."

"Do you want me to get Mrs. Booker?"

"No!" My voice is all shouty. "I mean, no. Thank you, but no." I turn and flee down the hall and burst into the waiting room. Ian and Sofía stand, eager for information. They look at me like I'm one of them, and for the first time all night, I understand why.

I wake up disoriented. Late-afternoon sunlight slants through my window, heating my bedsheets. I kick them off, sweaty and sticky all over, glancing at the clock.

Four thirty p.m. The day after Beau's accident.

I bolt upright and sit in silence for several breaths as the memories come flooding back, each one more horrible than the last.

"You puked on me."

"He's in a coma."

"Gemma is Beau's girlfriend."

My hands fly to my mouth as I realize the horrifying truth. *I'm Lizzie Spalding.*

The relevant facts about Lizzie Spalding are that she spent her whole senior year bragging about the modeling contract waiting for her in New York and the British boyfriend who'd fly in to take her to prom. None of it was true, but that didn't stop her from creating fake social media profiles for him and sending herself flowers on Valentine's Day. When prom rolled around, she tried to claim he'd been "unavoidably detained" in London, but by that time a PowerPoint presentation called "Lizzie Spalding Is Full of Shit" had spread like wildfire. The masterpost contained every shred of evidence that Lizzie had lied about New York *and* the boy. Naturally, she was canceled: lunch table privileges revoked, party invites rescinded, dignity in shreds. And now, three years later, she's never once been to New York and she spends her days turning hot dogs at the Maverik gas station.

I send Nina a panicked text. No response. *Ugh.* I drag myself out of bed and head to the kitchen. The house is quiet and empty, and I find a sticky note on the microwave with a blocky hand-written message from Dad.

TOWN HERO, SAVER OF BOYS,
LATE NIGHT. DON'T WAIT UP.

I smile; it's a typical Dad note. He's the silent type. Never uses two words when none will do. The kind of guy who can sit on a boat and fish in silence for hours. I'm talking literal silence, literal hours. As someone who also hates small talk, I am both impressed and relieved.

Lonely too, I suppose. Now that I think about it.

I realize with a twinge of sadness that Dad will probably sleep on the boat tonight. He does that a lot during the summer, when his schedule is packed with boat tours and jobs at the marina. I could bike to the marina to meet him, but the thought makes me exhausted, like my legs are filled with lead.

I text Nina again. Still no reply. Embarrassment creeps in. I wish Nina and I had the sort of ride-or-die friendship that I never question. As it is, she has another group of friends, people she hangs out with from student council. I used to wonder if she ever brought my name up, casually asking them, "Should we have invited Gemma?" on their way to grab slushes at the Sonic after school. And then I imagine every single hypothetical time they said no, and I want to light myself on fire. Or worse, what if they offered to invite me for Nina's sake, and *she* was the one to say no? I get a shaky stomach just thinking about it, but I can't bring myself to stop. Some days, it's practically all I think about.

I grab an armful of cereals (something chocolaty, something frosted, and something with marshmallows) and eat them dry while watching Netflix and scrolling through Instagram. Most of the kids at the party last night posted throwback pictures with Beau along with "thoughts and prayers"–type captions, which makes me wonder if I should post something.

I keep scrolling, nearly choking on Chocolate Marshmallow Mateys when I see Beau's feed. He posted the picture of the two of us on the beach, minutes before his accident. The caption reads *Starting the summer off right!* My wide, disbelieving gaze looks like one of total adoration. I'm the heart-eyed emoji personified. No wonder people in the ER were whispering about us, although it's strange that one Instagram picture was powerful enough to erase years of seeing me walk down the halls alone. One lie— *misunderstanding*, if I'm being technical—was enough to earn me a seat next to Sofía Lopez in the hospital waiting room. (It's not exactly an invite into her girl squad, but it's not nothing.) Imagine what would happen if I never told her the truth!

No! I mentally reprimand myself. I can't let this situation continue. It's unethical, unbelievable, and unsustainable.

Then again . . . it's not like I'm hurting anyone. If I squint and view the situation from a different angle, it's almost like I'm *helping* Beau's mom by giving her some peace of mind. So maybe it wouldn't be the worst thing in the world to allow this misunderstanding to continue, just until Beau wakes up.

I'm about to send Nina an SOS text when I realize she's likely busy with orientation and the new campers, and I feel a bit better about the fact that I haven't heard from her. Except now I have no idea what to do to kill time. I wander around the house for a while, feeling restless and claustrophobic. I need to get out of the house, out of town, off the land. I need to be on the lake. Instead, I keep the TV on, *The Island* reruns cutting through the silence. I fall asleep that way, the sound turned all the way up, and try not to think about the long summer ahead.

My phone beeps early the next morning, and I assume that Nina finally got back to me. Instead, I have a text from an unknown number.

We're visiting Beau. You should come!

I take a deep breath and consider a response. I want to sound breezy and easy and *normal*. I type and delete a response at least half a dozen times; the longer I take, the more awkward I feel about how long it's taken. Those three floating dots have been suspended in cyberspace for an agonizing length of time.

Okeydokey!!

I hit send, and as I stare at that mind-blowingly stupid word with not one but two (!!) exclamation points, I realize I may have overthought this.

Sorry, that was super weird! Don't know why I wrote okeydokey! And I just did it again! Haha. Who are you?

Hmmm. I might have overcorrected.

It's Sofía. Beau would want you there. I'll pick you up. Where do you live?

My stomach twists. I doubt Beau would want me there; he thought my name was Jenna.

But he did take that picture, and I *do* want to visit him. There's no harm in that. I want to see his face, to make sure he's okay. And that's fine, that's normal! This has nothing to do with the fact that I'm finally being included by a group I've envied for years. *Nothing!*

I text Sofía my address, then text Dad the plan. He replies with a GIF of Keanu Reeves giving a thumbs-up. Dad is a total meme guy. Anything that requires fewer words from him is solid in his book.

Sofía replies: **See you soon!**

One exclamation point. *I knew two was weird.*

I wait on my front porch, anxious and nervous and nauseous. All Sofía has to do is ask me one fact about Beau's life and she'll realize I don't know him at all. If I'm caught, it's going to be mortifying. Worse than a hundred karaoke parties in which I'm the only entertainment. I'll be doomed to a Lizzie Spalding life—no friends, no boyfriend, and grease stains on all my clothes. I shudder at the thought.

Right now, no one thinks about me as much as I think about them. There's still the possibility—however minor—that my fortunes could change. That this summer and this school year might be different from all those before it. But if they find out I lied about dating Beau, I'll become a cautionary tale, Gemma Wells synonymous with: liar, freak, desperate.

And yet—I can't bring myself to cancel, or go back inside, or even think of a plan to clear up the misunderstanding. In literally any other circumstance, the risk wouldn't be worth it. But if nothing goes wrong, I could potentially end up with friends. (Okay, so maybe that's a *small* part of the reason I'm doing this. Tiny. Minuscule.)

A car pulls up to the curb, the door opens, and I realize my mistake. It's full of balloons and flowers, and I'm empty-handed: the worst, most unthoughtful girlfriend in the history of Page High. I'm not really a girlfriend and I'm already failing at it. I reach into my messenger bag and scrounge around, pulling out a half-empty tin of mints. I hold it up and shake it for absolutely no reason that I or anyone else in the car can fathom.

"For Beau," I say. "They're his favorite." I'm met with blank stares from Sofía, Shandiin, and Kodi, all girls I know *of* from school, none that I've ever hung out with. They're all on the swim team together, and so is Beau.

Shandiin is in the passenger seat. She's from the Navajo Nation, and today she's wearing pigtail braids, bright pink lipstick, and a turquoise necklace. I look down at my cutoffs and tee, feeling underdressed.

Kodi leans forward to look at me from the back seat. "So, are you and Beau, like, dating?" She's hunched over, her white six-foot frame barely fitting into the back of Sofía's car. Her rainbow-dyed pixie cut is a mess, and she's wearing plaid pajama shorts and a white tank top. Looking at her makes me feel *overdressed*. (The irony is not lost on me. There's no boundary my insecurity won't cross.)

I shrug, thinking of the picture Beau posted. *Pretend that we're close. That you like me.* I don't understand why he said what he did or posted that picture, but it seems clear that he wanted people to believe something was going on between us. (Clear-ish, anyway.) When he said *people will believe anything*, it's because that's what he wanted them to believe. Right?

"We've never really labeled it," I say.

"I've never seen you two together," Shandiin says.

"We don't hang out at school."

"Leave her alone," Sofía says, smiling at me in the rearview. "She's shy."

I cringe internally. *Shy* is the main characteristic people ascribe to me. *Jenna Wells? Oh yeah, she's shy.* The word feels like a pair of jeans that have just been run through the dryer. A little too tight, a lot uncomfortable. *Shy* isn't the wrong word, necessarily, but it's inadequate. I've been labeled shy my entire life, and for a long time, I assumed that was the beginning and end of my story. And then I became friends with Nina, who *is* shy, and I couldn't help but wonder if I'm something else. Something *worse*.

"No flowers or balloons in the ICU," Nurse Andi says as we round the corner to Beau's room.

"Are we allowed to see him?" I ask.

"Leave the gifts outside the double doors and you can have five minutes," she says, smiling warmly. "His family would want you to see him."

I wonder vaguely if the only reason I was invited was to get "the girls" in. For the first time in the history of my life, I'm the cool friend who knows the bouncer at the club, the girl who can get you into the party. Except the club is the intensive care unit in the hospital, the bouncer is a nurse I accidentally lied to, and the party is a depressing hospital room where the boy I love is in a coma.

Wow, my brain is a fun place to be. No wonder I don't get invited to actual parties.

We ditch the gifts and enter the quiet room.

"I wish we could leave something to prove that he wasn't alone," Sofía whispers. For one agonizing second Kodi looks pointedly at my bag and I think she's going to ask about the mints, but she doesn't. *Halle-freaking-lujah.* I would have evaporated straight through the floor. They each take a minute to stand by Beau's bed and gaze quietly at him. Sofía pushes his hair off his forehead, squeezes his hand once, and ushers the others out of the room to give me "a few minutes alone with him."

"What do they think I'm gonna do, make out with you?" The only reply is the steady beeping and whirring of all the machines hooked up to Beau. Hospital rooms: the perfect place for inappropriate jokes.

With the room empty, I have no choice but to really look at him. Seeing the breathing tube stuck down his throat and the wires attached to his skull isn't any easier this time around, and my heart breaks all over again.

"Hi, Beau," I say, perching on the chair next to him. No response. Strangely, this makes me brave enough to continue. "It's Gemma Rae Wells. That's Gemma with a *G*, not Jenna with a *J*." I'm on high alert for any sort of movement or recognition. But his eyes stay closed, his deep breaths coming in and out. I relax into the chair and keep talking. "You don't know me that well, but everyone thinks we're dating. I honestly don't know how it happened. I think part of it was because people saw that picture you posted—not that I'm blaming you! I'm confused, I guess, about why you were talking to me when we've never been friends."

I pause, waiting for the familiar wave of self-consciousness to wash over me. It doesn't come. I'm in the presence of Beau Booker, and I don't have to worry about getting the words wrong, or embarrassing myself, or what he'll think of me when I'm done. I can just talk.

"Speaking of friends, I don't have many. Just Nina, really. Not that I should be complaining to you, considering you have bigger problems than I do. I just wish you were here so I could ask why you wanted me to pretend I like you."

I'm rambling now, but it's never been easier to talk to him. It's never been easier to talk to anyone. I take a deep breath and continue. "I've had a massive crush on you for years. And I hope that when you wake up, you can forgive me for getting you caught up in this mess—"

The door opens and I jump, startled by the sound. I turn, expecting to see Sofía or one of "the girls," and am shocked by the face of someone I haven't seen in more than a year.

It's Beau's older brother, Griff Booker.

Chapter 4

Griff crosses his legs at the ankle and leans against the door frame. "You're the girlfriend?" Beyond the barest note of surprise, his tone is impossible to decipher. His eyes cut into me, and something about the straightforward question causes sweat to pool in the center of my palms.

I'm a terrible liar. Genetics was unkind to me when it came to the blushing gene. I've never told a lie that wasn't evident all over my cherry-red cheeks.

I swallow the painful and panicked lump in my throat. "News travels fast."

"Apparently not." His shoulder is glued to the door frame. His eyes flash with emotion, but he glances at the floor and then back at me, and all I see in his expression is bone-deep exhaustion. Purple shadows and days-old stubble. The last I heard of Griff Booker, he abruptly left town last summer, just days before his senior year was supposed to begin.

"I'm Gemma." Silence. Uncomfortable under his scrutiny, I shift and clear my throat, hoping he'll say something. But he seems unwilling to put me out of my misery. "You're Griffin, right?"

"Griff," he says. I knew that, of course I knew that, everyone knows that. But I didn't want to seem strange for remembering. His gaze flicks over to Beau before he turns back to me with a grimace. "I guess Beau's told you all kinds of crap about me." His eyebrows are drawn, his face tense and sad.

"Nope." It seems like the correct answer until another flash of pain flickers in his eyes. Again, it's gone in an instant.

Griff shrugs. "He hasn't told me anything about you either." The words sound like a challenge.

My spine straightens as my insides wilt, and I'm hit with the paranoid suspicion that he somehow knows Beau and I aren't really a couple. It makes sense; the brothers are close in age, only a year apart in school. Griff could live on the other side of the world and still know the details of Beau's life. "I'll leave you alone with him." I duck around him to get out of the room, shutting the door quietly behind me.

The girls are waiting outside the door, their eyes wide.

"What did he say?"

"What was he *like*?"

"I can't believe he came back."

Sofía and her friends form a wall in front of me. It's officially my least favorite kind of wall. *What other kinds of walls are there?* Crap, why does my brain always do weird stuff when I'm supposed to be having a conversation? My cheeks flush, my heart hammers loud and fast, and my sweaty palms keep on sweating. The Gemma Wells trifecta. I swallow. "He didn't say much."

"But you heard why he left town, right?" Kodi asks.

"Everyone heard," Shandiin says. "And anyway, Beau would have told her."

"We di-didn't talk about it much," I stammer.

"I wouldn't want to talk about it if I were him either, considering." Sofía looks at me knowingly.

I have no idea what she's talking about. I'm struggling to figure out how to ask about it without seeming out of the loop as I follow them down the hall, our hands loaded with the ungifted gifts.

"I heard he was selling drugs in the school parking lot."

"Well, I heard he slept with Ms. Rose."

"She's, like, *thirty*."

"That's what I heard."

"That's not true," Kodi chimes in. "I heard—"

The elevator dings and the doors slide open. I turn just in time to see Griff duck out of Beau's room, his head down and his hands stuffed in his pockets. Not a long reunion for the brothers, then. Coupled with the rumors flying between Sofía's friends, I can't help but wonder about Griff's relationship with his brother.

I'm quiet as the girls laugh and chat on our way out of the hospital and back to Sofía's car. A few times I think of something to add to the conversation, a joke I could make or a way to relate, but I hesitate a moment too long and they're on to the next thing, leaving me scrambling up a sand mountain, the bottom continuously sliding out from under my feet.

Sofía pulls the car to a stop in front of a house and Kodi hops out. "See you tomorrow?" she asks, ducking her head back inside.

"After work," Sofía confirms. "I've got a new routine I want to try."

Kodi groans good-naturedly. "Again?"

"We're going to go viral by the end of summer," Sofía says.

Shandiin's dropped off next. They confirm plans to hang out tomorrow to film something for TikTok after Sofía finishes work, and it's silly, maybe, to feel left out when I'm not remotely part of their group. They've never invited me before. Why would they start now? Rationally, I know that. I'm not numb to the heartache, though, and I'm not sure I ever will be. All too often life feels like I'm wandering alone in the desert, tapping on windows, hoping for an invitation inside. I sink low in the back seat, feeling sad and small and impossibly lonely, flashing back to every weekend night sitting alone in my bedroom, watching real-time pictures and videos of everyone hanging out without me. It doesn't matter that I've never been friends with any of those kids, that I've never *expected* an invite. It all just hurts so much, every single time.

"Come up here!" Sofía says when it's just us left in the car. I crawl over the center console and into the passenger seat.

"I thought you'd use the door, but that works too."

I slide down, embarrassed. *Well done, Gemma. Perfectly normal.*

I fidget and bounce as she drives, nervous about how to act, miserable about acting nervous. I focus on the coconut air freshener hanging from the rearview mirror so I don't have to look at her. Sofía puts the car into park in front of my house. "Who's that?" she asks, nodding to the person standing on my front porch. She's tall, with dark skin, shiny black hair, and a stiff navy dress.

"I don't know."

Sofía rolls down the window and leans over me to call out to the stranger. "Can we help you?"

The woman smiles brightly as she approaches us. "Hello! I'm looking for Gemma Wells."

"Who are you?"

"I'm a reporter hoping to talk to Gemma—"

I roll the window up. "Why is a reporter at my house?"

"Teenage girl saves drowning boyfriend! It's a decent story in a sleepy tourist town."

"Oh." My mind scrambles over the last forty-eight hours, trying to remember who I lied to, who believes what, what I'm going to have to answer for.

"Do you want to talk to her?"

I shake my head, sick at the thought of giving an interview about my fake boyfriend. Not even Lizzie Spalding stooped that low. The reporter knocks on the window.

Sofía punches the gas pedal and we peel away from the curb. "Where do you want me to take you?"

I bite my lip, wishing Nina were still here. Wishing my dad weren't working all day. Wishing I had someone else, anyone else to turn to. Sofía looks at me, waiting. "I'd invite you to my house, but I'm on my way to work after this."

"Right. Yeah. Of course," I say quickly. I wish *I* had a job I could go to. Somewhere I could disappear for a few hours and not think about this mess. "Where do you work?"

"Gift shop at Wahweap. The one next to boat rentals."

Lake Powell has several marinas. Wahweap is at the south end of the lake, closest to Page. "My dad's working down there today," I tell her. "We can head that way."

"I heard Beau and Ian talking about you," Sofía says as we turn off my street and onto the main boulevard in town.

"When?"

"Before the accident."

My stomach clenches. "What were they saying?"

"You know, guy stuff," she says. My eyes widen in horror. "No 'locker room' crap. Ian was asking questions about you and Beau was smirking and silent, confirming without confirming. We all know he's had a secret for months."

Intrigued, I lean forward. I want to know more, but I can't pry too much without giving myself away. "Oh yeah?"

"His nose was constantly in his phone and he would freak out if anyone touched it. I'm just relieved to know his secret is you and not drugs or something."

"Sounds like a campaign slogan," I deadpan. Sofía cocks her head. "Gemma Wells: Better Than Drugs!" I spread my hands out like I'm reading from a marquee. Sofía's brow contracts. *Nice. Well done, Gemma.*

"Well, if Beau thinks you're cool, you obviously are, so I'm glad I'm getting to know you now." Her smile is summer bright; she thinks she's just given me the ultimate compliment. And maybe she has. Having the Beau stamp of approval certainly would feel that way. I remember how I felt when he took that picture with me on the beach: nervous and nauseous but also special and noticed.

"So how'd you two get together?" she asks.

I shrug noncommittally. "It's a boring story."

"I doubt it. You don't have to tell me now, but I will get it out of you," she teases. It feels vaguely threatening. I glance out the window as we cross over the bridge next to Glen Canyon Dam, staring at the seven-hundred-foot concrete structure, feeling like the biggest fraud. This was a terrible idea. Do I honestly think I can successfully scam my way into a friendship group by pretending to date a boy in a coma?

Sofía pulls into a large dirt parking lot at the north end of the marina. Wahweap is Lake Powell's largest marina; it's a sprawling operation that straddles the Utah-Arizona border. On the Utah side is the boat rental office, the marina center where Dad works, a campground, a picnic and fishing area, and Sofía's gift shop. On the Arizona side is the resort, the main launch ramp and marina store, more fuel docks, and a couple of restaurants.

"Sorry I didn't drop you at the service center," Sofía says, opening her door. My feet crunch on gravel as I step out of the car and into the blinding sunshine.

"No worries," I answer automatically.

"I was supposed to be in by ten," she explains as she puts her giant sunglasses on. They make her look like a glamorous bug.

I check the time. "You're good. It's only nine fifteen."

"Arizona time. The store is on Utah time."

"I bet that never gets confusing," I deadpan. Because Arizona doesn't participate in daylight saving time, for six months of the year we're on mountain time, which is the same as Utah. The other six months, we're on Pacific time with California and the rest of the West Coast. Summer is when we're on Pacific time. As if that's not confusing enough, the buildings at Wahweap literally split the border. The resort operates on Arizona time, but the boat rental dock and Sofía's gift shop operate on Utah time. It's about as stupid as daylight saving time in general, which I've never understood.

"Never," she agrees with an eye roll. "What are you going to do now? Hang out with your dad at the service center?" She wrinkles her nose at the suggestion as I fall into step next to her on the way to the T-dock that stands between boat rentals and the gift shop. I guess I'm walking her to work.

I shrug. "Do you like working at the gift shop?"

"It's boring, but I get a good view of all the hot guys from the fuel dock at the beginning and end of every shift. Speaking of—" She nods to a college-aged guy walking past us in khaki shorts and a red T-shirt that says LAKE POWELL FUEL in bold white letters. "Not that you need a cute guy when you already have Beau, but a little eye candy never hurt anyone." She sighs wistfully. "Hey! I know." She grips my arm. "You should apply to work with me in the gift shop! You need something to distract yourself from Beau's accident."

As usual, my gut instinct is to say no. "Maybe—"

"Trust me, you do. You do not want to spend the whole summer in bed, unable to remember the last time you showered."

I glance down, worried I look like someone who doesn't shower.

"Distractions are essential when life is garbage." Her hand slides to my wrist as she tugs me the last few feet to the gift shop. She's a toucher. Maybe even an octopus girl. I've never been friends with one of them before. The possibility of a different kind of summer unfurls in front of me, one where I'm busy and needed instead of alone and forgotten.

"How much would I have to talk to the customers?"

"Don't worry. It's easy." She pushes open the glass door with her free hand and pulls me inside the small shop. Sofía waves to the woman behind the cash register, but my eyes are stuck on the boy in front of the standing drink cooler, his hands shoved into the pockets of his jeans.

No. No no no.

He turns and I freeze in place.

"Griff Booker!" Sofía smiles widely.

Chapter 5

My heart seizes when I see Griff, more from surprise than anything. I loathe surprises. As someone who is prone to hyperventilating in public, I don't appreciate when human interaction is sprung on me. I also suspect that of everyone I've lied to, Griff is the person most likely to reveal me as a fraud.

"Funny running into you again," Sofía says, eyeing Griff with nosy interest.

Griff furrows his brows. The dark circles under his eyes look like twin bruises. "Do I know you?" he asks Sofía, his eyes flicking to me in obvious confusion.

"I saw you at the hospital this morning. Where have you been, anyway?"

"At the hospital," he says flatly.

"Before that. Where'd you disappear to? Kodi swears you've been hiding in your room all year, but Drew said—"

"Ohio." Griff cuts her off. "I've been in Ohio." His drawl is bored, but the clench of his square jaw gives him away. He hates this conversation.

"Is that the one with the potatoes?"

"No."

Unflustered, Sofía drops her bag behind the counter and pins a name tag to the front of her powder-blue polo. "Sorry again," she tells the woman at the counter. "Did you hear about Beau Booker? I was the one who called nine-one-one. Blood was gushing from his head and he was, like, dying. It was horrible. Anyway, I just came from the hospital. That's why I'm late."

Griff's scowl deepens more the longer Sofía talks about his brother. When he notices me noticing him, his expression smooths out. He holds it like that, carefully blank.

I glance around the shop, trying to imagine myself working here. The selection isn't as large as at the marina store inside the resort, but it has the basics. On the right side of the shop is sunscreen, snacks, batteries, and fishing gear. To the left is a rack of clothing with everything ranging from swimsuits and tank tops to sun hats, flip-flops, and sweatshirts. Because we're way at the end of the marina, I bet foot traffic is minimal, which means fewer people for me to deal with.

The door swings open. I duck out of the way, stepping on Griff's toe in the process. "Sorry!"

He looks at me like he's seeing me for the first time, then looks down at his toe. He rubs his eyes with the heels of his hands and shakes his head.

What are you doing here? The question claws to the surface, but I swallow it back. Griff looks dead on his feet. *You should be sleeping.* Another unsaid thought. He glances back at the drink cooler. I reach around him to slide the door open and grab an energy drink. "Do you want one?" The offer slips out easier than it would if it were Beau standing next to me.

"No," Griff scoffs, seemingly snapping out of whatever daze he was in. "That stuff's radioactive."

"Shh!" I clasp the giant can to my chest. "It can hear you."

One half of his mouth tugs up: the ghost of a smile. "Energy drinks make my heart feel like it's going to explode," he says, picking a bottle of water from the cooler instead.

"That's highway robbery." I point to the price tag.

"At least it won't kill me."

"It's bad for the environment."

His jaw clenches. He looks me dead in the eye and twists the top, taking a long swig from the frosty bottle.

"Wow," I mutter, sidestepping him to stand in line to pay for my drink.

He stands behind me. "What?"

"You are nothing like your brother," I say, my eyes forward. It's the kind of retort I usually wouldn't think of for several hours, but he surprised me into defensiveness and it just flew out of my mouth.

If Griff has a reaction to this statement, it's inaudible. I'm desperate to glance over my shoulder to see his expression, but I don't want to give him the satisfaction. I'm also terrified he'll notice the red splotches creeping up my chest. They happen whenever I get nervous or stressed out. I hate them even more than I hate surprises. If Arizona weren't one of the hottest places on the planet, I'd live in turtlenecks all year.

When it's my turn to pay, I run my hands over a spinning rack of personalized key chains while Sofía rings me up. Next to the clothes are the name-inspired souvenirs, racks and racks of magnets and mugs and key chains all lined up from Aaron to Zoe. "My name is never here."

"There are two spellings of Sofía," she says.

"Lucky bitch."

Behind me, Griff snorts loudly. My hand flies to my mouth. "I'm sorry, I shouldn't have—"

"Relax. It was funny." Sofía grins. "Who knew you were funny?"

"The summer after third grade I was so frustrated with the injustice of it that I took a black Sharpie with the intent of adding a *G* to one of the Emma souvenirs. Except when I walked inside the shop that Sharpie felt like a handgun in my pocket. I was sick with guilt and so nervous about getting caught that I ran out crying."

Sofía laughs. "Why didn't you just buy it and add the *G* after the fact?"

I feel the heat on my neck spread as she laughs at me. "I don't know." I pay for my drink and she hands me an application with my change.

"Are we hiring?" Sofía calls to the front of the store, where the woman in a matching polo is folding sweatshirts.

"No."

My stomach sinks. I could have enjoyed myself here, laughing with Sofía and plotting revenge on those lucky enough to have a souvenir name. "No worries." I shrug, stepping to the side so Griff can pay for his stuff. He does so silently, leaving without so much as a nod. *Whatever.* Beau must have gotten all the good genes in the family. The fact that Griff is here buying drinks instead of supporting his family in a crisis tells me all I need to know about him.

"You could see if the resort is hiring," Sofía offers after the door swings shut behind Griff. "Then you'll be close enough that we can still hang out."

"Yeah, maybe."

"Do it." She looks at me seriously. "I don't want you getting sad."

My stomach squirms as I avoid eye contact. I must be wearing my loneliness like a neon sign. It was a mistake to get invested in this idea so quickly, but every hour that passes without a text from Nina makes me feel even worse about the summer ahead. I turn to leave.

Sofía grabs my wrist. "Hang on. You could take Beau's old job."

I freeze, racking my brain for info on Beau.

"I'm sure they'll be looking to replace him—" She sees my panicked expression and backtracks. "I didn't mean that! You wouldn't be replacing him—you'd be filling in. And it'll only be for a short time. He has to wake up soon." She picks up a phone receiver and pushes a few buttons. "Hey, this is Simi in the gift shop." The woman folding sweatshirts with the Simi name tag raises an eyebrow at Sofía. "Are you hiring?" She waits for an answer and then gives me a thumbs-up. "Good. I'm sending you someone right now. She'll be there in five minutes." She hangs up the phone and looks at me expectantly. She must have called the Bookers' restaurant. I'm almost positive that's where Beau works. "Gus is waiting for you," Sofía says, throwing a massive wrench into my thought process. Beau's dad is *not* named Gus.

"Can you remind me how to get there?"

She gives me a funny look. "Turn right and walk down the dock. If you fall in, you've gone too far."

"The fuel docks?"

She nods slowly. "Didn't you know Beau was working there?"

"Yeah. Yes. Totally! The accident must have scrambled my brain a little."

She frowns. "There's a one-room building down there with a grumpy-looking old guy named Gus. Tell him Simi sent you." She moves from behind the counter and nudges me toward the door. "You'll love it! Good luck!" Two thumbs-up this time. It's confusing how excited she is by this idea, but I go with it, following her instructions down to the fuel dock.

I pop the top off the energy drink and take a long gulp. It tastes like battery acid. Griff's right about these things being terrible for me, but I can't help myself. I pay attention to my pulse, though. It's a little fast, but I'm sure that's just because I'm about to go to my first job interview in cutoffs and hot-pink flip-flops. (Technically, my first ever job interview was with Dad, but I bombed it on purpose. No amount of pleading can convince me to work with him running tours.)

I easily locate the building at the end of the dock, glancing down at the sparkly water as I walk. My heart soars. (And *not* in an overcaffeinated way, thank you very much.) I'd willingly spend every day here if they'd let me. I knock once and then open the door. The temperature drops as I step inside, thanks to the swamp cooler in the corner. In the three minutes it took to walk here, beads of sweat are already rolling down my neck. My eyes take a minute to adjust to the dim lights, but when they do, I see a white man with leathery skin and a gray ponytail sitting behind a desk, one foot up on his knee. A book of sudoku puzzles sits open on the desk.

"Simi send you?" he asks, not looking up.

"So I'm told."

He glances up. "You ever have a job before?"

"No, but I know my way around a boat."

"It's not rocket science. All you have to do is work a gas nozzle."

"I can do that," I promise, encouraged by the prospect of a job that lets me work right on the water and requires zero socialization. This is looking better than the gift shop all the time.

"All right. Let's give you a shot." He opens a desk drawer and passes me an application. "Fill this out before you leave today."

I sit in a folding chair in front of the desk and pick up a pen from a cup sitting near the edge. "I don't have to interview?" I was worried he was going to hit me with formal questions about my strengths and weaknesses or whatever.

"We're short-staffed because of Beau's accident. I hired someone else twenty minutes ago, but between you and me, he doesn't look that reliable. I wouldn't be shocked if he fell dead in the water on his way out of here. Tell me if you see a body when you leave." He picks up his sudoku book and settles back into his chair.

My brain prickles with awareness. *He can't mean*— "What's his name?"

"Hell if I remember. Some kind of bird? He's related to the Booker kid."

My stomach sinks. "Griffin?"

"That sounds right."

"I think a griffin is a lion-bird hybrid," I mumble. My excitement at getting the job fizzles. I only know two things about Griff: First, that his name inspires gossip, drama, and rumors. Aka: attention. (Thanks, I hate it.) And second, that he doesn't seem to like me. The possibility of having a low-key, under-the-radar job feels unlikely if he's stomping around.

Gus taps his foot against the edge of the desk. "What's wrong with parents these days? What happened to normal names like Tom and Joe and Sarah? Every baby now is named something insane like Rifle or Bexley, and if they have a normal name, the spelling's all jacked up."

"You like souvenir names."

"Huh?"

"Never mind." I sigh and slip my completed application across the desk. Extended proximity to a member of the Booker family is the last thing I need right now. Even the smallest slipup could out me as a liar. And there was something in the way Griff looked at me at the hospital. No, *look* is the wrong word. He *glared*. And now I'm going to have to work next to him all summer long. I worry my lip, tempted to call the whole thing off.

Without so much as a glance at my application, Gus drops it in in his desk drawer and slams it shut. He rummages through a cardboard box in the corner of the room and tosses me a red Lake Powell Fuel T-shirt. "Come in at seven tomorrow. I'm already training this Eagle kid, so I may as well get you both done in one shot."

I burst out laughing. As reluctant as I am to work with Beau's older brother, I cannot pass up the opportunity to see Griff's reaction when Gus calls him "Eagle." He's going to *hate* it. I try to imagine his annoyance, but I'm tripped up by the memory of the dark smudges under his eyes and the rumors swirling around his disappearance.

What's your story, Griff Booker?

If nothing else, working with him this summer will give me plenty of time to find out. As long as he doesn't find out my story first, expose me as the new Lizzie Spalding, ruin my social life for the rest of time, and doom me to a friendless existence. No pressure, right?

Chapter 6

I wake to the sound of my phone buzzing somewhere in my sheets. Thinking it's Nina, I scramble in the dark, pull back a blanket, and hear my phone thud against the wall. I crawl toward it and stick my hand in the crack between the bed and the wall, my fingers grasping it just as it stops buzzing. A missed call from a number I don't recognize. Awesome. So glad I woke up before dawn and got all worked up for nothing.

I'm sliding back under my blanket when I hear creaking bedsprings and a knock on the wall by my "room." I don't have a door, just a curtain I pull across the small cubby where I sleep on the boat. "You okay? I heard a thump." Dad's raspy voice carries easily through the thin fabric.

"Yeah. My phone got stuck in a blanket and I accidentally flung it against the wall."

He pulls the curtain aside, and in the dim moonlight spilling in from my window, I see Dad raise an eyebrow. "Since you're awake, do you want a blueberry muffin?"

"Blueberry muffin" is our code phrase, a callback to the prepackaged, processed baked goods we ate on our first sunrise boat ride when I was five years old. Before that, my parents were always telling me to stop waking up before the sun, begging me to sleep in and let them have some rest. So when Dad woke me up Christmas-morning early on the day after Mom's funeral and took me to the boat, it was the beginning of a new era.

It could have been the worst day of our lives, and in some ways, it was. But I was only five and didn't fully grasp what it meant that she was gone *forever.* What I remember most strongly from that day is that we were on an adventure, he and I, and we were in it together. We may have lost Mom to breast cancer, but we had each other.

We also had blueberry muffins. He bought two from the marina shop and let me eat both as he eased the boat onto the glass-smooth water. We watched the sunrise together, my salty tears running into the oily muffin, his running down his cheeks and into his beard. At the end of the ride I asked if we could go every day that summer. Surprise of my life when he said yes. (The only good surprise I've ever had.) If he ever got sick of it, if he ever wanted to sleep in or leave me with a babysitter or run away from being a single dad, he never let on. We don't go as often anymore, but we try to get in a few early morning trips every summer.

As we pull onto the water thirty minutes later, the lake is deep navy in the early light, the color of midnight skies and childhood dreams. Tourists are surprised to discover that Lake Powell is a chameleon, the water constantly evolving, adapting to its surroundings. Over the course of my life I've seen entire rainbows under my feet, the color variations shifting with the time of day, the season, the weather, and something distinctly magical I wouldn't want to nail down.

"Do you want to drive?" Dad asks as we float leisurely past the no-wake buoys, the ones that mark how far from the shore you must be before putting the boat in gear.

My phone buzzes in my back pocket. "Yeah. Hang on." I pull it out and see that it's the same number from earlier. I silence it with an eye roll. Scammers are getting more persistent.

As soon as the nose of the boat hits the buoy line, I take the wheel and push the throttle forward, bringing the bow of the boat up out of the water as we accelerate. When the boat evens out, I ease up on the throttle, keeping us steady around 4,000 rpms, my favorite cruising speed. I'm not quite tall enough to see over the windshield, so I stand, one knee up on the pilot seat. Cool wind rushes over every inch of me, billowing through my clothes and tangling my hair. I feel alive all the way down to my pinkie toes, an experience I've never been able to replicate anywhere else.

As we cruise down Antelope Canyon, stone walls rising six hundred feet above us on both sides, my phone buzzes again. I look at those now familiar numbers with a sigh. Dad doesn't ask but his glance makes me feel guilty anyway. "I'm putting it away!" I promise, just as my phone buzzes me again, alerting me to a new voice mail. "This person won't leave me alone!"

"Time to head back for your new job," Dad says abruptly.

I check the time. We don't have to turn back for another five minutes, but Dad seems impatient, so I do what he says and turn the boat back the way we came.

"Are you nervous?" he asks stiffly. He crosses his arms, and the movement reveals my name on his right shoulder blade, peeking out from the edge of his sleeveless shirt. His skin is dark from twenty years of running boat tours out of Wahweap Marina, and both of his arms are covered in a chaotic swirl of tattoos.

"A little," I admit. In contrast to Dad's omnipresent beach bum appearance, I'm in still-creased khaki shorts and a T-shirt that smells like chemicals. I finger-comb my hair into a high ponytail, yank it tight, and put on a gray baseball hat that says LAKE POWELL across the front. Camp counselor chic. All I need is a fanny pack.

"My offer to work with me always stands, you know," he says quietly.

"Dad." I sigh. "I don't want to talk about it." He wouldn't understand why the thought of taking my favorite activity in the world and combining it with strangers and small talk causes my anxiety to skyrocket. Cruising the lake is just for me. I don't want it to become something I hate.

My phone buzzes again. I barely have service, but I hit the answer button anyway. "Hello?"

"Hi, I'm looking for Gemma Wells!" a voice chirps across the line.

"Who's this?"

"My name is Karly Wallace and I'm a reporter with the *Lake Powell Chronicle.*"

"You were at my house yesterday."

"That's right. I saw the story about you saving Beau Booker's life and I'd love to interview you."

"Are you the one who has been calling me all morning? Did you leave me a voice mail?"

"I'm sorry to be a bother, but I was hoping to get ahold of you as quickly as possible."

"What do you want to know?"

"I've been doing some research—"

"What kind of research?" My palms turn slick on the steering wheel.

"This could be an inspiring human-interest piece," she says, which I hate. Interest equals attention. I've spent my entire life trying to make myself uninteresting to other humans. "I'm looking through your social media page now to get a better sense of your relationship, but I'm not seeing anything on your page, and only the most recent picture on Beau's—"

The boat sails through a dead zone and the call drops. I shove my phone back in my pocket with shaky fingers. Beau's and my "relationship" is so flimsy it'll never stand up to research. I can see the masterpost now. "Gemma Wells Is a Lying Freak."

I'm a trembling, anxious mess for the rest of the ride to the fuel docks. Dad asks enough questions to prove he cares but doesn't push the subject when I refuse to talk about the phone call. He waits with me at the dock until seven, when the sound of marching footsteps approaches from behind. I wave him off as he promises to pick me up after work. A white woman with a large mass of light brown curls and baby-blue glasses approaches, temporarily knocking Karly from my mind.

"Gemma, right?" she asks. I'd guess she's in her early twenties. Our tan shorts and red shirts are the same, but that's where the resemblance ends. I almost squeal in delight when I see her white fringed fanny pack. I *knew* I was missing something. She's also sporting a large crystal hanging from a hemp necklace. Combined with the fanny pack and the stiff uniform, her whole look is a vibe. I'm not sure what vibe, but it demands attention. She extends her hand to shake mine. "I'm Violet. I'll oversee your training."

"What happened to Gus?"

Violet rolls her eyes. "Did he say he was training you? He hasn't left the shack in years."

"The shack?"

She motions to the small building where I met Gus and checks her watch. "We're waiting on one more, but Gus said not to be surprised if he doesn't show up."

I wonder if she realizes the person she's waiting for is Beau's brother. We stand in silence long enough for it to morph from tolerable to uncomfortable to agonizing. It's a physical weight, pushing me down. I press up on my toes and check the time for the tenth time in three minutes.

"We'll start now," Violet says at ten after. "I'll tell Gus to fire the Booker boy if he ever bothers to grace us with his presence." She must take in my surprised expression because she follows this with a small lecture about the importance of punctuality that is strangely at odds with her fringe and crystals ensemble.

As Violet talks, Griff's weary face flashes in my mind. He looked wrecked at the hospital. Dazed in the gift shop. It occurred to me briefly in bed last night that he might have been on drugs. (I wouldn't know. Despite what I was promised in middle school health class, I've never been offered any.)

So maybe Griff was high, or maybe he was just spiraling from Beau's accident. My heart tugs and I find myself saying, "He might be on Arizona time."

Violet sighs. "Do you know him?"

"Not really. Just that he's Beau's brother."

"You know Beau?"

"Um . . . I sort of pulled him out of the water after he fell."

"Hang on—*you're* the girlfriend?" I wince as she cocks her head to the side and studies me. I feel that stare in my bones. "You're not who I expected." I'm mentally scrambling, attempting to articulate a response to such a loaded statement, when she checks her watch again. "Listen. Call Griff and find out where he is. If he's not here in twenty minutes, he's fired, and tell him that I'm only doing this because I like his brother."

I jog toward the shack, confused by my own motivation for defending Griff. I have zero reason to stick up for him. Except—those shadows. I've seen the same ones in the mirror on the mornings after I tortured myself by reliving every embarrassing thing that ever happened to me or almost happened to me or might happen to me in the future.

"Wait!" Violet calls to my retreating back. "If he's on Arizona time, he would have been here an hour ago."

I pretend I didn't hear her as I pull open the door to the shack. Gus finds Griff's phone number on his application and types it into his own phone before handing it to me. My finger hovers over the call button. Gosh, I hate talking on the phone. Why would any sane person talk on the phone when texting exists? But he doesn't have a lot of time, so I close my eyes, take a breath, and hit call.

It rings four times. I'm about to hang up when Griff answers. "Is something wrong?" he mumbles, his voice raspy from sleep.

"You're late for work."

"Shit." Hurried, rustling sounds carry over the line. I imagine he's getting dressed, and then I forcibly stop imagining that, because what the hell, brain? "Who is this?" he finally thinks to ask.

"Gemma."

"Who?"

I scuff my foot against the dock, embarrassment souring my stomach. "Beau's girlfriend."

A long silence. Then finally, "What?"

"I work at the fuel dock. Our trainer says you have twenty minutes—fifteen now—to get down here."

The sound of a water faucet fills the line, and then the unmistakable gargle of Griff brushing his teeth. *Gosh.* Why hasn't he hung up yet? He spits. "Is that it?"

"She also said that the only reason she's giving you a second chance is because she likes your brother."

The line goes dead.

Chapter 7

"Griff Booker?"

"The one and only." He strides toward us, his hands shoved into his front pockets, his footsteps causing my anxiety to spike. My phone is suddenly heavy in my pocket, a reminder of Karly's phone call and how easy it'd be for anyone even halfway interested to realize that Beau and I weren't close. I back up until my heels hit the edge of the dock. Griff's brows furrow slightly as he watches my retreat, but otherwise he ignores me. A small mercy.

Violet makes a show of checking the time. "You're lucky I like your brother."

He throws her a careless grin. "Seems to be a running theme in my life."

"Maybe because he's nice to people," I mutter. The corner of his mouth twitches. Despite everything in my body telling me to fly under Griff's radar, I can't help what I say next. "How's he doing? Any updates?"

"Not yet," he says stiffly. His mouth forms a grim line as he focuses his eyes on the water behind me.

Violet unzips her fanny pack and retrieves a white crystal. She presses it into Griff's palm. "Quartz is a master healer. Leave this in his hospital room."

Griff's eyes meet mine, and I bite back a laugh at the "WTF" expression on his face. When Violet turns to the nearest gas pump, he chucks the stone into the water.

Violet walks us through training. I pretend not to look at Griff while she talks, but I can't help myself. I'm strangely relieved to see that the purple shadows under his eyes are less prominent than yesterday. He's also clean shaven, which makes him look not only younger but also less like he's about to keel over.

The job is as easy as Gus made it sound: A boat pulls into the watery parking slip and we fill it with gas and send the customer on their way. Repeat for eight hours. "These pumps are really old, so you might have to work the nozzle to get the flow going." Violet demonstrates by squeezing and shaking the gas nozzle. I make the mistake of glancing at Griff in this moment and his eyes are as wide as mine. I cover my smirk with my hands while he clamps his lips together.

"No dirty jokes," she warns.

"Wouldn't dream of it," I say while Griff shakes with suppressed laughter next to me.

"Oh my gosh!" I say when Violet leaves us to work pump three on our own. "She must know how that sounds."

Griff's eyes are still shining with amusement. "Your cheeks are bright red," he says.

My hands fly to my cheeks and I close my eyes and groan. "Don't look at me."

"What?"

"Turn around! Seriously, don't look at me." I peek one eye open and to my surprise, he's turned around. How surprisingly decent of him.

He clears his throat. "Uh . . . how long do I have to stay like this?"

I press the backs of my fingers against my cheeks. Still warm. "A few more minutes. I hate when people see me blush."

"Even Beau?"

"Especially Beau."

He's quiet for what feels like a long time before he asks, "How long have you two been together?"

I'm an idiot for not having invented a plausible explanation for this inevitable question. I *knew* I should. It's one of the things that kept me awake last night. And yet the idea flooded my stomach with so much anxious dread that I couldn't bring myself to do anything beyond worry about it. "I don't want to talk about him."

Griff glances over his shoulder with a frown. "Why not?"

"It makes my stomach hurt," I say truthfully.

His face falls. "Mine too." He waits another beat and I feel like absolute garbage. Time to change the subject.

"Why were you late this morning?"

"Slept in. I drove two days straight to get here."

"I thought maybe you were high."

"My reputation precedes me," he says with such a straight face I don't know what to make of it.

He inches closer. "You were the last person he was with. Tell me one good thing about that day and I'll leave you alone."

My heart beats uncomfortably hard as I rack my brain for something to say. "He was going to do a tubing competition with his friends. He's competitive, you know?" I say finally, grasping for any memory to give Griff to hold on to. He rolls his eyes like he *does* know, which makes me feel like an idiot. Obviously he knows his brother better than I do. As I stare at his guarded expression, I've never hated myself more.

I can't lie anymore. I dig my fingernails into my palms and search for the words to explain how this misunderstanding happened. Maybe if I come clean now, the last few days will slip from the town's collective consciousness by the time Beau wakes up. Or at least by the time school starts again in the fall.

"There's something you should know—" I say at the exact same time Griff asks, "What about before the party?"

A bead of sweat drips into my eye. My mind is blank. Tumbleweeds blow across my empty brain. "I didn't see him."

Beau lifts an eyebrow. "My mom said he was with you all day."

"I need to tell you the truth."

"About what?"

"Gemma Wells?"

A zip of fear climbs my spine at the now familiar sound of that chirpy voice. Griff and I swivel in unison toward the shiny-haired woman striding up the dock. It's Karly Wallace, the reporter from my porch and the phone call this morning, here to blow up my life.

"Griff—" I turn to him and grab his wrist. "I have something to tell you." Better coming from me than some reporter.

But not even my plea can pull Griff's attention from Karly. "Who's that?" he asks loudly enough for her to hear.

"Hi, I'm Karly, reporter from the *Lake Powell Chronicle*

dot-com. Nice to speak to you—for the third time," she says pointedly. She sticks out her hand to shake mine. Her shiny black hair is pulled back into a low ponytail and she's wearing Birks, jeans, and a gauzy tank top. She doesn't look as threatening as she did in her stiff dress, but I still don't want to have anything to do with her.

I shake her hand anyway. I can't *not*. It's a compulsion. "Are you following me?"

"Your dad told me you work here." Her wind-chime voice is friendly, but I can't forget the memory of her telling me she's been doing research. On Beau. On *me*.

I have to get her out of here—*now*.

"I told you I'm not interested."

"Why are you here?" Griff asks.

"I want to do a human-interest piece on Gemma and Beau. The story is so inspiring. Not a lot of girlfriends can say they've saved their boyfriend's life."

"She said she's not interested."

"Everything okay over here?" Violet strides toward us and it gets harder for me to breathe.

"She's just leaving," I insist.

"I'm the manager. Can I help you with something?" Violet asks.

"Did you know you have a local hero working here? I'm hoping to do a quick interview with Gemma." Karly smiles brightly and I feel trapped. Heat blooms on my cheeks.

"I can't. I'm at work."

I need more time so I can figure out how to explain this to Griff. And Sofía. And Mrs. Booker. And Kodi, Shandiin, and

Ian. *When did the list get so long?* My stomach flip-flops like a dying fish. I wish there were a way to tell everyone at once. Preferably a method that doesn't involve me having to explain myself half a dozen times. I'm so bad with words, I'll only make things worse. If only I could correct this misunderstanding once and someone else could make it sound good.

Someone like a reporter, I realize with a flash of brilliance. Karly is the answer to my problem. This interview is my chance to get ahead of the story. No one can accuse me of being Lizzie Spalding if I go on the record with the truth.

"Actually—I will do the interview. If that's okay with you," I say to Violet.

She shrugs. "We're slow today. You can do it now."

"Excellent!" Karly leads me up the dock. She takes a seat on a small bench outside the shack and motions for me to do the same. We awkwardly angle our bodies toward each other, and I cringe when my knees bump into hers. She pulls a small, thin computer out of her bag. "All right! Let's talk about Beau Booker."

Chapter 8

"When did you and Beau start dating?" Karly's fingers hover over her keyboard. In the distance, Griff pretends not to watch.

I take a deep breath. It's time to set the record straight. "There's been a misunderstanding."

"Can you explain what you mean by that?"

"People have been making a lot of assumptions about our relationship. The truth is, Beau and I—" I wipe my sweaty palms on my thighs and my eye catches sight of someone approaching us. Sofía waves, sunshine glinting off her sharp, neon-green nails. My stomach drops as she walks right up to us.

"Is that the reporter?" Sofía stage-whispers.

I reluctantly introduce Sofía and Karly. "I *so* did not mean to interrupt," Sofía gushes. She turns to me. "I was wondering if you wanted to get lunch with me on your break . . . but I'll come back later?" I don't miss the question mark on the end of her sentence, and neither does Karly.

"I'd love to ask you a couple of questions too if you have a minute!" Karly says.

"Sure!" Sofía motions for me to make room on the bench, and while I'd normally welcome someone who can take the attention off me, I'll never be able to explain this misunderstanding with Sofía freaking Lopez sitting next to me.

"No!" I shout. They both stare at me. "I, um, I only have a few minutes to talk. I'm still at work."

"I got you." Sofía winks before addressing Karly. "You can put me on the record saying that Gemma and Beau are the cutest couple *ever.*"

"That's not true—" I choke out, desperate to get her to stop talking.

"It is! Gemma won't say it herself because she's shy. Did you know she *never* comes to our beach parties? No one knew why she was there until she saved Beau's life and admitted that they've been dating in secret. It feels like fate brought the two of them together to save Beau's life."

"A secret relationship?" Karly's grin widens as her fingers fly over the keyboard. If misery could kill a person, at least I wouldn't have to sit through this excruciating moment.

"Yeah, but thankfully now she's telling everyone the truth about her and Beau."

"I'm not telling everyone!"

"Sorry!" Sofía winces before turning to Karly. "See what I mean? Gemma doesn't like attention. You should put that in the article! People need to know she's not using Beau's accident to get publicity for herself."

"Sofía!" I screech, panic building in my chest. I can barely breathe.

"I'm leaving! Lunch later?" she asks. I nod just to get her to leave. She's not twenty feet away before my phone beeps with a text from her.

Sofía: **sorry if I said too much** 😞

I groan and sink lower into the bench. Sofía made this so much harder for me. How can I come clean now, with her on the record saying that I'm "telling everyone" that Beau and I are dating?

Karly taps away on her keyboard for several seconds as I grip the bench underneath us and fight to keep my breathing steady.

"A secret relationship certainly explains why there's no evidence of you two online," Karly muses. "Now, where were we?" She stops typing and scans the screen in front of her. "I asked when you and Beau started dating, and you said, 'The truth is' . . ." she prompts, her fingers drumming lightly on the keyboard.

"The truth is . . ." I swallow the painful lump in my throat. "I don't want to say anything that will make Beau feel uncomfortable," I say, buying time. This is it. This is how I go. On a hard bench, under a hot sun. Cause of death: total mind-numbing paralysis.

"Why would you?" Her brow creases in confusion. My heartbeat is *painful*. "You are dating Beau, aren't you?"

Never in my life have I experienced a moment that I *knew* would change everything. If I lie in this moment, I can never, ever take it back. The realization knocks the wind out of my chest; it's scary enough I almost say no. But when I meet Karly's eyes, they're full of wary skepticism, and it breaks my resolve. Her expression is my biggest fear personified. Every decision I've ever made has been to keep from embarrassing myself like this, to save myself from being looked at like *that*.

I glance to the dock. My eyes easily find Griff. If I tell the truth, I'll have to quit this job. Sofía will never talk to me again. I'll be the new Lizzie Spalding: a public embarrassment. Griff's head lifts, his gaze moving to Karly and me. I avert my eyes as my heart thunders in my chest. He will eviscerate me when he finds out I'm a liar who used his brother for social clout.

Nope. Telling the truth is not an option.

New plan: perpetuate this lie until Beau wakes up and then make him fall in love with me. *(I'll worry about the details later.)*

"Yes!" I breathe, making my choice. I force an unnatural laugh. "Can you imagine if I wasn't?"

She shakes her head. "I've heard of girls doing desperate things for attention, but never anyone stooping so low as to lie about a comatose patient. Now, tell me how long you and Beau have been dating."

"Not that long," I say quickly.

"Can you give me a time frame?"

"I don't—I'm not sure."

"Not even a rough estimate?" Her eyebrows rise in surprise and I realize that if I'm going to sell this story, I need to be decisive.

"February."

"Tell me about Beau."

"He's competitive."

"That's all?"

"No! He's shiny. I don't know how else to describe it. Beau's the type of person you can't help but stare at. When he's in the room, no one else matters," I say. I'm relieved to be able to tell the truth about this, at least, but a nagging sense of dread fills me as I fall deeper and deeper into what appears to be a bottomless hole.

Karly tilts her head thoughtfully. "What do you and Beau like to do together?"

"We cruise on the lake. We swim and jump off cliffs and watch sunsets." My cheeks heat and I pray Karly chalks it up to the temperature. The truth is, I got too close to revealing my most frequent daydream. The one where Beau kisses me under the stars and promises I'll never be lonely again.

"When was your first date?" she asks as she types furiously.

"Valentine's Day."

"What did you do?"

"We had dinner at R.D.'s and watched a movie at my house." *(Is that believable? Do people even go on "dates" anymore?)*

"What movie?"

"One of the Avengers." *(Why did I say that? I've never seen an Avengers movie in my life.)*

"Tell me about the day of the accident."

Sweat runs down the backs of my knees. I take in a slow, shaky breath. "It was the last day of school. We were excited to spend the summer together. Now that he's—he's—" Tears form behind my eyes and a sharp lump appears in my throat. "I hope we get more time together." My hands are shaking so bad that I sit on them to calm down. Karly asks questions—about where I learned CPR and how I felt seeing Beau fall into the water—and then she wraps it up.

"I think that's all I need for now," she says as I swipe the tears from my cheeks. "Thanks for talking to me, and I hope Beau wakes up soon."

"Me too."

"I'll reach back out if I have any more questions. Oh—and can you text me a few pictures of you and Beau? Nothing professional, just shots of you hanging out."

"There's one on his Instagram you can use."

"I saw that one, but I'd like to include a few more."

"I don't have more."

Skepticism flashes across Karly's face and I wither under her scrutiny. "You don't have any photos after more than three months of dating?"

"My phone fell in the lake and I didn't have anything backed up." The lie slips easily and believably from my lips. Sometimes I get lucky.

"I'm sorry to hear that. I'm sure you'll have more opportunities to take pictures with Beau." Her head tilts with a sympathetic nod, and then she leaves.

The knot in my chest slowly loosens. The hard part is over, at least for now. I have an official cover story and, until Beau wakes up, no one to contradict it. After all, if I can handle an interview with Karly, I should be able to manage Beau's family and friends.

"How'd it go?" Griff drawls as I return to our dock.

"Good, I think!" I say as adrenaline pumps through my blood. Maybe Sofía was right about fate bringing Beau and me together. "Was the dock slow while I was gone?"

"Dead," he confirms.

"Let's make a bet on when we'll see our first customer!" I sit next to Griff on the edge of the dock and lean back on my hands, my heart lighter than it's been for days. "Winner buys Popsicles."

Griff glances sideways at me with a strange expression.

"What?" I smooth my hair, self-conscious under his scrutiny. "What's wrong?"

"Before your interview, I asked about Beau, and you said, 'I have to tell you the truth.'" He angles his body toward mine and looks at me evenly. "The truth about what?"

"Did I say that?" I swallow my nerves. I feel bad for lying, but I don't owe Griff anything. Beau told me to pretend we're close, and he's the brother I care about. I shrug and tip my head back, closing my eyes in the bright sunshine.

"I don't remember."

Chapter 9

The truth about what?

I stand in the corner of the shack the next morning at our mandatory team meeting and try to blend into the wooden paneling. Griff is sitting against the opposite wall, his feet propped up on the messy desk, his toe mindlessly drumming against a Tina Belcher Funko Pop.

The truth about what?

I can't get his earnest tone out of my head, or the way his expression hardened when I claimed memory loss. I shouldn't care so much what he thinks of me, but who am I kidding? I care what everyone thinks of me.

"Take water breaks as needed. We don't want anyone else getting dehydrated—" Violet drones on about safety protocol, but I'm only half listening. I sneak a glance at my phone and refresh the *Lake Powell Chronicle* front page. No story yet. I hope it'll be a fluff piece that everyone forgets about in twenty-four hours, but I'm desperately curious about which of my lies will make it to print.

"Gemma? Are you listening?"

"What?" I startle, pushing myself off the wall.

"No offense, Vi, but this is boring as hell." The blond guy

sitting next to Violet yawns and tips backward in his chair. He's a nineteen-year-old rock climber from Colorado who introduced himself as *Cannon*. I felt the ghost of Gus's indignation enter the room when he said his name out loud.

"Fine." Violet abandons her clipboard of announcements and checks her watch. "We have a few minutes before we open. Let's play a game to get to know one another."

I glance at Griff. His face mirrors the unfurling horror in my gut. Get-to-know-you games are a nightmare on par with surprise parties. The odds of humiliation are approximately one hundred percent. It's like—let's put people on the spot, give them zero prep time, and expect them to sum up their entire personality while also being witty and interesting. Icebreaker games are The Actual Worst. They should have been outlawed by the Geneva convention.

"Two truths and a lie!" Violet declares. "Gemma—you go first."

"I—uh—I don't think—I'm not good at—" My heart thumps hard in my chest.

"I'll go first," Griff says, giving my poor heart a break before it explodes. I doubt he realizes that he's saving me, and when I glance at him to show I'm grateful, he's staring at the ceiling. "I was high during my job interview, I'm my parents' least favorite child, and as of today, I'm officially a high school dropout." He ticks them off on his fingers.

Cannon shrugs while Violet's eyes turn to me.

"H-how should I know?"

"You're dating his brother," she points out.

That shuts me up. I look at Griff and am flustered to find him staring back. It makes me desperate to fidget. I tug hard on the bill of my hat. "The second one is the lie."

A lazy smirk spreads across his face. "Wrong. And I wasn't high. You shouldn't believe everything you hear."

"Parents don't have favorite children."

"Spoken like a favorite child."

"I'm an only child!"

He tips his head to me. "There you go."

Violet glances out the window. "Looks like we're opening early; boats are pulling into slips two and four. Cannon, that's us." She motions for him to follow her outside, leaving Griff and me alone in the shack. And even though the game is over, I can't smother my curiosity. For years I've wanted to know more about Beau's life, and here Griff is, full of intriguing answers. "Who's the favorite child?" I ask.

He quirks an eyebrow. "Who do you think?"

Beau. I smile at the thought that even Mr. and Mrs. Booker aren't immune to their son's charms. "I'm sure they *love* you two the same, but you have to admit that you've—" I cut myself off, my cheeks burning in embarrassment.

"It's all right. You can say it. I've made their lives hell." He shrugs, his dark eyes unreadable before he shoulders open the door. A strip of sunlight falls across the floor as my phone buzzes in my pocket.

"You coming?" he asks.

"In a minute." I grab my phone and glance at the unknown number. I normally wouldn't answer, but after accidentally insulting him, I'd rather put some space between Griff and me.

"Hello?"

"Hi, is this Gemma Wells?" a low, unfamiliar voice asks.

"Who is this?" I hope it's not another reporter. Just because I survived one interview unscathed doesn't mean I can do it again.

"I'm the fact-checker for the *Lake Powell Chronicle*. I'm calling because I have a few questions about the interview you did with Karly Wallace. Do you have a minute to talk right now?"

I bolt to my feet and press my back against the door of the shack to prevent anyone from entering. "Sure! What's wrong? I mean, what are your questions?"

"I'll be honest, we don't heavily fact-check our human-interest pieces, but this came across my desk, and when I noticed an inconsistency with your statement, I couldn't help making a phone call."

"Okay?" My breathing turns shallow as I prepare for the worst. *This is it.* He knows I'm a liar and he's gonna tell Karly to publish the world's most embarrassing story about the girl so desperate to have a boyfriend she claimed the one in a coma.

I should have told her the truth when I had the chance, but instead I leaned so far in the opposite direction I no longer have plausible deniability when it comes to this misunderstanding,

"You told Karly that you and Beau went on your first date to R.D.'s on Valentine's Day, correct?"

"Is—is that a problem?" My voice is shaky and unsure.

"Only because R.D.'s was closed on Valentine's Day."

My heart drops. "I, um, that's right! I had too much homework on Valentine's Day to go out, so we went the day after. I can't believe I forgot."

"You went to R.D.'s on February fifteenth, are you sure?" His tone is doubtful. I have no idea what to say. "I called the owners to verify. They had a leaking pipe that flooded the dining room. The restaurant was closed from the thirteenth through the fifteenth.

"Gemma? Are you still there?" the fact-checker has the nerve to ask, as if he can't hear my erratic and panicked breathing through the line.

"Did I say R.D.'s? Oh my gosh, that's so embarrassing. I meant Sonic! We one hundred percent went to Sonic on Valentine's Day."

The fact-checker pauses for a beat too long. "You went to Sonic on Valentine's Day or the day after?"

Wow, I suck at this. "The fourteenth."

"Are you sure?"

"Definitely!"

"Hmmm."

"Don't—don't you believe me?" I swallow heavily and wipe my sweaty palms on my shorts. "I'm not lying! Why would I lie about my date with Beau Booker? Only a crazy person would do that!"

"Right." He clears his throat.

"When will the story publish?" I ask with forced cheerfulness.

"Karly was hoping to publish it tomorrow, but it could take longer."

"Why?"

"Any number of reasons. She might want to follow up with her other interviews."

My heart stumbles. *Other interviews?*

"I think she's still looking for pictures to accompany the article on our website," the fact-checker continues.

"I'll send them! Today after work." I'll do anything to get this article published before Karly interviews anyone else.

"I'll tell her to expect them. Good to talk to you, Gemma." He hangs up.

I bang my head against the wall and groan.

Time to learn Photoshop.

Chapter 10

By the time the dock closes at five, the tangy scent of gasoline wafts off my hair and clothes, my shirt is soaked through with sweat, and I have an unopened text from Karly Wallace telling me where to send pictures. As the last boat leaves, I let my body sag against the side of the pump and pull out my phone. Between the steady stream of customers and my total lack of material to work with, I'm no closer to possessing a picture of Beau and me.

I'm scrolling through Beau's social media feeds looking for a picture I could plausibly insert myself into when a shadow falls across my feet. "You really miss him?" Griff asks, glancing at my phone over my shoulder.

He doesn't seem upset that I implied he deserves to be the least favorite child, and I'm not going to bring it up. "It feels unreal more than anything."

"I get that."

"Any word from the hospital?" I cross my fingers and toes for good news. As much as it would suck for Beau to tell everyone I'm a crazy liar (oh my gosh that would *suck*) I'd make that trade in a second if it meant him waking up today. The world doesn't feel right without Beau Booker in it.

"Not yet." Griff scowls.

"Do *you* miss him?" I ask. He ignores my comment and crouches beside me. He pulls a wad of cash out of his pocket and starts counting the bills.

"What are you doing?"

"Giving you half."

"Of what?"

"Our tips. Violet said we split it evenly because we're working the same pump."

"I'm sorry, this job makes tips?" I ask indignantly. Griff waves a wad of cash in the air as if to say, *Yes, you absolute dimwit.* "No one said anything about tips!"

"Violet did at the meeting this morning."

"I didn't get any tips."

"But you did half the work, which is why you get half the tips. Take it." He attempts to push the money into my hand.

I swat the bills away. "Does *everyone* tip?"

Griff's eyes shift to Cannon on the next dock. I follow his line of sight, and sure enough, Cannon is thumbing through his own stack of bills.

"Was I supposed to ask for the money?" Griff laughs and fire burns over my skin. "*Well?* What did you do that I didn't?"

"You could stand to be a little—" I glare daggers at him, and he swallows the last word of that sentence.

My mouth hardens into a line. It's easier to pretend I'm furious with him than let him see the truth, which is that I'm mortified. After years of avoiding working with Dad for fear of being too awkward, I thought I'd found something that I could do. But nope. Turns out I suck at this too.

"I can teach you."

"No."

"It's not a big deal." Griff shrugs. "It's easy."

"Not for me."

"Look up from your shoes every once in a while, and you'd be surprised." He puts his finger under my chin and nudges my head up. Our eye contact is physically painful. I feel like my insides are turning to liquid. "I'll teach you," he says.

"Why would you help me when I basically said you deserve to be the least favorite?" I guess I *am* bringing it up.

He folds his arms across his chest, his biceps straining against the clingy fabric. I tear my gaze away, grateful my face and chest were already matching my uniform. He clears his throat. "Personal reasons."

"You have personal, mysterious reasons for wanting to help me?"

"Yes. And you'll just have to trust me that they're good," he says. I raise an extremely skeptical eyebrow. "Don't I look trustworthy?" he asks darkly. He doesn't even have the decency to smile. *No*, nothing about him looks remotely trustworthy.

"You also helped me today during two truths and a lie. I didn't want to play, and you volunteered."

He shrugs. "That was payback for saving my job."

"What's your explanation for this offer?"

He sighs and runs a hand through his hair. "My brother likes you. Loves you, maybe. I don't know." He shrugs, looking as uncomfortable as I feel.

"Fine," I breathe, just to end the moment. "Teach me. Go ahead."

"It's as easy as making small talk."

"Well—that's my problem. I don't make small talk. Physically can't do it."

"Okay," he says slowly. "Compliments are helpful. People love to be complimented."

"Wow, really? That's so insightful. You must be, like, a genius or something." I flutter my eyelashes outrageously.

He glares at my sarcasm. "It doesn't matter what you say, it could be total bullshit. You'll never see them again."

"You don't strike me as a guy who gives out fake compliments," I say.

"I don't. I go with option two—questions. People love to talk about themselves."

"I still don't understand why that would compel someone to give me money."

He laughs. "Take it from someone who's worked as a server for the last five years. Making a 'personal connection' is the fastest way to earn money." He uses extreme scare quotes.

"I'm bad at connecting with people."

"It's not real. It doesn't matter."

"But I can't make my brain or my mouth work around strangers! I get—" I cut myself off. No need to spill all my problems to him. "It's awkward." I smooth my shirt and fix my eyes on a fish in the water behind him.

"Let's practice," he says. "Pretend I'm here for gas."

I groan.

"No! This is a good idea." He slips off his shoes and socks, walks to the end of the dock, and dives in the water. I watch, openmouthed, as he pulls his arms up onto the dock and crosses them, resting his chin on the backs of his wrists as he treads water.

"You're insane."

"I'm here for gas! Can you help me?"

I stare at Griff, waiting for him to laugh at me or announce this is a big joke to make me look like an idiot. When he doesn't, I finally give in. "Are you done for the day?"

He looks less than impressed with my efforts. "Yes, ma'am."

Ma'am. I shudder. "Okay. Well, cool."

"Ask if you can get in my boat."

"Excuse me?"

"Ask permission to get in the boat, then sit on the back while you fill it."

"No."

"Then ask something else." His cocky grin completely transforms his face; he almost looks happy. It's impossible to reconcile this boy with the one from all the rumors. *Drugs. Fights. Affairs with teachers. Mysterious disappearances.*

"I don't know what to ask."

"Anything. It doesn't matter. Just ask the first thing that comes to mind."

His liquid dark eyes make it impossible to think. "Do you have a girlfriend?" I blurt.

His whole body freezes. "I don't."

We stare at each other for several breaths. "Your advice is terrible. I asked a question, and it didn't lead to sparkling conversation. If you'd been my customer, you never would have tipped me."

Smirking, Griff lays his hands flat on the dock and pulls

himself out of the water. The red shirt is clingier than ever. I should talk to Gus and get him a new one. Something that fits properly.

"Gemma!" Sofía waves from the top of the dock. She untucks her blue polo and unties her braid as she waits for me to join her. "How's life as a working woman?"

I throw a glance at Griff, who's walking behind us. "I think my coworkers hate me and I made zero dollars in tips."

"Screw them," she says fervently. "Hey! Have you heard anything about Beau?"

I shake my head and Sofía turns her eyes to Griff. He ignores her implied question.

"A bunch of us are going to the fundraiser at Booker Brothers' before visiting him at the hospital. You should come."

For the space of three exhilarating heartbeats, I'm the happiest girl in the whole town. I construct an entire universe in those breaths, one in which I'm friendly and outgoing, the kind of girl who lives a life of infinite possibilities. *Pizza at Booker Brothers'. Friday nights at The Bowl. Stolen kisses on the beach.*

The girl in my imagination is me—but not.

She's me—but better.

Gemma Rae Wells 2.0—*now sold with zero social anxiety disorder!*

Smiling at my own absurdity, I glance up and realize we've arrived at the shack. Cannon is leaning against the side talking to Violet, a vape pen hanging from his lips. "I heard you might need this." He holds a five-dollar bill in his outstretched hand. "Try smiling one of these days, and you might earn your own." He winks.

"Go to hell, man," Griff says tightly.

"Ignore him. The rest of us do," Violet says, shoving Cannon up the dock.

Sofía turns to me. "So that's a yes to the fundraiser?"

"No thanks." I duck my head, hoping to hide the disappointment in my eyes.

"If this is because of what that Cannon said, ignore him. Just 'cause a guy is eye candy doesn't mean he's worth speaking to. No offense," she says to Griff.

"It's not Cannon's fault," I say. And it isn't. I just can't handle that much unplanned social pressure. I'm not Gemma 2.0, the girl who kisses Beau in my Fourth of July fantasies. Not to mention the fact that I get to spend my evening manufacturing evidence of a relationship that doesn't exist. "I just—can't." My voice cracks as emotion makes my throat ache.

Griff's uncertain eyes flick to my face. He frowns.

"Are you sure?" Sofía asks.

"I'm sure. No worries. You guys have fun."

Sofía jogs to catch up with Violet and Cannon while Griff and I sign our time sheets. After, we amble out of the shack and into the early evening sun. I wait a beat, giving him time to leave without me so we won't be stuck in one of those are-we-or-aren't-we-walking-together nightmares. But he also waits a beat, probably trying to avoid the same thing. And then we end up walking near each other, and despite our height and leg-length difference, we reach the parking lot at the same time.

We split with a mildly awkward head nod and I trek to my car at the back of the lot. Inside Sunday's sweltering cab, I crank the air-conditioning and wait for the steering wheel to cool down. Once upon a time I had an electric-blue steering wheel cover that looked like it came straight from the back of a *Sesame Street* character, but I tossed it when it started to shed. Fortunately, I still have a pink fuzzy pom-pom on my key ring, for flair. It has a monster face and everything.

My eyes wander to Griff's car as Sunday churns toasty air straight into my face. To my surprise, it hasn't moved. Curious, I watch as he exits the car and lifts the hood. I gingerly touch the steering wheel, relieved to find that it's now just *hot* instead of *blistering*.

I ease off the clutch, drive over to him, and crank the window down. "Everything okay?"

He kicks a tire and growls in frustration. "Car won't start."

"What's wrong with it?"

He shoves both hands into his already messy hair, clasping his fingers on top of his head. "It's twenty years old and I drove it across the country on a bad battery and no oil?"

"You need a ride?"

He kicks the car again, swearing when it hurts. "I'm working in fifteen minutes. The restaurant will be packed tonight."

The fundraiser is the last place I want to be, but I can't leave him here alone in the heat. Especially not after he tried to help me. I reach across the center console to manually unlock Sunday's passenger door and push it open. "Hop in."

Chapter 11

The population of Page, Arizona, is about 7,500 people, and from the looks of it, every single one of them is at Booker Brothers' Pizza tonight. The parking lot is filled with cars and—I notice with a shock of dread—two giant news vans. Posters with Beau's face are taped to the restaurant windows. They read HELP PAY BEAU'S MEDICAL BILLS!

"Wow," I breathe. Tears prick the corners of my eyes as the awful reality of Beau's situation hits me for the hundredth time. "People love your family."

"People love my brother," Griff corrects me as he opens the door. "Thanks for the ride."

"Now we're even again. You taught me how to make tips—or tried to anyway. I gave you a ride."

"You don't sound very happy with my performance."

"I'm not blaming you. It's my faulty wiring."

"Come on." He rolls his eyes.

"What?"

"Stop fishing for compliments."

I bite my lip as my cheeks—terrible, traitorous cheeks—turn red. "I will when you stop whining about how people like Beau more than you."

He laughs. "Can't. Sorry. It's part of my DNA." He holds the grab handle above his head and leans into the truck to touch the fuzzy pom-pom hanging from my keys. "This is hideous."

"I like it."

"What's to like?"

"I never lose my keys in my purse. Plus, it has a face." I turn the ball of fuzz so Griff can see the googly eyes. One is hanging on by a very thin strand of glue.

"That's the ugliest thing I've ever seen in my life. Please tell me it at least has sentimental value."

"My dad won it for me from one of those claw machines after my mom died. He spent twenty dollars in quarters trying to win it because he thought it'd cheer me up."

Griff winces. "I'm so sorry—"

I laugh. "I'm messing with you. I bought it last summer from the Maverik."

He frowns and gives me a knowing look. "From Lizzie Spalding?"

My stomach tightens. "Yeah."

He reaches out to touch the fuzz ball again and my stomach sours with disappointment. It's clear he doesn't want to go to the fundraiser, but he wouldn't want to kill time with me either if he knew the truth.

"BOO!" One of the little Booker boys appears under Griff's arm. It's Noah, the younger one with the mess of blond curls and a pizza-sauce grin. I jump in my seat, which he *loves*. He laughs like I'm John Mulaney. "Who are you?" He cocks his head to the side, curls falling across his face.

"This is Gemma—Beau's girlfriend," Griff says.

"Is she staying?"

"No," Griff answers quickly.

Beau's other little brother knocks on my window and waves with both hands. I roll the window down. "I have a new Pokémon card. Do you want to see it?" he asks.

"Sure!"

"That's Bennett," Griff says as his brother passes a Pokémon card through the window. The creature on it looks like a black mop with a pumpkin for a butt. "And this is Noah." He ruffles the curls of the little one.

"I know that!"

"Right. I forgot about you and Beau for a second."

"Very cool," I say, handing the card back to Bennett.

"I traded for it!" He puffs his chest out.

Mrs. Booker steps up to the window, her hair pulled back into a tight ballerina bun on the top of her head. "Gemma! You came!" She leans in to hug me through the open window. She smells like yeast and pizza and I'm almost disappointed when she lets go. "Everyone will be so happy to see you!"

"To see me where?" I ask uneasily.

"At the fundraiser."

Noah opens my door and impatiently tugs on my hand. "I'll come back when you're less busy—" I say, but somehow, I'm out of the truck with a little Booker brother hanging off each arm.

"Nonsense!" Mrs. Booker says as she closes Sunday's door while the boys drag me through a maze of parked cars.

Griff strides easily behind us, smirking at my desperation.

"It's hard for me to talk about the accident," I call over my shoulder.

"We won't talk about that. Tonight is a celebration; no tears allowed," Mrs. Booker insists. "Beau will wake up soon and he'll kill me if he knew the whole town was sitting around crying over him."

"Have you met your son?" Griff asks.

Bennett pushes the door open, and the intoxicating smell of cheese and garlic knocks me out. I inhale; I can't believe no one has bottled this to sell as perfume. I'd have more friends if I smelled like this. The air is cool, and the lights are dim; checkered tablecloths and red brick give the place a homey, old-fashioned vibe.

"Gemma!" Mr. Booker's voice booms from the corner booth of the crowded restaurant. He's standing on the bench seat and waves me over to him. "Get up here!" The buzz of chatter hushes. From the corner of the room, a news camera swivels my way, and I want to die.

I turn, desperate for help, but Griff is gone. A wave of nausea rolls through me and my knees tremble as the boys lead me over to their dad. Mr. Booker holds out a hand to help me onto the bench opposite him. I climb on unsteady legs and wipe my sweaty palms on my shorts.

He claps his hands for attention and addresses his patrons. "Welcome to Booker Brothers. My wife and I are incredibly thankful for the outpouring of love and support we've felt since Beau's accident. You've kept our small family business running for the last fifteen years, and we're so grateful for the continued support, especially as we face the enormous challenge of Beau's medical bills. He's not out of the woods yet, but his team is happy with the reduction of swelling they're seeing in his brain." A cheer goes up from the crowd. I bite my bottom lip and do my best not to pass out. "Before you get back to your dinner, I want to say a public thank-you to this young lady on my left." He points to me, and the restaurant breaks into a round of applause. "That's right—" He points to the news camera, and I noticed Karly freaking Wallace standing next to another reporter, watching me with interest. "She's not only a hero, she's also Beau's girlfriend." Laughter, whistles, and applause ring through the building. From a table in the middle of the restaurant, Sofía waves with both hands.

"And finally, as a thank-you to the community, the Beau Booker special is twenty-five percent off tonight. Gemma, do you want to tell everyone about the Beau Booker special?" He motions to me. I can hardly breathe.

The crowd quiets in anticipation. I spot the second news camera on the other side of the restaurant, and it's also pointed at me. Tears burn behind my eyes. I shake my head. "I don't know," I whisper.

"What's that?" Mr. Booker booms.

"I don't know," I say louder. Tears spill over my cheeks, and Mr. Booker's eyes widen with alarm.

"That's okay!" He laughs awkwardly. I don't blame him. Dads don't know what to do with tears. "We'll let you try again. Tell everyone Beau's drink of choice and we'll let them have that for twenty-five percent off in addition to the spaghetti calzone, which is Beau's favorite, by the way."

I squeeze my eyes tight and search for any memory of Beau drinking. Nothing. My mind is a void. I shake my head again. "I—I don't know." Tears spill over my molten-hot cheeks. Two hundred people, including every member of the Booker family, Sofía, Violet, Cannon, and two news cameras are all here to witness my humiliation.

Whispers spread through the crowd, which makes Mr. Booker uneasy. "Why don't you tell us something you *do* know about my son!" His laugh is strained. "His favorite video game? Ice cream flavor? His time in the hundred-yard butterfly?"

"54.43," Ian yells from a table in the back. "He never shuts up about it!"

Mr. Booker looks at me expectantly.

"I—I—the thing is—" A wave of nausea crawls up the back of my throat. "I'm gonna be sick." My hands fly to my mouth.

Mr. Booker's eyes widen in horror. "Bathroom's that way!" He points to the far corner of the restaurant. It's too far. I'll never make it.

"I need a bucket!"

Customers at the closest tables leap up from their seats and back away. A cleaning bucket is thrust in my face and I double over it and vomit into the dirty water. Gasps and groans ripple through the restaurant.

A hand lightly holds my hair back. "Cherry Sprite on the house, in honor of Beau!" Griff's rough voice carries easily through the crowd. I wipe my mouth and glance up to see him standing above me holding my hair with one hand and the bucket with the other. He smiles grimly. "Follow me."

He leads me back to the kitchen and opens the door to a small, crowded office. "You can wait in here until the cameras leave. Give me a few minutes and I'll bring you food." I'm too mortified to do anything but collapse in the padded chair behind the desk and let Griff shut the door on his way out.

I sink into the soft leather as a wave of exhaustion ripples through me. I text Dad to let him know that I'll sleep at the house tonight because the idea of driving all the way to the houseboat makes my brain numb with exhaustion. I lean my head against the chair and yawn, my eyelids growing heavy.

"Gemma." A whispered voice sends shivers over my skin. I open my eyes and lift my head, wiping a dribble of spit from my chin.

"What time is it?"

"Ten thirty." Griff is sitting on a chair on the other side of the desk, a dish towel slung over his shoulder. He pushes a steaming pizza toward me. "Sorry it took so long."

I push myself up as my poor overworked heart spasms with yet another wave of embarrassment. A hoodie slides off my body and lands in my lap. "Why didn't you wake me up?"

"You looked tired. I know what that is like." He stretches his arms above his head and yawns. "I also felt guilty for forgetting to take your dinner order, but I never had the opportunity to stop, wake you up, and actually take it. I was swamped all night."

I shiver as a blast of air-conditioning hits me from the vent above the desk. I pull the hoodie up around my arms. "Where'd this come from?"

He shrugs. I pull the black jacket around my torso and slip my arms inside. "Was I on the news?"

Griff grimaces and I bury my face in my hands. "How bad was it?"

"You looked nervous . . ." He hesitates, and I glance at him through my fingers. "And a little bit like you've never spoken to Beau in your life—"

I groan and pull the hoodie over my face.

"No, no, no. I'm just kidding. You looked fine."

"Liar."

"You looked . . . sad and overwhelmed. You looked honest." One corner of his mouth lifts, and I've never hated myself more than I do at this moment. "Eat," he says, nudging the plate toward me again.

"Did they at least cut out the vomiting?"

"Don't make me answer that." He lifts a slice of pizza and takes a bite. I study him from under my eyelashes. It's strange, the way he looks like Beau but also doesn't. They have the same shade of dark brown eyes, but Griff's are guarded in a way I've never seen in Beau. As if sensing my thoughts, Griff looks up at me. Unacceptably, blood rushes to my face again, and I break eye contact. I hate how often my body betrays me like that.

He leans back in his chair and rests an ankle up on his knee, and I can't help but think it should be Beau next to me instead of Griff. My heart sinks at the thought of him lying alone in a cold hospital room.

If Beau were here right now—I grimace as I realize the truth of the situation. If Beau were here, I'd be an absolute wreck. The anxiety I'm feeling now, times a million. He took all my neuroses and magnified them, making me feel the worst kind of wrong in my own body. There wasn't a word I spoke to him or a gesture I made that didn't make my skin feel turned inside out. I feel nervous and a bit awkward around Griff, but at least I'm not hopelessly in love with him.

Unable to stop myself, I glance up at Griff again. As always, his almost-black hair is falling into his eyes. He pushes it off his forehead, revealing dark brows underneath. I bite back a smile; he's constantly messing with his hair at work too.

I've passed the socially acceptable amount of time to stare at someone's face, but I can't quit. Griff has a sharp jaw, and a light dusting of facial stubble that does something funny to my stomach. Suddenly, sitting so close to him, it seems impossible that I never paid attention to him before. But I know why it happened; my eyes were always fixed on his brother. Beau has the open smile and easy-to-read expression of a boy who sails effortlessly through life. He makes high school look enviable, and maybe that's why I fell for him. Because he's everything I want to be. Griff, on the other hand, is impossible to read. He's either sporting a cocky smile or pretending to feel nothing at all, and each conversation we have makes me more curious than before.

He chews slowly, not looking at me. "Why'd you say no when Sofía invited you here tonight?"

"I didn't want to go."

He scoffs. "You're lying. I saw the way your eyes—" He clears his throat and shifts in his chair.

"What did my eyes do?" I demand, both curious and horrified.

"They—I don't know," he sighs. "They sparkled."

I burst out laughing and almost choke on a glob of greasy cheese. "They did not."

"Swear on my life." He laughs. "When Sofía asked you to hang out with them, you looked like you'd been named prom queen." He rolls his eyes, his tone dropping into one of derision.

My laughter dies in my throat as embarrassment burns through me. That eye roll told me everything I need to know about his opinion of me. "I bet you hate all that stuff. Prom king and popularity. High school dances and football games."

"Why do you say that?" He sets his plate on the desk and pulls a guitar pick from his pocket. He plays with it absentmindedly.

"I've heard things," I say.

His face darkens. "People in this town talk too much."

"I assumed you don't care what people think."

"I don't," he says quickly. "I really, *really* don't care what my dad or anyone in this patch of dirt thinks about me," he says with more conviction than I've ever said anything in my entire life. Goose bumps speckle my arms as I'm flooded with envy. I'd give *anything* to be wired that way. "I don't care what people say about me, but that doesn't mean I don't notice the stares and whispers."

"I'm sorry."

"That's not—" He shakes his head. "It's fine. Seriously. But I'll put my cards on the table right now: I'm not my brother. I'm not in the habit of charming anyone, or winning people over. If you've listened to the rumors and already made up your mind about me, that's fine."

I can't look at him. My face is burning. My whole body is burning, the tension in the air simmering uncomfortably. A long silence passes as we finish the whole pizza. I grow more desperate with each passing second.

When Griff stands to take the dirty dishes, I still haven't answered his unasked question.

"I haven't," I blurt, climbing awkwardly to my feet.

He cocks his head to the side, confused. *Brilliant, Gemma.* Maybe he'd forgotten. "I haven't made up my mind about you . . . yet."

He nods, stuffing his hands in his front pockets. "Anything you want to know?"

"Are the rumors true?" I don't know why I ask that. It's not even the thing I want to know. I guess it's just the easiest thing to ask, the most obvious. Anything else would betray my curiosity about him and Beau.

His smile is wry. "The rumors are terrible and cruel, but honey, most of them are true."

"Why does that sound familiar?"

"It's Taylor Swift. The girl can write a mean lyric."

I blink back my surprise. I'm not sure which shocks me more: the fact that he basically just admitted to sleeping with Ms. Rose, Page High's science teacher, or that he quoted Taylor Swift.

"And now?" he asks, eyes narrowed.

"Still deciding," I say, stifling a yawn.

"You should go home before your parents call the cops." He opens the door, and we walk into the kitchen. Griff quickly washes our dishes by hand and stacks them on a drying rack.

"My dad. And he won't. No one's home." I shrug one shoulder, aiming for nonchalance. I realize I'm still in the black hoodie, so I unzip it and drop it in a lost-and-found box sitting on the bottom shelf of a large rack of dishes. "I can pretty much come and go as I please, especially in the summer." I hope to sound breezy and cool, but my voice is strangled.

"Sounds like heaven," Griff says, without a hint of irony. He must see something on my face because his brow furrows. "Did I say something wrong?" He props open the back door and programs the alarm.

I shake my head as I step through the door, a gulp of warm air filling my lungs as we step out into the night. Dad's truck is in the parking lot, waiting to take me to a lonely house, and my chest aches at the thought. "We could not be more different, that's all."

Griff gives me a half smile and follows me to the truck. "Sounds like you're perfect for my brother, then."

Butterflies dance in my stomach as I remember the doodles I used to scrawl in the corner of my binder. *Beau and Gemma: MFEO.* Even Griff thinks so.

I climb into the cab and glance at Griff one last time over my shoulder. His face is in shadows, his body silhouetted by nearby streetlights.

"One more thing." His hand shoots out to hold the door open.

"I helped you at work. You gave me a ride. I made you dinner."

"Okay . . ." My word stretches into the still night air, unsure of his meaning. My eyes have adjusted to the dark enough to just make out his expression, but it's as inscrutable as always.

He winks. "That means you owe me one."

Chapter 12

For the next few days, all I care about is the article. Worrying about what the fact-checker will dig up on me becomes as natural as breathing. I set a "Gemma Wells" Google Alert to email me when it's posted, but that doesn't stop me from refreshing my browser every other breath. Whichever FBI agent is assigned to stalk my internet history must be flummoxed by the number of times I've visited the *Chronicle*, a website so dull that their current top article is the *Lake Powell Fish Report*. The government is likely flagging me for closer inspection now: *Teen girl has fish fetish. Watch closely.*

Yesterday, Karly sent a text asking about pictures I promised to send.

Tomorrow! I lied. **I'll send them tomorrow!**

Tomorrow turned into today, and I have nothing to show for these last twenty-four hours except an outbreak of stress canker sores and a handful of Photoshop fails. I look at my phone screen with a resigned sigh and call Nina.

Given our lack of recent communication, I'm shocked when she answers. She catches me up on camp counselor drama (a long, emotional saga revolving around two boys named Brayden and Jayden), and then tries to hang up.

"Wait! I'm sending you a picture and I need your honest opinion." I text her the least terrible of my edited photos and hold my breath while I wait for her to open it.

She cackles loudly at the doctored image of Beau and me on the beach. "What in the fresh hell is this?"

"Can you tell it's edited?"

"You're kidding, right? Why is your head so big? It's twice the size of his!"

"It's the closest match I could find!" I pull the phone away and inspect the picture again. Nina's right. My head looks like it's filled with helium.

"Why did you create this monstrosity? Are you that bored without me or did the sun finally fry your brain?" Nina asks.

"I did something stupid."

"I know. I'm staring at it."

"Not that. Something worse." Against my better judgment, I tell her everything that's happened between Beau's accident and now. I'm relieved to come clean about my new life, but as the story spills out, I'm overcome with the desire to crawl into the shower and pull the curtain over my head, even though she's hundreds of miles away.

"Gemma," she says seriously.

"I know." I hold my breath, waiting for the inevitable freak-out.

"You're the new Lizzie Spalding!"

"*I know!*" I bury my face in my hands, mortified. Nina is my only friend in the world and even she thinks I'm insane. That's got to be a bad sign.

"How are you pulling this off?"

"He's in a *coma*. It's not like he can call me out for lying."

"But it's *you*."

"Is it *that* unbelievable that I'd have a boyfriend?" I regret the words as soon as they're out of my mouth. I can barely maintain eye contact with Beau, let alone hold his hand or make out with him or whatever it is that functional couples do together.

"Come on, Gemma," Nina says. "This can't end well for you. What happens when he wakes up?"

He falls in love with me. The words appear unbidden. I've tried to ignore them, but it's happening more and more lately. Sometimes I spin elaborate fantasies about Beau waking up and learning that I saved his life. That I visited him in the hospital and spent time with his family and am friends with the same people as him. If I'm already part of his world, it's not so hard to imagine that our fake relationship will become a real one and no one will have to find out the truth. We *will* go to the Fourth of July party together, and he'll kiss me under the fireworks—

"Gemma? You still there?" Nina asks.

"Sorry!" I say, snapping out of the daydream. I know better than to say any of that out loud. "I'll worry about it when it happens."

"Whatever you do, you can't send that picture to the reporter. If she's already suspicious of you, that freaky photo will only make things worse."

I groan, furious with her for being right. "I know."

"Where'd you get the picture of him anyway?"

"The 'Family Camping' album on his mom's Facebook page."

Nina laughs. "If you try to Michael Scott your way into Beau's family vacation pictures, I'm never talking to you again."

That's fair, I guess. I wouldn't ditch her if *she* became the town laughingstock, but I don't blame her for wanting to avoid the controversy. I mentally add Nina to the list of people I'll lose if this goes south.

"You could always take a picture of you sitting next to him at the hospital," she says.

"Doesn't that feel slimy? Like I'm taking advantage of his injury?"

"Whatever. He won't know the difference. Anyway, I've gotta go. Keep me updated when this thing blows up in your face," she says, and suddenly I'm queasy for a reason that has nothing to do with the gentle sway of the floor beneath my feet.

Chapter 13

"How do I make you fall in love with me, Beau Booker?" I curl my legs under me on the chair next to Beau's bed. It's been almost a week since Nina told me to send Karly a hospital room selfie, but I haven't been able to do it. I'm not always a good person, but there are some lines I won't cross; Karly will have to do without her pictures. I stopped answering her calls, so I don't know if she plans to run the article without them.

Every day after my shift at the dock ends, I visit Beau in the ICU. On my days off (like today) I come in early. At first, I only stayed for a few minutes, but at each visit I've found it harder to pull myself out of the pleather chair next to his bed and face the real world.

The ICU nurses recognize me by now and have no problem with my visits, but they refuse to answer my questions about his progress. From what I understand, because Beau's coma is medically induced, it's up to the doctors to decide when to wake him up. No one will tell me when that's going to happen. Mrs. Booker is so relentlessly optimistic about Beau's condition that it's hard to trust what she says, and Griff doesn't say anything at all. I pester him for answers every day at work, but it's obvious he hates to talk about his brother. I suspect he's sad and doesn't know how to deal with his feelings. (A thought he did *not* enjoy hearing.)

I lean toward Beau, resting my arms on the side of his bed. "What am I going to do about you?" I ask. The beeping drone from his monitors is my only response.

Pretend we're close.

Those were his words. I cling to them like a life raft, hoping that one of the last things he said before the accident will be one of the first things he thinks about when he wakes up, and that when he realizes what I did for him, he'll fall in love with me.

"I realize that's a lot to ask," I say, transitioning the conversation in my head to one with Beau. "I'm awkward. I cancel plans at the last minute and get overwhelmed in crowds. Meeting new people makes my stomach hurt. I'm not the kind of girl anyone wants to bring to a party. I'd be a disastrous girlfriend."

My heart aches as I hear the truth out loud. Even if Beau agrees not to tell everyone I'm a liar, the chance of us having a successful relationship has never felt so far away. How am I supposed to be his (or anyone's) girlfriend when I'm plagued with constant anxiety?

How do I get rid of my anxiety when the world is just so damn scary?

"How do I fix myself?" I whisper to Beau. I open my phone and pull up Google with shaking fingers. I type the words that have been ricocheting around my brain for months.

Social anxiety disorder.

I tick all the boxes on the National Institute of Mental Health website:

Do you avoid meeting new people? *Yes.*

Are you very self-conscious in everyday social situations? *Absolutely.*

Are you extremely afraid of being judged by others? *Yes x infinity.*

The list of signs and symptoms is even more telling: blushing, sweating, mind going blank? *Check, check, check.*

I read articles about how SAD (the irony of that acronym should be illegal) is more than just shyness, and I feel vindicated. *That's Gemma; she's shy.* I've heard those words my entire life. I've said those words—but I knew in my bones it was more than that. The label "shy" was never one that felt right. Social anxiety feels better, like changing out of a damp swimsuit into dry sweatpants. And now that I have the language to describe what happens to me when I leave the house, I can fix myself.

And once I fix myself, I'll be ready to make Beau fall for me.

My heart beats hard with possibility as I swing my legs over the arm of the chair and settle in for more research. I read everything I can about the treatment for social anxiety disorder. Cognitive behavioral therapy, or CBT, is often recommended. I veto that as an option, as it would require not only an awkward conversation with Dad but also a pile of cash we don't have.

Antidepressants are sometimes recommended, as they can treat certain anxiety disorders. I don't bother reading much about that option. Dad's always been wary of medicine. We don't have anything stronger than 200mg Tylenol in our house, and he won't even take it when he has a headache. It took me a full four years of suffering from period cramps before I realized that I could take medicine to help. Dad sees the virtue in gritting your teeth and suffering through the pain. So no, he's not going to take me to a doctor and get me a prescription just so my palms are less sweaty when I'm in social situations.

Which leaves one option: facing my social fears head-on. Everything I read says the same thing: Avoidance makes it worse. The more I put myself in social situations, the more comfortable I should become.

The door opens, startling me out of my research. In walk Mrs. Booker and Beau's little sister, Winnie. Winnie's hair is hanging in her eyes and tangled like it hasn't been brushed in a week. Her shoulders are freckled from the sun and her knees are dirty, and I'm positive if I were closer, she'd smell of sunshine. I get a sick swoop of nostalgia in my stomach for a time when things were easier, when the scent of sunscreen and boat leather filled my days.

"Did you see that the article published?" Mrs. Booker asks. "They quoted me!"

"What?" My heart spasms and I check my email. Nothing. I'm never trusting Google Alert again. I refresh the *Chronicle* website and there it is. I wince at the headline. *Boyfriend*. My fingers tremble as I scroll.

TEEN GIRL SAVES BOYFRIEND FROM DROWNING AT LONE ROCK BEACH

PAGE, Arizona—Seventeen-year-old Page resident Gemma Wells saved fellow Page High student Beau Booker from drowning at Lone Rock Beach after he fell off the back of a friend's boat and hit his head on the motionless propeller.

"Gemma is our guardian angel. We're so grateful for her relationship with our son," said Mrs. Booker. "Not to mention her quick thinking and CPR skills," added Mr. Booker, owner of Booker Brothers' Pizza, located on Lake Powell Boulevard.

"No one else saw him fall. He probably would have died if Gemma hadn't been there," Beau's friend Ian Radnor said.

"[Gemma] never comes to our beach parties. No one knew why she was there until she saved Beau's life and admitted that they've been dating in secret. It feels like fate brought the two of them together to save Beau's life," said Gemma and Beau's classmate Sofía Lopez.

Gemma and Beau started dating this February, as confirmed by Gemma. They had their first date at Sonic on Valentine's Day, and since then they've been known to cruise the lake together on Gemma's family's boat. "I never imagined anything like Beau's accident would happen," Gemma said.

Even though Gemma and Beau were keeping their relationship under wraps, it seems young love may have saved his life. He's currently sedated at Page Hospital while swelling in his brain is monitored, but doctors say he has an excellent chance at making a full recovery.

(Image Left: Beau and Gemma at Lone Rock Beach;

Image Right: Gemma at a fundraiser to help with Beau's medical bills.)

I drop my shoulders for the first time in days, and the muscles ache from the tension I've been holding there. I feel instant relief. It could have been so much worse. There's no mention of the Valentine's Day mix-up *or* my refusal to send photos.

I might be getting away with this. *(Take that, Nina!)*

"How's our boy doing?" Mrs. Booker asks brightly as she crosses the room and pulls open the curtain to allow sunlight to flood the room.

"The nurses won't tell me anything."

"He looks good, though, doesn't he? His color looks better than yesterday!" Mrs. Booker smiles brightly and turns to me for confirmation. I glance at Beau; he looks the same to me, but I nod anyway.

"Did you bring this?" She points to a new Get Well Soon card on the table next to Beau. I shake my head. She picks it up. Her smile slips as she reads.

"Who's it from?" Winnie asks.

"It's not signed," Mrs. Booker says, and puts the card facedown on the table. "Has Griff been here today?" she asks me.

"I haven't seen him."

"I better check with the nurses," she mutters to herself. "Winnie, grab something for you and Gemma from the vending machine." Mrs. Booker hands Winnie her credit card before leaving.

"My favorite food in the world is this strawberry pastry thing that they only sell in the hospital vending machines.

I lived on them a couple of years ago," Winnie says.

I'm only partially listening; I'm dying to pick up that card and find out what knocked the determined smile off Mrs. Booker's face. "What happened a couple of years ago?" I ask absently while glancing at the card.

She fixes me with a look that makes it clear I'm the biggest idiot on Planet Earth. I shrivel under her condescending stare and wait for death. "How long have you been dating my brother?" With her hand on her hip like that she's a formidable opponent.

"Not—not that long."

"Huh."

I swallow. "What?"

"It's just that I only had a crush on Kyson Reyes for a week and I knew more about his family than you know about ours." Again, *the look*. Geez, she's terrifying.

"How old are you?"

"Nine."

I need to distract her. "Aren't you too young for crushes?"

"How come you don't know anything about me?"

"I, um, I didn't—"

"I had cancer." She wrinkles her nose and I feel my face fall. "Leukemia. It's the most common kind. I'm fine now."

"I'm so sorry, Winnie. Beau never told me."

She narrows her eyes. She doesn't believe me. I wipe my sweaty palms on my shorts, which she one hundred percent notices. The girl could be a detective.

"I'll be back." She follows her mom into the hall, leaving me alone. With one eye on the door, I pick up the card.

Beau,
I'm sorry for the beginning and the end,
but never for the middle. Wake up soon.
Love always, D

Why did Mrs. Booker say the card was unsigned? Is it because she doesn't know who "D" is?

The door opens and I put the card facedown on the table again. Mrs. Booker is all smiles. "If Beau's vitals stay stable and his swelling continues to go down at the current rate, they plan to wake him up in three weeks!"

My heart spasms at the sudden deadline.

I have three weeks to turn myself from a socially awkward potato into the kind of girl Beau will want to date. Twenty-one days to face all my biggest social fears. No biggie!

"Come to dinner tonight to celebrate!" Mrs. Booker insists. "We still need to properly thank you for saving Beau."

Every instinct in my body tells me to say no. Which is how I know that if I'm going to get over my anxiety and win Beau's heart, I need to say yes.

That evening, I slide open the glass door and walk to the deck of the houseboat. Dad is sitting with his feet on the rail, fishing rod propped against it, a paperback spy thriller in his lap. "Going somewhere?"

"Dinner at the Bookers'."

"How's he doing?" he asks. "They think he'll wake up soon?"

"If his stats stay stable, he should be awake in a couple of weeks."

"Will I get to meet him?" Dad looks at me now, and he appears so viscerally uncomfortable with the prospect that I can't help but laugh.

"Maybe. Eventually."

He nods again, looking slightly relieved. "I had to ask. It's my job as your parent."

"I know." I hold my fist out for a bump. After he does, I turn to leave.

He clears his throat, stopping me in my tracks. "I've had an offer to buy the business."

"What?" Panic makes my head spin. "Since when do you want to sell the business?"

"It'd go a hell of a long way toward putting you through college."

"I don't want to go to college!"

He raises both eyebrows. "What *do* you want?"

"I don't know! Maybe college—but I'll find another way to pay for it. You can't quit your job!"

"I'd work full-time at the marina. We'd be fine."

"This makes no sense. You love running boat tours more than anything!"

"Not more than you," he says quietly. It's so sincere I can't even look at him. "I built this business for you. I thought you'd work with me and eventually take over, but if selling is a better way to secure your future—"

"It's not!" My throat swells painfully. How do I tell him that the thing I want more than anything—to spend every day of my life on the water—is also the thing that scares me the most? The lake is the only place where I'm not plagued by anxiety. I don't want that to change. "When do you have to decide?"

"By the end of the summer. I'll be honest, kid. I'm considering it."

I dig my fingernails into my palms as a bead of sweat drips down my back. "I'm nervous about tonight. I'm nervous a lot. Whenever I meet new people or am in a big group. It makes it so I don't like to do things," I confess, hoping he'll understand that I'm talking about not just tonight but also his business. My heart is a jackhammer in my throat as I wait for his response. *I need help* are the unsaid words that stick in my throat.

"Chin up, sweetie. I used to be like that, but look at me now." He gestures to his fishing rod and his book. "You'll be fine."

My sandals slap against the dock as I leave, and when I get to the end, I turn again. I'm not sure what I'm expecting to see, but the familiar sight of Dad sitting alone on the deck causes a lump to rise in my throat, and it occurs to me, for maybe the first time in my life, that Dad might be as lonely as I am.

Chapter 14

"Gemma!" Little Noah Booker throws his arms around my legs after he opens the door. His curly hair obscures his eyes, and his gap-toothed smile is smeared dark purple.

"Let me guess," I say, crouching until I'm eye level with him. I take his chin in my fingers and gently inspect his face. "You ate berries today."

He grins. "You're wrong!"

"Am I, though?"

"I had a smoothie!"

"With berries in it?"

His eyes widen in surprise and he freezes for a second before laughing and nodding. He takes my hand and drags me into the family room, where Bennett is sitting next to a mound of paper airplanes. Mr. and Mrs. Booker wave from the kitchen, and Winnie is sitting upside down in an armchair, her legs stretched out over the back, her head hanging by the footrest, a tablet in her hand.

"Hi, Winnie!"

She flips right side up and eyes me skeptically. She's obviously still thinking about our disastrous conversation at the hospital, and I have a plan for that. "I brought you something!" I open the messenger bag I brought for this purpose and pull out a pack of chunky, sparkly hair clips that I bought at Walmart on my way here. I'm not above a little bribery.

Her eyes widen as she runs her fingers over a fake crystal the size of a penny. "Are these real diamonds?"

"Uh . . . no." I hold my breath while she appraises them. After a beat she pulls her hair out of her eyes and secures it with three clips.

"Do I look fancy?"

"Very fancy."

"Thanks! I love them!"

"You're welcome."

"Gemma Gemma Gemma!" Bennett throws an airplane at me and it bounces off my stomach. "You're on my team! What color airplane do you want? Pink because you're a girl?"

With one last look down the hall, I kneel on the carpet with the boys. The Booker home is small and cozy, filled with furniture that looks like it's been well loved for the last twenty years. My house never manages to feel like anything other than the place where we wait during the months it's too cold to sleep on the houseboat.

"I don't want pink just because I'm a girl." I survey the sea of planes and my eye catches on one at the bottom of the pile. "But yes, I would like this one, please." I pick up a hot-pink plane with the name PINK POWER written in shaky letters across one wing and toss it into the air.

"That one's mine! You can play with it," Noah proudly declares, and my heart warms. In the first years after Mom died, I was happy not to have siblings because it meant that I didn't have to share Dad with anyone. And then eventually, I stopped thinking about it altogether. But now I realize I should have been parent-trapping him this whole time, scheming to set him up with someone who could have given me an adorable little brother or sister who would worship me. If nothing else, siblings have got to be good for the self-esteem.

"I won!" Bennett declares.

"No, I won!" Noah says.

"You're a butt!"

Noah bursts into tears. "I hate you!"

Then again, maybe not?

"Dinner's ready!" Mr. Booker calls from the backyard after twenty minutes of plane noises and races and breaking up fights.

"Is Griff coming?" I whisper to Winnie as the kids and I head to the backyard.

"Griff never eats with us." She picks up our conversation where we left off before my shameless bribe. "Not since he broke Beau's nose."

"Excuse me?" I hiss under my breath.

"Last year Griff punched Beau in the face and knocked out two of his teeth." She mimes the punch and points to the two front teeth. "His nose is all crooked now. Mom and Dad took Beau to the doctor and when they came back, Griff was gone."

"Why were they fighting?"

She shrugs. "No one would tell me because I'm 'too little.'" She punctuates the sentence with angry air quotes.

We step into the backyard, where an angry-eyes Mr. Booker mans the grill. "Where's Griff?"

"Leave it alone." His wife puts her hand on his arm.

"If he can't get his act together, he can find somewhere else to stay. We have company!"

"Which is why you need to let it go," she says tightly. I close my eyes, wishing for something to put me out of my misery. A meteor, maybe. It's bad enough to witness confrontation; it's even worse when the subject is me.

Mr. Booker fumes through dinner, but it's not such a bad time now that he's stopped talking. We eat hamburgers on the back patio around a charming, uneven firepit. Bistro lights crisscross overhead between large citrus trees, and the yard is strewn with water guns, broken pieces of chalk, and a fleet of toy dump trucks. I'm enchanted by the cozy business of it, but I can't stop myself from glancing back at the house, wondering why Griff never eats with his family.

"Gemma, have you ever played cornhole?" Bennett asks me through a mouth of barbecue chips.

"I sure have."

"Have you ever played Cover Your Assets?" Noah asks.

"Nope."

"Have you ever played swamp spies? We made that one up."

"Never!" I exclaim, and the boys shout over each other as they explain how to play. It has approximately five thousand rules and as far as I can tell, there's no way to win.

"No one cares about your stupid game!" Winnie announces loudly.

"Nice words only!" Mrs. Booker admonishes. "Gemma, tell us something about yourself."

I shudder involuntarily. I hate that question as much as I hate icebreaker games. "I have to use the restroom. Excuse me." I abandon my plate and rush inside. In the bathroom, I splash lukewarm water on my face (tap water doesn't get cool in the summer) and lean over the sink, praying they'll forget about me while I'm gone. While I wait, the sound of music floats through the crack under the door. I turn off the faucet and stand still, straining to hear. The smooth, wistful melody draws me in, and before I know it, I'm tiptoeing down the hall. At the end of the hall, a door is open a crack, and I peek inside. Griff is playing the guitar, his fingers dancing over the strings, his head down, hair falling into his eyes.

Griff's sad song ends, and he picks it up with something else. Still mellow. Still in the same steady style, with a slight country twang, but it lights up all the nerves in my body, making me want to dance. Instead, I watch. Riveted. My eyes are glued to Griff. Only his profile is visible, a pick stuck between his teeth.

"Are you gonna come in, or just stand there and listen?" Griff asks around the pick, his eyes never rising to meet mine.

Blood rushes to my face, and I want to melt into a puddle and evaporate into the atmosphere, never to be heard from again.

He removes the pick and tucks it swiftly in his pocket before resuming his song. "Either is fine, but a guy could get self-conscious, with you hovering like that," he says, his fingers still strumming, looking undisturbed. *He's* self-conscious? I'm embarrassment personified. The living embodiment of awkward shame.

Griff stretches out a leg and nudges the door open with his foot, leaving me with only two choices: accept his invitation, or run from the house, quit my job, leave town, change my identity, and never look him in the eyes again.

I choose the former. *Barely.*

I step over the threshold, and my plan ends there. There are two beds in the room, and my stomach sinks with the realization that this is also Beau's room. One side of the room is decorated with a few foreign-to-me sports posters and a calendar still show-ing May. Must be Beau's side, then. That calendar and the layer of dust on his nightstand is crushingly sad. I glance at Griff's bed, and the wall above it. It's empty, and somehow almost as sad. Now that I'm in the room, the only place to sit is on either Griff's bed or Beau's bed, both of which make me want to *die.* So I stand, arms wrapped around myself. *Should I lean a shoulder against the wall?* I do, and then just as quickly—I don't. *No. Nope. Not gonna do that.*

Griff watches this all with an expression of mild interest and/or amusement, his fingers still strumming.

"Sorry I was listening," I say.

"You apologize a lot."

"I do?"

He nods.

"Is that a bad thing?"

He shrugs. "Up to you. But you don't have to apologize to me."

"Ever?" I roll my eyes.

"Ever," he says confidently.

"What if I do something terrible?" *Like lie to you and your whole family.*

"Trust me, I've done worse." He tips his head back, his eyes closed and his strumming growing louder, his fingers skipping across the strings. It's relaxing enough that some of the tension eases out of my muscles. Still avoiding his bed, I sit on the floor, my legs tucked up under me.

Watching him play like that feels like an invasion of his privacy. Emotion swells inside me, and it feels like embarrassment, but it's not that. I don't have a name for it, but it makes my insides feel squirmy, so I close my eyes and lean my head against the wall. The music washes through me, slow and steady, somehow electrifying and relaxing at the same time. I feel like all my bones have fallen loose. When Griff starts humming, hope squeezes my heart. *Please sing.* I'd give anything to know the lyrics to this song. But he doesn't sing, and too soon, the song ends.

When I open my eyes, Griff's hand is resting on his guitar and he's watching me. I fiddle with the unraveling hem of my T-shirt, staring at it like it's the most fascinating thing in the room. Sharing this small space with him feels so different from laughing together on the dock. I don't know if it's the walls or the beds or the music, but something between us shifted when I stepped in here. "What are you playing?"

"Jason Isbell."

"I liked it," I say honestly.

Interest sparks in his eyes. He leans forward. "Do you know him?"

"Should I? Is he from here or something?"

Griff shakes his head with a laugh, and my cheeks burn as I realize my mistake. "He's pretty famous. One of the greatest songwriters working today," he says.

"Him and Taylor Swift?"

Griff's eyes spark again. "Him and Taylor Swift," he agrees, his fingers absentmindedly strumming.

"Beau's a fan of Post Malone, and you're more of a singer-songwriter guy. Is that what you meant about being opposites?"

Griff's fingers still at the mention of his brother. He sighs and sets the guitar down, rubbing his hands over his face. "That's one of many examples, sure." The lightness from before vanishes from his face. I should drop the subject, but I find I'm desperate to know more. "What else is different about you two?"

"I'll tell you some other time," he says, and it sounds more like a promise than a brush-off. He picks the guitar back up, and I wonder if he's also confused about what to do with himself in this situation.

"I wish I could sing," I confess. I blame the music. It makes me feel uncharacteristically brave.

"Who says you can't."

"Trust me. I can't and I don't. Except when I'm alone in the car, pretending I'm in front of ten thousand screaming fans." I stop short of telling him that I'm usually belting love songs, and that his brother is always front and center in the crowd. The cheesiest of all the cheesy rom-com clichés.

"I do that too," he says.

"Sing something now!"

"No."

"Does it make you nervous?"

"Sure, but that's not why." He brushes it off, like nerves aren't a good reason to avoid something. Or *all the things*.

"Are you waiting for me to guess, or . . . ?"

"I'm not letting your first Isbell exposure be through my fumbling filter."

"You didn't sound fumbling to me," I say, my face hot.

"No?" He smirks. "How'd I sound?"

"Proficient."

He tips his head back, laughing. "Fair enough. I'll play for you later, but only after you've heard his songs the way they were meant to be heard."

I bite back a smile, excited by the prospect. "Where do I start?"

"I'll text you my suggestions. What's your phone number?"

We pull our phones out of our pockets and exchange numbers, and I'm hit with the memory of standing next to another Booker brother while he used his phone to take a picture of us. On an awkward scale of one to ten, that was a twenty-five. Talking with Griff is a measly seven. Seven is nothing. My hands aren't even sweating.

Maybe there's something to this exposure therapy after all. I'll practice with Griff, and if—no, *when*—Beau wakes up, I'll transfer all my newly acquired social skills to him. *What could go wrong?*

"How many songs is too many? I wanna send you all the good ones, but maybe I should just start with the three *best* ones. This is going to be impossible. What do you—" Griff's excited grin slips when he looks at me. "What happened?" he asks, frowning. "Your face just got all sad." He leans in and I make the mistake of eye contact. Guilt explosion.

"Nothing. I—" I don't mean to do it, but my eyes flick to Beau's bed. His gaze follows mine, and I feel more than see the moment Beau's memory enters the room.

"Oh." Griff rocks back on his heels. "I almost forgot, for a second."

"Forgot what?"

He releases a breath. "That you're his girl."

My heart stops. And then my phone—still clutched in my hands—buzzes.

"Answer it," he says.

I look at the text from Sofía. "Sofía and a bunch of people are going cliff jumping."

"You have to go."

"No way."

Griff looks at me, one eyebrow raised. I open my eyes wide and stare back. "Zero sparkle," I say.

He squints and leans in close, pretending to inspect my eyes for this mysterious sparkle he swears he saw. "If you say so." One side of his mouth kicks up. It's a shot of serotonin straight to my bloodstream.

I wrestle with my own grin and remember my new goal to do the things that scare me. "What the hell. Let's jump off a cliff."

Chapter 15

Griff and I said quick goodbyes to his family, changed into swim-suits (I always have at least one in the truck), and left. Just like that! I'm being spontaneous and social! There's a good chance I'm going to be sick to my stomach in the next ten minutes, but for now, I grip the steering wheel hard, savoring the feeling of blood thrumming through my veins.

"Why didn't you eat dinner with your family?"

"I don't want to talk about it," Griff says.

"Your dad seemed kinda pissed that you weren't there."

"And I *really* don't want to talk about that."

I search for another topic of conversation. My eyes land on my messenger bag in the back seat.

"Oh! I got you something!"

"Consider me intrigued."

"It's in that bag."

He turns, grabs it, and pulls out his gift: a new red LAKE POWELL FUEL shirt. He shakes the T-shirt open and holds it up in front of him. It's an XXL, and at least two sizes bigger than the bicep-hugging one he wears on the docks. He cocks one eyebrow and looks at me, waiting for an explanation.

"You made me dinner; I bought you a shirt that actually fits.

Now we're even again." I wink and in the ringing silence that follows, my heart spasms. But then Griff bursts into laughter and the sound pops the bubble of anxiety in my chest.

"You know what this means?" he asks seriously.

"What?"

"You just admitted to checking me out in my perfectly fitting shirt." He flexes and my cheeks turn pink.

I'm still flushed when we pull off the road and the tires crunch on gravel ten minutes later, although my stomach is in anxious knots for an entirely different reason. I assumed we'd be meeting up with Sofía and a few of her friends, but the cliffside is crawling with people. At least a dozen cars are parked in a line on the edge of the road. Any of these people could be the mysterious "D" who left a note by Beau's bedside. The bravery I felt back at Griff's house vanishes, leaving me filled with preemptive regret.

I groan and let my head fall to the steering wheel. My forehead slams on the horn and a loud blast sounds. "I can't get out of the car."

"You don't want to—or you can't?"

"Can't. Physically. This was a terrible idea. I could easily name a hundred things that could go wrong."

Griff rolls his eyes. "If you can name one hundred things that could go wrong, I'll happily leave with you."

"One—I jump off the cliff and my swimsuit falls off in the water and sinks before I can find it. Two—I belly flop and break all the blood vessels in my face. Three—my top falls off when I jump, but I don't realize it until I've climbed out of the water and showed everyone my naked . . . chest." (I cannot say the word *boobs* in front of Griff Booker.) "Four—a fish touches my foot underwater. Five—"

"Hang on! What's wrong with a fish touching your foot?"

"I hate fish. If a fish touches any part of my body, I *will* freak out."

Griff grins. He's *loving* this. "Continue."

"Five—I slip on a rock and knock out a tooth. Six—I get so nervous that I throw up. Seven—" *I start my period. Everyone realizes it but me.* "Trust me, you don't want to hear seven. Eight—I try to make a joke that is so unfunny everyone immediately goes silent. Nine—I fart in the water and bubbles appear next to me." Griff howls with laughter. "Ten—I get a bad swimsuit wedgie and my choices are either let everyone see my butt or witness me picking my own wedgie. Eleven—my swimsuit is unexpectedly sheer when wet. Twelve—my swimsuit is unexpectedly glow-in-the-dark and has the word *tasty* written across the butt."

Griff doubles over with laughter. He holds up his hands to stop me while he wheezes. "Half of these things would never, ever happen."

"Thirteen—I get lost in the dark and have to call my dad to come save me. Fourteen—I come up from the water and have snot running down my face. Fifteen—I scream way too loud when I jump, and someone records it. Sixteen—everyone else goes skinny-dipping and I have to decide between being naked and being the outcast. Seventeen—a scorpion crawls into my swimsuit and I pull it down to get the scorpion off me."

"A lot of these revolve around you being naked."

"Correct. Eighteen—"

"Okay, okay, I surrender! I have full confidence that you could imagine one hundred terrible scenarios."

"Thank you." I turn the key in the ignition.

Griff covers my hand with his. "Wait. How did you do that?"

"I'm always doing that."

His brows contract. "How do you have time to think about anything else?"

"I don't." We stare at each other for a beat too long.

"Stay," Griff says. "It'll be fun."

I glance out the window with a sigh. I hate this. My brain reacts to every social event the same way. *Danger!* it screams. *They might not like you. Danger! You might feel alone. Danger! You're safer at home.*

And what has a lifetime of safety earned me? Nothing but loneliness. I pull the key out of the ignition with a sigh. "If anyone sees me naked—"

"You never have to speak to me again," he promises as we climb out of the truck.

"You made it!" Sofía trots over.

"There are so many people here." I rub my hands up and down my arms even though it's not cold.

"Isn't it great? Have you jumped here before? There's an amazing spot just down that way." She points to a worn path leading over the edge of the cliff. A splash echoes through the canyon, followed by cheers. "Let's go! I'm sweating to death."

Griff and I follow her to the edge of the cliff, where Cannon is eyeing a group of girls. He raises an eyebrow when he sees me. "Who invited you?"

My cheeks blaze in the dusky light as all my fears are confirmed. No one wants me here. Griff mumbles something to Cannon low under his breath and places a hand on my elbow. "Ignore him. He sucks."

I fight the urge to run; the last thing I want to do is give Cannon the satisfaction of scaring me off. Griff and I turn and climb backward ten feet down, until we stop on a sandstone ledge jutting out over water the color of gunmetal. The sun is low over the horizon, casting shadows against the rocks. We join the line of people waiting to throw themselves over the edge.

"What is Griff doing here?" Sofía whispers with a glance over her shoulder.

"I was having dinner with the Bookers when you texted me."

"How's Beau? Any update?"

"If his vitals are stable and his swelling keeps going down at its current rate, they'll try to wake him up in three weeks." My stomach lurches at the new deadline. It feels simultaneously like an eternity and like a blip in the timeline. Only twenty-one days to make myself into a new, non-anxious person. The kind of girl he'd be interested in while conscious.

"Who are all these people?" My unease grows as I vow to keep my mouth shut around anyone and everyone. I dodged a bullet with the fact-checker, probably because a few busy adults don't care that much about whether I did or didn't go on a date with Beau on Valentine's Day. But high school students? If I slip up and say the wrong thing, they *will* care. Outcast girl lies about dating the most popular guy in school (while he's in a coma!) will be the juiciest gossip Page High has ever heard.

Sofía rattles off the names of everyone here tonight, including several people from school and a bunch who work at the marina. The name that catches my attention is the one that starts with *D*.

Deja Jackson. She and Kodi are perched at the top of the cliff, their legs hanging over the edge as they observe the jumpers. I wonder if she left the card in the ICU.

"Did Deja and Beau ever date?"

Sofía laughs. "I doubt it, considering Deja's gay. She's dating Kodi. I can't believe you didn't know that!"

My cheeks burn. Mental note: *Don't try to figure out who D is. I'll only embarrass myself in the process.*

I spin away from Sofía to cover my embarrassment. "Will you tighten my top?" I pin my swimsuit to my chest with my forearms while Sofía reties the top. "A few years ago, I was tubing and lost my top and bottoms when I wiped out. I've been paranoid ever since." There's no panic quite like scrambling through dark water for lost swimsuit pieces.

"If you lose your clothes, I'll lose mine in solidarity," Sofía says as she pulls the strings of my bikini top into a tight bow.

"Please don't." My body shudders in revolt. The idea of seeing anyone else naked is the opposite of comforting. I might spontaneously combust.

Sofía and I step to the edge of the outcropping and I glance over. My head sways. Thirty feet, easy. Maybe closer to forty. Despite the slight vertigo, my stomach zips with anticipation. This part of it—the actual act of jumping—is the least nerve-racking element of the evening. As long as my swimsuit stays in place, I could do this forever.

"NOW!" Sofía's scream echoes off the canyon walls as we fling ourselves over the edge into the freezing water below. When I come up (snot-free, swimsuit in place), I'm relieved to see that no one has a GoPro or a cell phone shoved in my face, lessening the chances of something embarrassing ending up on the internet for the rest of time.

We jump again and again, getting colder and laughing louder with each jump. By the time I pull myself out of the water after our sixth jump, the muscles in my arms shake with the effort of climbing onto the rocks and every inch of my skin is covered in goose bumps. I collapse on the sandstone to catch my breath.

"I can't remember the last time I had this much fun," I gasp. How many nights did I sit alone on the top of my houseboat when I could have been doing something like this? I've been so scared for so long.

"When Beau wakes up, we'll throw a huge party to celebrate. It'll be way more fun than this," Sofía promises.

I swallow the lump in my throat and look down at the water. I let myself forget that this is all pretend, but now I can feel the ticking clock in my bones. Barring some miracle, I only have three weeks left of nights like this. If and when I'm banished back to my houseboat—alone—I won't even have fantasies and day-dreams to keep me company. I won't be able to trick myself into thinking I'm one perfect moment away from a different life.

"My lips are numb. I'm done." Sofía's teeth chatter as she wrings out her hair and wraps a towel around her shoulders. She climbs up wet rock and disappears over the edge of the cliff toward the bonfire smoke curling into the night sky.

Lounging on a small, jagged rock between me and the top of the cliff, Griff sits with his back against smooth sandstone. He looks down at me, his expression unreadable in the dark.

"You're not jumping?"

"Nah." He pushes his hair out of his eyes.

"Are you scared?"

He rolls his eyes and slips a guitar pick between his teeth. "Coming up?"

"Yeah." I'm losing feeling in my toes and the smell of a campfire has never been so inviting. Griff stands and places one foot on the step below him. He reaches out a hand to help me climb the slick sandstone. He hauls me up the last few rocks and I crash into him, knocking him back a step. My foot slips out from under me, my knees slamming into the rock as I slip backward. Terrified I'm about to fall backward off the mountain, I reach up, scrambling for anything to grab on to.

"My hand!" Griff shouts, but I grab hold of the only thing I can reach—the hem of his swimsuit. I pull, but instead of lifting my body up, it yanks his shorts down. The last thing I see before I crash backward into the water is a naked Griff Booker.

Chapter 16

When I come up for air, laughter echoes through the canyon. I'm shaking from the cold, but my insides boil. I want to swim away and never come back. I want to disappear. I want a time machine so I can go back to before Sofía, Griff, Beau, and that night on the beach. I'd take a thousand invisible days over this public humiliation.

Everyone stares as I swim quickly to shore.

"Well," Griff says with a grim smile as he offers me his hand, again. "At least I didn't see *you* naked."

I can't speak. I can't even *look* at him. My eyes burn as I ignore his offered hand and push past him. I climb as quickly and carefully as possible, tears mixing with lake water running down my cheeks. People move aside to let me through, but I hear every whispered word and gleeful taunt as I pass.

"Damn, Booker, your junk is so ugly it makes girls cry!"

"She's crying?"

"Why is she crying?"

"I bet it reminded her of Beau's."

"Is she hurt?"

"I bet she wanted to know who's bigger. Who is it, Gemma? Beau's taller, but Griff's hands . . ."

"You can't have them both!"

More laughing. So much damn laughing. I gulp air, but I can't get enough. My head spins.

Sofía steps in front of me, blocking my escape route. "Are you okay?" I can feel everyone staring at us. I've never wanted to climb out of my own skin more than I do right this moment.

"I can't breathe." I swerve around her, half blinded by tears as I stub my toe on a rock and limp into the dark. I'm dripping wet and freezing cold but don't stop to dry off before yanking open Sunday's door and diving inside.

"Shit. You took her breath away. Nice work, Booker." I slam the door, silencing the howls of laughter. I lean my head against the window, furious with myself for thinking I could be normal. *I hate this I hate this I hate this.* I suddenly know exactly where I want to be tonight, and it's in a quiet hospital room with Beau.

The passenger door opens and shuts quickly. I cover my face with my hands. "I'm so sorry. It was an accident. I didn't mean—"

"It's not a big deal," Griff cuts me off. "It was almost dark anyway."

I curl my legs up under me and open one eye. Griff looks fine. Worried, maybe. But he's not losing his mind the way I am. He was naked in front of everyone, and I'm such an anxious mess that *I'm* the one freaking out. "It was an accident, I swear."

"I know." He looks at me evenly.

My face is on fire. "Please don't look at me."

He laughs. "Gemma—"

"I'm serious. Don't look at me. Don't talk to me. Never, ever touch me."

He chokes on thin air. "Why would I touch you?"

"You wouldn't!" *OMG, is there no end to this humiliation?* "Please get out of my truck."

"Are you serious?"

"Can you find a ride with someone else?"

"You pulled down my pants in front of all your friends, and you're mad at me?"

"I'm not mad; I'm mortified. I can never speak to you again."

I've seen him naked. Everyone laughed at me. Worse—they think I did it on purpose, like some kind of pervert with a brother kink. It's too awful. I can't fathom ever having a non-awkward conversation with Griff again. My skin is lava and my bones are rubber.

"They're being stupid, but they'll all forget about it by tomorrow. Look at me, Gem—"

"I'm one excruciating minute away from puking my guts out in your lap, at which point my shame will be so overwhelmingly massive that I'll have to kill you and sink your body to the bottom of the lake."

"Wow."

"Get. Out."

He does.

I sit for a minute, frantically gasping for air. The tips of my fingers go numb. The feeling in my lips goes next. I start the truck and a spray of gravel kicks up beneath my tires as I peel away from my utter and complete humiliation. I manage to keep myself together as I make the short drive to the marina, but as soon as my feet hit the dock, a dam bursts in my chest.

I'm sobbing as I fall into bed.

"Gemma?" Dad knocks on the wall outside my cubby the next morning. My eyes are swollen and sore from crying myself to sleep.

"Go away."

"Is this about me selling the business?"

I want to shout that not everything is about him, but I also want him to feel bad for considering the offer. "Yes."

He leaves me alone after that.

I call in sick to work on Monday. And again on Tuesday. By Tuesday afternoon I'm filled with self-loathing, tired of my own internal monologue, and two days closer to facing a conscious Beau Booker. If I can't be in the same room as his brother, how will I ever convince him that his family loves me and therefore he should too?

(The plan still needs work.)

In addition to all that, a line from my SAD research keeps coming back to me.

Avoidance makes it worse.

I believe it because the thought of talking to Griff makes me feel sicker now than it did on Monday morning. I wander to the top deck and sit with my feet on the railing and stare at the fuel dock in the distance. I wonder which red dot is Griff, and whether he'd ever want to speak to me again after Sunday night. I'm almost as embarrassed for kicking him out of my car as I am for pulling his pants down. At least the pants thing was an accident.

By Tuesday night, I'm restless in my own skin. I've ignored two more calls and three texts from Karly saying she wants to do another interview, this one filmed. My hair is greasy, my brain is foggy, and I feel that specific, intense kind of stomach-ache that comes from too many days of laziness and self-loathing. It's a preview of a Lizzie Spalding summer, and I hate every second of it.

I'm convinced there's no feeling as desperate and painful as hoping someone likes you.

Do they? Could they? Maybe . . . if magic strikes, if you make yourself funny enough, and pretty enough, and interesting enough. If you tell the right stories, know the right people, dress the right way. Maybe then?

Experience has taught me there's no worse feeling than wishing, desperately, that someone sees you, accepts you, *likes* you—except the confirmation they don't.

(Why don't they?)

I've constructed my whole world in an effort to avoid that confirmation. Not just with Beau, but with everyone else too.

Every party I didn't go to. Every conversation I didn't start. Every text I didn't send, for fear of not knowing when to end the conversation. All of it, every decision I've made, to avoid a feeling I'm already drowning in. *Loneliness.*

I don't understand the way my brain works, or why it treats social situations or hard conversations like an actual physical attack. But if I don't *try* to change this, then I'm scared I'll spend the rest of my life stuck in this place of painful wishing, waiting, hoping. Backing out of chances instead of embracing them. Running from danger that might not exist.

I can't do it anymore.

I scour the internet for every account of exposure therapy for social anxiety.

And then, in the predawn hours on Wednesday morning, with a deep breath and a shaking hand, I make my own list.

I include parties and social events and purposely humiliating myself in public. I'll expose myself to all the things that scare me until I'm no longer terrified. I'll make a better version of myself. And then, when Beau wakes up, I'll explain what happened, ask him not to out me as a liar, and hold my breath that maybe he wants to date me for real.

(I didn't say it was a *good* plan. But it's all I've got.)

I write every scary thing I can think of, and at the very top of the list, I write the thing that feels equally terrifying and possible.

Become friends with Griff.

I need one real friend in my life, and he's as good an option as any.

I start on Thursday, armed with an apology milkshake. I considered baking him something—cookies or whatever—for ten unpleasant seconds, and then I bought the shakes. No use trying to be something I'm not. He's already seen my weirdness (and I will *not* think about the parts of him that I've seen); a plate of bad cookies isn't going to change his mind about me.

I push the door to Booker Brothers' Pizza open in the late afternoon, milkshakes in hand. As I'd hoped, the restaurant's dead. A sign on the empty hostess stand tells me to wait to be seated. Noah scoots through the empty waiting area on his knees, driving a Transformer vehicle in each hand. I see the moment he sees me, and a mischievous grin spreads across his messy face. He holds very still for three seconds and then jumps up and yells, "BOO!"

I gasp. "You scared me!"

He doubles over in a fit of giggles and moves on.

"Sit anywhere," a girl in a black T-shirt tells me. Her name tag says Thea. "I'll be right over to get your order."

"Can I sit in Griff's section? Is he here today?"

She checks her watch. "He's between shifts, but he'll be back on at four thirty if you want to wait."

"Where is he now?"

She motions to a booth near the back of the room. I move toward it, but my steps falter when I see him. His legs hang over the edge of the bench, black high-top sneakers resting on the floor. He's stretched out across the bench with his eyes closed and wireless earbuds in his ears. His chest rises and falls in a steady rhythm. I turn abruptly and choose a booth on the opposite side of the dining room.

"We have milkshakes here, you know," Thea says as she plops a menu in front of me.

"Sorry." My cheeks flush. "I'll have a water." She scowls. "And mozzarella sticks."

I eat mozzarella sticks, drink my milkshake, and stare at my SAD Bucket List while I wait for Griff's shift to start. When my milkshake is gone, I drink half of his, hoping it'll settle my stomach. It doesn't. I'm sick with nerves. Instinct tells me to leave before I humiliate myself, but I promised myself I'd accomplish something today. I scan my list, looking for an easier task.

Send a text that scares you.

Easy enough, considering *all* texts scare me. Texting should be easier than talking, and in most ways, it is. But I'm still plagued with self-doubt. *What should I say? How quickly should I say it?* And the biggest hiccup in my texting game? *When do I let the conversation die?* Dad is terrible at this. The absolute worst. He'll send a bland text like, **Running late at work. See you in an hour.** And I'll respond: **ok.** And that's where it should end! But instead of getting the hint, he'll then text me a picture of Obama in sunglasses that says *See You Soon.* Followed by Baby Yoda, followed by Mr. Bean, followed by, like, a kitten. He doesn't even like cats! It's too much, and he's trying way too hard. The worst part is when I don't respond, and he asks me *if I got the messages.* Oh, Dad.

My biggest fear is that I'll be the equivalent of someone's uncool meme-junkie dad who just does not know when to quit. I shudder, glancing back down at my list. It's just one message.

I pull up Griff's number and take a deep breath. Across the restaurant, he adjusts his earbuds, which gives me an idea. **You never gave me any songs to listen to.** I glance at him out of the corner of my eye, surprised when he slips his phone out of the pocket of his dark jeans and holds it over his face. Because he's still lying down, I can't see his expression, and I don't want to. But then the worst thing happens! He sits up! I do the only reasonable thing a girl can do in this situation: dive under the table.

It's dark in my corner booth, and if there is any justice in this world, he won't see me.

He stands and walks to the kitchen. A few seconds later he reemerges, tying an apron around his waist as he approaches the front of the restaurant. As he nears my table, his feet slow. And that's when I remember I left my keys on the table, monster fuzz pom-pom with one eyeball in plain sight. My brain freezes, and all I can think, literally the only coherent thought in my brain, is that I should have brought monster fuzz into my bunker. I genuinely don't know if it'd be worse to crawl out from under the booth now or stay and hide.

Griff reaches my table in three strides. If the key chain didn't give me away, it would have been my thundering heartbeat. He crouches, meeting me at eye level, and holds up the monster fuzz. "What happened to its other eye?"

"It melted off," I wheeze.

"Sad," he muses. "Actually, no. He looks better like this. Do you have a piece of paper?" His mouth twitches like he's fighting a smile.

If an earthquake were to hit and turn this place to rubble, that would be ideal. "No."

"Give me a minute." He stands and rifles through the pocket of his apron. He leans over, placing something on the tabletop. I can't come out now even if I wanted to because he's boxing me in. He leans over, his head appearing upside down underneath the table. "All-time favorite songs or current favorites?"

"Current."

He straightens and leans over the table, and then crouches,

holding out a scrap of paper. "Can I ask what you're doing under here?"

"No, you may not." I take the paper from him, careful not to let our fingers touch.

This earns me a bemused head tilt. "You're kind of a weirdo, aren't you?"

My face falls, and despite the shadows, Griff sees it. "It's not an insult."

"Doesn't sound like any compliment I've ever heard," I mutter. "Let me out of here." Griff backs up and I make the mortifying crawl of shame back into the restaurant's soft lamplight. Cheeks burning with an embarrassment from which I'll never recover, I slide back into the booth and study the paper in my hand.

His handwriting is nearly illegible. "'Alabama Pines,' 'Speed Trap Town,' and what's this last one?"

"'Tupelo.' That's the best one, so listen to it last."

I nod and stuff the paper in my pocket.

"Who was here with you?" He points to the two R.D.'s cups and slides into the booth across from me.

"No one. One was for you. I drank half of it." I push the half-empty cup toward him. This is the part where I'm supposed to apologize for The Incident and the aftermath, but instead I blurt: "Now you owe me?"

He laughs, *hard*. I expect him to ignore the half-melted drink, but he picks it up and takes a long sip. And then he leans forward and picks up my SAD Bucket List. "What's this?"

"Nothing!" The edge of the paper slides across his palm when I yank it away.

"Ow!" he growls, pressing his other hand over the cut to stop the bleeding.

"Sorry! I'm so sorry!"

He shakes his head. "Don't worry about it." And I know it's just a paper cut, but I feel awful. And awkward. And oh my gosh, he must think I'm an absolute freak.

A bell jingles over the door and Thea wanders over. "You want this one?"

Griff holds up his hand. "I have to take care of this first." She winces in sympathy and goes to seat the first table.

"What did you see?" I ask. As much as I don't want him to confirm he read my list, not knowing would be worse.

His lip twitches. "Some kind of bucket list."

"Is that all?"

"It may have been sad?" His mouth twitches again. He's *laughing* at me. My chest burns as flames of embarrassment lick my insides.

"Don't tell anyone."

"Why was my name on it?" He leans forward, clearly enjoying this.

"Promise me that you won't tell anyone what you saw."

"Who would I tell?" he asks drolly. "I don't even like anyone in this town."

I feel prickly and defensive, and my mind immediately jumps to his brother. He knows Beau. He could tell him, and then I would have to move off the planet. But Griff can't know how embarrassed I would be to have Beau see this side of me, not when we're supposedly secret lovers or whatever. My face gets hot and I'm dangerously uncomfortable. It's not fair that my insides feel like they're boiling and he's sitting there smirking like we're in on a shared joke. I want him to leave me alone, to stop smirking like that, to feel an ounce of the hot, bubbling misery simmering in my gut.

I open my mouth and shoot to kill. "Not even Ms. Rose? I heard you *know* her."

Chapter 17

Ms. Rose. The Page High science teacher Griff supposedly slept with.

Griff's face darkens, his jaw going rigid. He appears for five seconds like he's going to snap, and then his face relaxes; his eyes lose their wild intensity. "Don't move," he says as he stands.

"Why not?"

"I have to work, but I'll be back. Stay here."

He leaves me sitting alone next to my plate of congealed cheese sticks. The uneasy misery coursing through my veins makes room for another emotion: guilt.

As the tables around me fill up, though, I realize it's only a matter of time before someone kicks me out for occupying an entire four-person booth by myself without ordering. Griff walks by and I try to get his attention so I can throw a real quick "Sorry I suck!" his way and then leave, but the old woman at the table next to me gets to him first.

"Excuse me, I asked for extra cheese," she says as Griff stalks by her table with a tub of dirty dishes in his hands.

His eyes flick briefly to the pizza on the table and then back to the tub in his hand. "That has extra cheese."

"The last time we were here, it really had a lot more cheese."

"No, it didn't," Griff says.

"I'm sure it—"

"It didn't." He walks away as the woman sputters indignantly. Thea takes Griff's place and tries to smooth things over.

I see an opportunity to apologize (without the awkward task of verbally apologizing). I jump out of the booth and follow him across the floor. "I can help you."

"No."

"I can clear dirty dishes."

"You don't work here."

"Stop being so stubborn." I grab the tub of dishes and yank it away, but he doesn't let go. We struggle over it for a few seconds before it slips out of our grasp and crashes to the floor. Broken glass and soggy pizza crusts spew fifty feet in every direction as I fall to my knees. The ringing silence that follows lasts for a heart-stopping second before the patrons burst into applause. I scramble to my feet, slicing both of my hands open on broken glass. "Crap. I'm bleeding!"

Soaking wet and shell-shocked, Griff gapes at me. Thea the scowling waitress arrives on scene, looking more furious than ever. "Kitchen. Now," she orders. We follow obediently. She wrenches the door of the walk-in refrigerator open and nudges us inside with a handful of Band-Aids and rubber gloves.

"I'm so sorry!" I say.

She ignores my apology. "Do you need a doctor?"

Looking at my hands, I see at least a few chunks of glass stuck in the skin. I pull out the first one, wincing in pain. "Don't worry about it."

"Good. Are you going to sue us?"

"I don't know any lawyers."

Her scowl deepens. I didn't think it was possible.

Griff rolls his eyes. "She won't. But Mrs. Weatherby might."

"Speaking of Mrs. Weatherby, what the hell is wrong with you? Why are you arguing with the guests?" She doesn't wait for an answer. "I don't know what happened out there, but you need to stay in here until you figure it out and can promise me it won't happen again. You're done for the night by the way."

A muscle in Griff's jaw twitches and he has fire in his eyes. I expect him to argue with her, but then his shoulders slump and his brutal expression smooths.

"Take it up with your dad if you're pissed," she says. The door swings closed behind her with an ominous thud. We're alone in a chilly room filled with shelves of cheese and vegetables.

"I will because this is bullshit!" Griff yells. He leans his palms against the door and hangs his head. "Damn it!" He punches the door and swears again when he sees his bloody knuckles.

"Does she hate me?" I ask.

"Most likely."

I groan. "Should I apologize again?"

"No. She hates everyone. It's not a big deal."

"But . . . I want everyone to like me."

"That's a terrible goal." He flexes his right hand and winces in pain.

"Bad day to be our hands," I say, holding mine up.

He swears again. "Let me see."

"No, I'm okay."

He scoffs and reaches for my wrist. The gentle scrape of his calloused fingers surprises me. My pulse quickens under the heat of his touch and I pull away.

"Guitar calluses," he explains, showing me the hardened pads of skin on his left-hand fingers. "Did I hurt you?"

I shake my head, heart in my throat. He picks up my hand again, moving with extra care, and leans over it. His head is too close to mine, his hair brushing my forehead as he pulls out a shard of glass. I don't register any pain: I'm too distracted by the smell of him. It's spicy and kind of smoky, the opposite of my dessert-scented body washes. I always smell like flowers or sugar. Boys, it turns out, smell like campfire and pine trees. The one with his fingers on mine does, at any rate. *What does Beau smell like?* The thought pops into my head, and I'm crushed to realize I don't know.

My heart will not behave, and it's obvious why. I'm not used to being touched, like, at all. Ever. This is the closest I've ever come to holding hands with anybody, and just my luck, we're both bleeding. Not that I want to hold hands with Griff. It's just an observation.

"All done." He drops my hands unceremoniously. We scoot to opposite sides of the walk-in and sit cross-legged, passing electric-blue bandages back and forth. It's cold, and I miss his breath warming the air around me.

"The blue color is so we can easily spot a bandage that drops in the food. We don't want anyone to get served a Band-Aid surprise," he explains. I pretend to gag. "We use blue finger condoms for the same reason."

My head whips up. He's holding up a small circle of blue latex and unrolls it over the finger. "Protects the Band-Aid." He winks.

Fire. I am made of fire, infernos of embarrassment swallowing me whole. Griff chuckles. "Officially called finger cots, but what's the fun in that?" He tosses one to me from the first aid kit. It bounces off my knee onto the floor. My SAD Bucket List says nothing about finger condoms, so I feel free to ignore it on the grounds of potential mortification.

He turns his attention back to his hand, flexing the damaged knuckles. "We make a pathetic pair," he says, and my heart skitters in my chest. Two hours ago, I'd have found this moment mortifying—sitting with a pile of neon Band-Aids, banished to the walk-in after an embarrassing meltdown in public. But I'm not the only one who lost my cool tonight, and that fills me with strange comfort. For the first time, Griff and I are on an even playing field: pathetic *together*. A team. One socially anxious girl and her comatose fake boyfriend's rebellious older brother.

"Why are you here, anyway?" he asks.

"To convince you to be my friend." I wince. "I'm sorry for pulling your pants off. And for kicking you out of my car. And I'm sorry for what I said earlier." I can't bring myself to repeat it.

"You're not selling yourself all that well." He smiles, and I writhe in well-earned misery. "I overreacted. It's not true, by the way. Most of the rumors are true, but that one isn't."

"Oh." I can't formulate a proper response. I want to breathe a heavy sigh of relief, to tell him how glad I am to hear that. (And not just because there's not a predator wandering the halls of our school.) But why should I be glad? Griff's sex life (past or present) doesn't have anything to do with me. Obviously. I attempt to shake my confusing thoughts away.

"It's not your fault I was pissed." Half of his mouth crooks up in an ironic grin. "Not all your fault, anyway. That cranky old lady sits in my section every single weekend and always has a new complaint. She's just trying to get a discount, and Dad knows that. He—" He cuts himself off, shaking his head and muttering something under his breath.

"What's the story between you and your dad?"

"We don't get along," Griff says eventually, as if that's answer enough.

"I gathered as much. *Why* don't you get along?"

Griff shrugs. "It probably has something to do with the time I stole petty cash and booze from this place, went on a joyride, and slammed my car into a telephone pole."

"Yikes."

"Does that help you make up your mind about me?" he asks, the poster child of self-deprecation. It's almost like he's daring me to hate him.

"I've never done any of those things."

He huffs a laugh. "No, I wouldn't expect you had."

I groan. I'm so tired of living up to everyone's expectations of me, especially because it feels more like I'm living down to them. *Gemma Wells, she's shy. Gemma Wells, she's good. Gemma Wells, she would never be involved in a DUI.* Okay, that last one is a point in my favor. But the point is, no one expects anything of little Gemma Wells.

As if reading my mind, Griff says, "That's a good thing. You shouldn't aspire to my level of screw-up."

"I don't. But sometimes I get tired of being what everyone expects."

"For what it's worth, I don't expect anything of you," Griff says evenly. "But since you're with my brother, I can make a few assumptions."

"*That* sounds bad."

"Trust me, it's really not."

I want to surprise him. I want to surprise *myself*. "I think I have social anxiety disorder," I blurt. I pick at the laces of my shoes, poking the ends in and out of the grommets, unable to meet his eyes. "That's what SAD stands for."

"That acronym sounds like a cruel joke."

"Truly. Anyway, I hate it. So I got this idea to make a list of things that scare me, and then do them. That's what the SAD Bucket List is."

I wrap my arms around my knees, eyes resolutely on the ground. If Griff doesn't say anything, I will go to my grave without knowing his reaction to this information because I can't look at him. Lifting my eyes to meet his feels Herculean. Impossible. *Dangerous.*

To his credit, he doesn't laugh. "What's on your list?"

"Irrelevant."

"Come on! Tell me one thing."

"I can't! That's the whole point. I can't talk about things like this! It's too hard and awkward and my mind will go blank and I'll say something embarrassing and you'll think I'm a freak!"

Silence rings out in the space following my outburst. *Cue regret in one, two—*

"I'm confident I won't," he says. And something about his tone makes me want to believe him.

"Ask me again when I'm done with my list, and hopefully by then I'll be a whole new person."

Griff scoffs. "A whole new person? How will Beau recognize you?" he says drolly.

"I'm hoping he'll like the new me even better."

"That's messed up."

"Is it?"

"It's not very romantic," he drawls, sounding bored with this conversation.

I lean against the shelf at my back and close my eyes. I can give him romance. "I've been in love with your brother for as long as I can remember. When he walks in a room, I can't look at anything else. It's absurdly easy to love him." I open one eye and sneak a glance. Griff's mouth is a grim line.

"Sickeningly easy," Griff agrees, and I can't help but smile at this description of Beau. It's nice to remember him like this instead of picturing him unsmiling and undimpled in a hospital bed.

"I don't make it easy to love me. I never put myself out there and I keep everyone at arm's length. I'm hoping that if I face down my fears this summer, I'll be the person he deserves when he wakes up."

Griff's quiet for so long that I'm convinced he's not going to say anything. But then he leans forward. "Show me your list."

My eyes snap up to meet his for the first time since we were unceremoniously shoved in here. After my embarrassing confession, I prepare to feel gut-wringing distress, the way I do on the rare occasions Dad talks about Mom. I have so little experience sharing my feelings that I bristle against anything heavy or raw; those conversations sit on my skin like a rash. Strangely, that doesn't happen now.

"She looks up," Griff says, the corner of his mouth twisting wryly. My heart stops, devastated. But then I notice his eyes are sparking, playful. *He's teasing me*, I realize with a start. And earlier, at the start of his shift, he wasn't laughing at me to be mean. He was being *friendly*. My belly warms, but unlike the painful heat that comes with humiliation, it's a pleasant feeling.

"Let me see your list," he says again.

"Fine." Groaning a little, I hand over my SAD Bucket List.

He scans the page. "Why do you want to be friends with me?"

I don't have a non-embarrassing answer. "You're Beau's brother."

He nods, pulls out a pen, and starts adding things to the bottom of the list.

"What are you doing?"

"I'm helping you."

"Are you leaving tips on how I can stop feeling embarrassed about everything I've ever said?"

This time he *does* laugh, and I smile triumphantly, feeling like I just won the lottery. "Is that what it's like?" he asks.

"More or less. The real problem—"

The door opens and Thea appears, looking startled. "What are you still doing here?"

"Planning my lawsuit," Griff says, holding up his hands.

"Self-inflicted injuries are not the company's fault."

"I didn't do this. Vouch for me, Gem."

"I didn't see anything," I say, which causes her to roll her eyes at Griff. She props the door open with her foot, motioning for us to leave.

"Give us a second," Griff says, nudging the door closed again. She gives up and lets him close it, but not before calling him a very rude name. He ignores her, pressing his foot against the door, leaning back against it with one knee up. "I'm going to help you with your bucket list." It doesn't sound like he's asking. "I owe you for the milkshake."

"I drank most of it."

"It's the thought that counts. When's your next day off?"

"Thursday morning."

"We'll hammer out the details then." He opens the door and moves to leave.

"Wait! What about my list?"

"Meet me here," he calls over his shoulder, "and you'll get it back."

Chapter 18

"She doesn't work here." Mr. Booker frowns at Griff and me on Thursday, stern lines creasing around his mouth. I shrink away from him, sweating in Griff's black Booker Brothers' T-shirt. He handed it to me when I walked in before opening this morning and I blushed fire at the thought of wearing his clothes.

"It's clean," he promised with a wink.

I put my nose to the shoulder now and inhale, mildly disappointed to discover it smells like laundry detergent instead of his smoky, spicy cologne.

"You didn't care about that when she stayed late to help me close," Griff says to his dad.

"Isn't she the reason we had to comp Mrs. Weatherby's meal the other night? No offense, Gemma."

Griff's jaw tenses. "It's just for one shift."

"If you're trying to get out of work—"

"I'm not. I'll be here the whole time."

Mr. Booker sighs. "She's not trained on the system."

"I'll be here to help her, and Monday afternoons are slow. She can handle it," Griff says. It's big talk considering he has no reason to believe in me.

"If you need a job, Gemma, we can talk—"

"I don't," I say quickly. I really, really don't. I hate this idea. My stomach is a tangle of knotted rope and my palms are sweating like ice water in July. I wipe them on the butt of my jeans. "This is for today only."

"I'm sorry, Gemma, but I can't put you on the floor unless you're an employee. Insurance reasons."

"No worries," I say as he walks away.

"It was a good idea—" I say at the same time Griff says, "Okay, so let's go over the ordering system one more time."

"But your dad said no."

"That's never stopped me before." He winks.

After our conversation in the walk-in the other day, I drove home with antsy anticipation in my blood. I hardly recognized what I was feeling. It wasn't embarrassment, exactly. It wasn't regret or fear or excitement either. I'd just had the strangest night of my life, in which I'd done and said things that would normally mortify me, but I was buzzing from my toes, up through my stomach and chest, all the way to the top.

Hope.

That had been the unnamed feeling sending shocks of electricity through my bloodstream. Hope that I could change, that things would get better, that there might be a future for Beau and me at the end of this complicated mess.

I clung to that hope as I walked in this morning. Griff handed over my list immediately, his own suggestions scrawled on the bottom. The first addition? Work a serving shift at Booker Brothers' Pizza. Now that I'm standing here, surrounded by tables and employees who know what they're doing, it feels like I'm being thrown into the deep end and no one taught me to swim.

When I say as much, Griff nods. "You're going to teach your-self to swim. That's the best way to learn." I grimace and he sighs. "I'll pull you out if you're drowning. Happy?"

Hardly.

Twenty minutes later, Mrs. Booker shows up with all the kids. The two little boys jump in their dad's car and he whisks them off to the hospital to visit Beau. If I survive this shift, the hospital is the first place I'm headed.

"See, it'll be fine. Dad will never know," Griff says.

"What if someone here tells him?"

"I've threatened everyone," he says easily. "As long as you don't screw up, Dad will never find out."

Don't screw up. I roll my eyes. "No pressure or anything."

The bell over the door chimes and both our heads turn. "My table?"

"Your table," he confirms. I move to greet the family.

"Wait." Griff's hand touches my elbow, stopping me in my tracks. He pulls a name tag out of his back pocket.

"Who's Marge?"

"You are." He clears his throat, looking uncomfortable. "If you want. I thought it might help with your anxiety if you could pre-tend to be someone else."

"How?"

"Let's say you screw everything up today—"

"Gee, thanks."

"No, listen. Let's say the kitchen messes up and this lady with the kids is furious and blames her server, which always happens, by the way. So she's pissed and in need of validation in the form of an angry Yelp review eviscerating the one employee she can single out. Who does she write about? Not Gemma Wells." He taps the name tag. "Marge."

He's thoughtful, I realize with a start. Not only did he set this up to help me, but he brainstormed ways to make it easier on my anxiety. He bounces up onto his toes, his eyes sparking. "Do you think I look like a Marge?"

"Is Marge bad?"

"Not if you're seventy."

"Fine. I'll be Marge." He pins the name tag to his own shirt.

"No! I want it." I lunge for the name tag, but he easily captures my wrists in his hands.

"Sorry, it's mine now."

"Give me Marge! I want to be Marge."

With a smirk, he unpins the name tag from his shirt and leans forward to pin it to mine. Like that night in the walk-in, I inhale a breath of his smoke-and-spice scent and have trouble thinking about anything else. His presence is a windshield wiper, swiping the nervous dread from me, replacing it with bubbly anticipation. He's done in a flash and steps away, clearing his throat. "Let's go, Marge."

"Marge is a terrible name," I mutter as I follow him across the floor. His shoulders shake with silent laughter.

My first few tables are rough. I stammer, I stare at my shoes, I apologize constantly. Griff hangs by my side, helping when I freeze up, watching when I don't. And somehow, the roof doesn't cave in. I'm struggling, but the world isn't ending. "Hi, I'm Marge and I'll be your server today" becomes my favorite sentence. It's delightful, the way I can pretend to myself that Marge is braver than I'll ever be. Between my name tag and my apron, I blend into the scenery as a Booker Brothers' employee.

At the peak of lunch rush, I have four tables that all need something from me at the same time and Griff has disappeared. "Diet Coke with lemon, two Dr Peppers, one root beer," I repeat under my breath as I fill drink orders. I should have written it down, but I was in a hurry. I'm called back to the table thirty seconds after I drop off drinks to try again. "Two Diet Cokes, one Dr Pepper with lemon, one root beer."

"Need help?" Griff asks as he wraps a paper ring around a bundle of silverware.

"Please," I gasp. "Table seventeen has been sitting forever and I haven't greeted them yet, and table nineteen's food has been in the window for five minutes. It's officially time to pull me out of the deep end."

"Hey," Griff says a little sharply. I look up at him, pausing for the first time in hours. His face is serious, but not in the fake-bored way it often is. He watches me intently. "You are not drowning."

"Tell that to table twenty, who just acted like I poisoned them when I got their drinks mixed up."

He steps closer. "This feeling you have—this incredible ball of stress sitting right in your chest? The feeling like you're doing fifty things at once and you're doing them all badly? That's food service. We all mess up drinks, we all get snowed under. I've been watching you, and you're doing fine. I promise."

Strangely enough, I believe him. I get back to work.

By the time my shift ends, I'm physically and mentally exhausted, but I'm also proud of myself. I did something scary and I survived.

"Nice job today, Gem," Griff says as he passes me with a tub of dirty dishes in his hand. I move to unclip "Marge," but he waves me off. "Keep it as a memento."

"Thanks for setting this up today," I say, following him into the kitchen. "Wait for me to wash my hands and I'll count my tips so we can split them."

He shakes his head. "You earned them. So, what do you think?" he asks, unloading the dirty dishes into the sink. "Have you found your new calling?"

"Definitely not."

He puts his hand to his chest. "That hurts."

"Too many people, too much stress, not enough sunshine. I need a hundred afternoons on the lake just to recover."

"I haven't been on the lake since I've been home," he says with a shrug.

"No!" I gasp, grabbing his arm. "I have to take you."

"Yeah?" One side of his mouth quirks up. "I have missed it."

"It's settled; you help me with my list, I repay you with boat trips. It's only fair."

"How soon can I expect repayment?" He folds his arms, and my eyes stray helplessly to the muscle in his bicep. "We may need to set up an interest plan." His face is grave, but his eyes are dancing.

"I'll have to check with Dad and see when the boat is

available. And I'm visiting Beau after work. But I'll let you know."

"Oh." His eyes widen in surprise, but it's gone in a blink. "Cool." He finishes with the dishes while I pull my list out of my pocket and cross off today's task in one satisfying stroke. In the span of one afternoon, my summer just got so much brighter.

Chapter 19

"You're late." Griff is stretched out on the dock with his feet up on the bow of my boat. He squints up into the sunshine to look at me.

"I know, I know. I'm sorry. I was with Beau." I now visit the hospital every day to search for anything else from "D," but there's nothing new. Ever since I saw the card, I can't shake the nagging suspicion that this person has information that could expose my lie. Searching for them feels too dangerous, though, so I'm just holding my breath and waiting. Been doing a lot of that lately.

I climb on the boat and kick it to life. "You ready?" I may have been the late one, but I'm impatient to get on the water.

Griff climbs to his feet and eyes my boat skeptically. "Permission to board?" His gaze lands on a small tear in the leather and he scowls. In addition to the frown, everything he's wearing is all wrong. Black Converse high-tops. Dark, tight jeans. A black Drive-By Truckers T-shirt. I can't decide what's worse—his outfit, or the fact that he's holding a guitar case.

"What are you wearing?"

He glances down. "What's wrong with it?"

"You can't wear that on a boat."

"Why not? Are you planning on capsizing?" He presses his toe to the front of the boat, pushing slightly.

"No."

"Then I don't see what the problem is. Besides, the last time I wore a swimsuit around you, you cried."

Splotches of red bloom across my chest. "I thought we agreed to never speak of 'The Incident' again."

"I don't remember that conversation."

"It's a 'tree falls in the forest' situation. If I don't bring it up, and you don't bring it up, did it even happen?"

He laughs and my stomach squirms like I swallowed a live fish. "Whatever. Can you untie the stern line when you get in?" I point to the rope tethering the boat to the dock. Griff presses his toe to the front of the boat again, as if testing its seaworthiness. "Are you stalling?"

"No."

"It won't sink."

"I know," he says too quickly.

"Are you nervous?" I ask, a slow smile spreading across my face.

He scoffs. "No."

"Then why won't you get in?" I fold my arms, enjoying this immensely.

"It's been a while since I've been on a boat," he admits.

"Guitar," I say. He hands it to me, and I carefully lay it across the worn leather seats. "Hand," I say next. I stretch mine out and he reaches for it, his rough fingers scattering goose bumps across my arms. He hesitates briefly and then steps into the boat. It wobbles beneath us and he grabs my hip with his free hand, his body tense.

The weight of his hand on my hip is an anchor, dragging my mind into a very unexpected place. *He is close enough to kiss me*, I realize with a start.

Our hands spring apart, both of us averting our eyes.

"How far away is your houseboat?" he asks, picking up his guitar case and glancing around like he's not sure what to do with it or himself.

"Why?" I fumble with the rope still holding us to the dock, my hands shaky.

His brow furrows. "You told me that you and your dad live on a houseboat during the summer . . ."

"Yeah?"

"And you said you wanted to take the boat out!"

"This boat! The one beneath your feet!"

Griff's eyes widen and he looks at himself again. "I wouldn't have worn this if I'd known we were spending the day on a speedboat. And I sure as hell wouldn't have brought this!" He holds up his guitar case.

"What were you planning to do with it on the houseboat?"

Bright spots of sunlight glint off the water and into my eyes, making it difficult to tell for sure, but it appears that Griff's cheeks flush.

"Where do you want to go?" I ask, eager to cover up his embarrassment. Vicarious humiliation is almost as bad as the real thing. When TV characters get embarrassed, I watch through my fingers. "This is your trip," I remind him. Technically I owe him multiple trips; in the days between promising him this ride and making it work with our schedules, I've crossed off two more items from my list. On Thursday evening we both had the afternoon off (but Dad had a tour scheduled) so we went for milkshakes at R.D.'s dressed in Halloween costumes. I didn't have anything that fit because I haven't gone out for Halloween in years, but Griff unearthed matching pirate costumes from his family's house. His was too small, the pants only coming to midcalf, and mine was too big, the shirt slipping off my shoulder every ten seconds. My stomach churned at the prospect of dressing so conspicuously in public, but being with Griff took the edge off my embarrassment.

"You're gonna have to talk to me," I said as we sat across from each other at a small table in the center of the restaurant. My fingers clutched my milkshake, creating indentations on the environmentally dubious Styrofoam. Nudges, pointed glances, and whispers came from the nearest table.

"About what?" Griff pulled at the too-tight sleeves of his shirt. I swear he wears them on purpose; when he saw me notice, his lips curled up in a smirk.

"Do you think those kids are talking about us?"

His eyes cut dismissively to the table. "Who cares?"

"I care." My voice wavered, and Griff's eyes snapped up from his milkshake.

"Did you know that the Scots have four hundred and twenty-one words for snow?"

"Why so many? It's cold, it's wet, it's white. What else is there to say?"

He leaned forward with curious eyes. "Have you ever seen snow?" I shook my head. "Do you want to?"

I shrugged. "Never really thought about it."

He frowned at me. A burst of laughter exploded from the nearby table. My fingers itched to take the feathered hat off my head. "That group of kids is still laughing at us. More facts, please, I need a distraction."

"Okay, um—" Griff turned to look at the group so obviously mocking us. "You know how animal groups have names? A school of fish? A murder of crows?" I nodded in response. "What do you think a group of teenagers would be called?"

"A terror," I said immediately.

He laughed and bumped his knee against mine under the table. "A dread."

"A *panic* of teens. No, wait—a judgment. A judgment of teenagers." I didn't move my knee and neither did he. It really was a small table.

The next evening Griff had to work at the restaurant, giving me time to tackle another task from my list without him. I sent a text to Sofía for no reason other than to strike up a friendly, casual conversation, in which I didn't once use the word *okeydokey*. Texting led to making plans, and I ended up meeting her and Shandiin at Booker Brothers', where we ate breadsticks and drank soda until ten minutes after closing, at which point Griff's laser eyes glowered at me, reminding me that he still had to clean up after us.

Now, Griff is sitting in the passenger seat of my boat dressed like he belongs on a stage, his guitar case settled between his legs. "Don't care. Surprise me," he says, in response to my earlier question about where we should go.

"You're the one who's been away for a year. You decide."

"I'm not a lake kid like you," he says.

"How's that possible? You grew up here. Put your guitar here, I'll cover it with a towel." I point to the floor. He follows my instructions and I make a splash guard for his instrument.

"We've never owned a boat." He shrugs. "I don't know where any of the good places are."

I eye his clothing again. It's easily a hundred degrees out here, and swimming is obviously off the table. "What are you in the mood to do? And how much time do you have? You're going to sweat to death in that."

Without a word he pulls his shirt off in one fluid motion. He wads it up in a ball and shoves it into one of the storage compartments in the side of the boat. "Happy?" he asks.

My throat goes dry. I turn, hoping he won't notice my red cheeks. "Sunscreen in the side compartment." I stow the rope and push us away from the dock. As we float toward the no-wake buoys, an uneasy silence settles over us. We talk every day at work, and we went on the milkshake excursion together, but this feels different. We're not working on my list, for one. We're half dressed, for another. If Griff were shirtless with swim shorts on, that'd be one thing. But shirtless in jeans? It feels different. I can see the waistband of his boxers sticking up half an inch over his pants.

I grip the steering wheel until my knuckles are white.

I see the moment Griff notices my mounting anxiety because his demeanor softens. "Why don't you take me to your favorite place? I've got nowhere else to be."

"Yeah?" I breathe, some of the pressure behind my ribs easing.

"I'm easy to impress," he says.

"I doubt that," I say, thinking again about what Winnie told me about him knocking Beau's teeth out. How can he be this thoughtful guy sitting next to me, the one giving up his summer to help me overcome my anxiety, *and* the kind of person who punches his little brother in the face? It's the same thing I've wondered every day for the last week and a half. I don't know how to reconcile those two different versions of him.

Griff notices me staring at him and gives me a funny look. "What?"

"At least run the soundtrack," I say, handing over my phone.

Griff scrolls through my Spotify as I push on the throttle.

"Hey!" he yells over the roar of the wind in our ears.

"What?"

He turns my phone around so I can see the screen. He points to the Recently Played section of my profile. "You listened to Isbell!"

"You told me to!" I pulled Griff's hastily scrawled list out of my pocket as soon as I climbed into my truck and hit play on "Alabama Pines." I planned on listening on the way home, but as soon as that locomotive rhythm hit my bloodstream, I was stuck. I let the keys fall to my lap on the side of a midnight road and listened to the story of a rootless wanderer longing for home.

I listened to the other songs he recommended, and I recognized "Tupelo" as one of the songs he played for me in his room. The melodies are intoxicating, the lyrics heartbreaking. Isbell sings about a suffocating small town, about the desperation to be somewhere, anywhere else.

I played them again as I drove home and again as I crawled into bed. I fell asleep to the twangy, drifting heartache of Jason Isbell, hoping it'd help me untangle the mystery of Griff Booker. There's still so much I don't know about him. I don't know what happened between him and Beau, or why he left town, or why he's so intent on helping me with my list.

"Why didn't you say anything?" Griff asks now.

Why *didn't* I say anything? Maybe because the more I listened, the more personal it felt. "Why didn't *you* say anything?"

"I almost did! I almost texted you so many times, but I—" He cuts himself off, running a hand through his hair.

"You what?"

He blows out a breath, wrestling with his answer. When he finally says, "I didn't want to bother you," I can't help but wonder if he's telling the truth. It's his turn to refuse eye contact, and the role reversal is disconcerting. We drive by Castle Rock, slowing to a crawl through the Castle cut. (The water level has dropped so low over the last several years that a section of rock was bulldozed to create a passable route from Wahweap to the main channel.) We cruise around towering sandstone walls, each bend revealing a new stretch of water. It feels like another world, nothing visible but water and sandstone and sky. Blue, red, blue.

"What'd you think?" Griff asks eventually, and it takes me a second to realize he's asking about Isbell. It's so quiet I almost don't hear it. I ease up on the throttle, slowing the boat down.

"I listened to your songs first." I don't tell him that I fell asleep with them in my ear and made them the new soundtrack of my life. I don't tell him that they make my chest ache with a feeling I don't have words for.

"And?" He holds his breath. The tension in the air feels heavy enough to hold up this eroding sandstone for another thousand years.

"They're all about leaving."

He nods, his eyes fixed on the water. "I guess that's true."

"You don't like it here?" It sounds like a silly question with an obvious answer, but I can't help myself.

He runs his hand through his hair again and leans forward, his elbows resting on his knees. He studies me intently with dark, curious eyes. It makes it hard to breathe; my chest feels smothered and panicky and I'm overwhelmed with the sensation that he can hear every thought in my head. It's the most uncomfortable feeling of my life. Worse than the party on the beach or serving tables in the restaurant or drinking milkshakes in full pirate garb.

This outing suddenly doesn't feel so low stakes.

Griff's eyebrows are pulled together like he's debating something. As if deciding, he finally says, "I don't see a future for myself here."

Here rolls from his lips with more than a hint of disdain, reminding me of the time he referred to Page, the hometown I love almost more than anything else in this world, as a "patch of dirt." I should have known then.

"I don't understand that," I admit. He has more family in this "patch of dirt" than I have in the entire world. If I had two parents and a bunch of adorable siblings who loved me and a restaurant that always felt like home, I'd never feel lonely again.

"You don't ever dream of taking a midnight train away from here?"

It's such a Griff thing to say. "There aren't a lot of train stations in Page."

"You know what I mean. Do you ever want to disappear in the middle of the night and start a new life somewhere else?"

My gaze strays off him and settles on the lake around us. I don't think I'd ever leave. My heart belongs to this water. "Why would I? Everything I love is here. The lake and my dad and—"

"My brother," Griff says, cutting me off.

"Exactly," I whisper. My stomach sours in protest, though I'm not sure why. I *would* miss Beau if I left.

"Unlike you, I don't have anything anchoring me here," he says, sounding sad instead of bitter. The guilt of my lie is intense, but it's not the only uncomfortable feeling sitting in my gut. "You know I left last year, right?" he asks.

I nod, my curiosity burning like a wildfire.

"I've never felt more relief than the second I crossed that state line."

"Oh." *Well done, me. I'm a conversational savant.*

What I should have said is *Why'd you leave?*

Three words. He brought it up. He's practically begging me to ask.

Why is it so hard to say three words?

I know the answer to my own question. Because the conversation that follows might make me like this gorgeously sad boy more than I already do. Which is a huge problem because he believes I'm dating his brother. And because I'm *in love with* his brother, who is supposed to wake up from his coma in eight days.

"What's the deal with you and Beau?" I blurt, unable to smother my raging curiosity for another second.

He sighs, and for a long couple of seconds, I don't think he's going to answer. I've cut the engine by this point, and we're rocking gently in an otherwise empty channel, just us and the water and the sky. We could be the last people on earth. We could be the first people on earth, for all the signs of civilization.

"Beau and I are Irish twins," Griff starts. "Born less than a year apart. We basically grew up like twins, and absolutely everything was a competition. Who could eat faster, who could get dressed first, who could do the most jumping jacks in a row, stupid stuff." He pauses to think, and I suspect this is a story he's told a million times in his head, but maybe never out loud. "Dad was always egging us on, getting in the loser's face, encouraging them to be better, faster, stronger. I know he thought he was encouraging us. He still thinks that, despite everything.

"Beau and I were evenly matched for a long time, trading wins back and forth. But then around my freshman year he just . . . outpaced me, I guess. He won every competition. He was taller, and stronger, and played every sport. He always won, and he always gets, *got*, what he wanted."

"He does that," I admit, thinking of Golden Boy Beau and his Instagram abs.

Griff sighs and tips his head back. "Exactly. Anyway, it took me way too many years to realize that the thing we were really competing for was Dad's approval, and Beau was and always will be the ultimate winner. In Dad's eyes, Beau was the perfect son.

And I was . . ." He grimaces. "More sensitive? Shit, that sounds stupid."

"No it doesn't," I say. But I don't know if he believes me because I still can't bring myself to look at him.

"I used to cry every time I got hurt."

"Kids do that," I argue, feeling defensive for little Griff. "Hell, I do that. I stubbed my toe yesterday and cried for like two minutes!"

Griff sighs. "It's not what 'men' do, according to my dad. Beau *never* cried. Dad was always there, in my ear, saying, 'You're tough, right? You're strong.'" His voice strains, and he clears his throat. "By the time I started sophomore year, I was angry, like, all the time. And I didn't know what to do with that, or with the fact that Dad gave Beau all the best shifts, or the fact that I felt like I was drowning here in Page. I had no idea how to deal, so I lashed out at everyone. Started fights. Stole booze and money from his restaurant, stayed out too late, hurt people I cared about, made my mom cry. If I couldn't be happy, I didn't want anyone else to be."

My heart breaks to hear the regret in his tone when he talks about hurting people he cared about; he must mean Beau. "Is that why you left?"

"More or less. Mom shipped me off to live with her parents in Cleveland—"

"And you've never felt more relief than when you crossed that state line," I finish for him. I've been staring ahead at the water, but when I finally turn to look at Griff again, his eyes are open and honest in a way that steals the breath from my lungs. He looks younger like this, vulnerable in a way that makes my palms sweat. "There's really nothing in this town you'd miss?"

He smirks, his eyes dancing in the sunlight. "Other than my family, I can't say there is."

I'm baffled by his lack of awareness. We're sitting in one of the most beautiful places in the world, and he doesn't appreciate it. I want to grab his shoulders and shake him.

He's still shirtless, though, so I better not.

I'm not good at conversation, or talking to boys, or being vulnerable. But I do know this lake, and I can show Griff a good time. I turn the key in the ignition and kick the engine to life. "I'm going to make you fall in love with this place so that when you leave again, you'll have something pulling you back home." I say this while secretly thinking that I'll make him love it here so much he decides to stay. *How could he not?*

Griff's eyes darken as any hint of a smile vanishes from his face. "Do your worst."

Chapter 20

Griff's shirtlessness becomes a problem. His skin is turning pink. I slow the boat down and reach across him for the bottle of sunscreen. "You're getting roasted." I squirt a large amount of coconut-scented lotion into my palms and massage it into my arms.

"Am I?" He presses two fingers against his pink shoulder and lifts them up again, watching his skin flood with neon color.

"It's going to be painful," I say, applying the lotion to my shins, my heart thundering at what inevitably comes next. "You want to know the worst thing about a sunburn?"

"The skin cancer?"

"Okay, the second worst thing."

"The pain?"

I roll my eyes. "The *third* worst thing."

"Enlighten me."

"Every single person you encounter *will* point it out. There's no escaping it. You could be a bright red lobster, wincing in pain as you walk, and someone—*everyone*—will stop you on the street to say 'You're sunburned,' as if you didn't already know."

"Remind me again why you love this place so much?" He raises a skeptical eyebrow, and I know he's just teasing me, but I'm compelled to answer him anyway.

"I grew up here."

"So did I, and I've never loved anything half as much as you love this lake."

"I'm not talking about Page. I'm talking about the water. I was born on this lake. These stone walls are the building blocks of the happiest memories of my childhood. My mom is dead, school has always sucked, and summer is lonely. So, Dad and I spent all our time out here. I can't even count the hours I spent in the bow of the boat, making up stories in my head."

"You were literally born on the lake?"

"On a houseboat in Gunsight Canyon."

"That's pretty badass." He smiles, and I smile back until my cheeks hurt.

"Sunscreen!" I eventually say, tearing my eyes from him.

"Will you get my back?" He hands over the bottle of sunscreen and turns.

"Sure." I swallow heavily. *It's only weird if you make it weird. It's only weird if you make it weird. It's only weird if you make it weird*, I chant inwardly.

Griff smells like coconut and sunshine, and my fingers tremble as I smooth the lotion over his broad back. Without him looking at me, I finally work up the courage to ask the question that's been nagging at me for days.

"Did Beau ever date someone whose name starts with the letter *D*?"

"You two haven't had the past relationship talk?"

"Is there a reason we should have?"

"It's a pretty common relationship milestone."

My fingers freeze against his warm skin. I clear my throat, hoping I sound casual when I say, "I wouldn't know."

"Beau's your first boyfriend?" Griff looks over his shoulder, but I avert my eyes.

"Yep. Must be why he didn't feel the need to ask about my exes."

"Why are you bringing it up now?"

"There was a card in the hospital from someone who called themselves 'D.' I'm curious, that's all. All done!" I announce. Griff turns to face me, his expression blank. My heart falls a little; he must not recognize the initial, which is understandable. He *has* been gone a year.

"What do the two of you talk about?"

My heart rate increases. "Everything."

"Not your social anxiety. Or his past relationships, or favorite food, or swimming times, which is a little unbelievable because he brags about those to literally everyone."

"What's your point?"

Griff rakes a hand through his hair and sighs. "I don't know."

"Is it so hard to believe that your brother likes me?"

"That's not what I'm saying—"

"Some people think I'm hot."

Griff's eyes widen. "I'm not disputing that—"

"So we don't talk that much. Who cares?! Not every couple has to share all their feelings."

"You're right. I shouldn't have—"

I hold my hand to the side of my mouth and talk in an old-timey newscaster voice. "News flash: I'm an awesome kisser!" Unable to stop myself, I add jazz hands.

Griff looks like he'd rather be anywhere in the world other than on this boat with me.

"News flash! Your brother likes making out with me."

He tilts his head, looking miserable. "What's happening right now?"

I'm completely panicking, that's what's happening. I'm turning weird. I can't help it. I shrug and dance a little jig.

"Uh . . . Do you want me to do your back?" he asks.

"Boy do I!" I say. I turn, wondering if it's possible to put sunscreen on a creature who is no longer human. I'm an amorphous blob of self-loathing.

I sweep my tangled and windblown hair off my neck. I hold it up, practically vibrating with humiliation. I want Griff to touch my back *and* I want to throw myself off the edge of the boat and never speak to him again. I contain multitudes. A splotch of warm lotion hits my skin, and Griff's fingers slide against my back. My knees go weak, but I'm rooted in place; it'd take a hurricane to get me off this boat now.

"Can I—" His fingers hesitate.

"What's wrong?"

"Nothing," he says quickly. "I just—uh—can I move this back tie thingy to make sure I get sunscreen everywhere?"

"Mm-hmm." I don't trust myself to speak. Griff's calloused fingers gently nudge the back string of my bathing suit top and his other hand quickly slides under, massaging the lotion into my back. I hold my breath the entire time as heat and butterflies surge through me.

"All done," he says. I can't look him in the eye. I whisper a strangled thanks and drown myself in gulps of cold water.

We drive to Rock Creek Canyon; it's a large canyon filled with deep sandstone caves. I pull into an enclosed grotto, where the water is glass clear. Streams of sunlight shine through teal, and I follow the anchor with my eyes for several feet before it finally disappears.

Griff whistles as he rotates a full 360, taking in the scenery. "Damn. Okay, Gemma, you came to play." We're surrounded by high red rocks that slope up and inward, creating a dome. Kind of like an upside-down bowl with a hole in the top. Only a small patch of sky is visible above us.

"It's good, right?" Now that he's focused on something other than me, my limbs relax. I can't hide my satisfied grin.

"It's good," he agrees.

"If you were dressed to climb, we could swim to the outside, climb up the rock, and jump in the middle."

"Who says I'm not dressed to climb?"

I raised an eyebrow at his skinny jeans. He must be sweating to death in there. Oh geez. I avert my eyes. Don't think about "in there."

"Turn around," he says.

"Why?"

"Because I'm going to take my pants off, and I don't want you to spontaneously combust from embarrassment."

Yeah, no. Turning around is not going to be enough. I turn, quickly slipping off my own shorts, and think about the fact that swimsuits are basically underwear. My stomach does something weird and unfamiliar, and it feels like my insides are turning to lava. I place my foot on the edge of the boat and fling myself into the cold water. I roll onto my back, floating under the patch of graying sky. I swim freestyle strokes to the edge of the cave and look up. Clouds are gathering on the horizon, a warning sign for an incoming monsoon.

We should leave. It isn't smart to stay. But I can't bring myself to care, not when I'm finally in my happy place, and for once, I'm not here alone. I grin up at the gray sky.

A splash breaks my reverie and Griff pops up a few feet away from me, pushing his soaking hair off his forehead.

"Please tell me you're not naked." I glance up, wondering at the chances of this dome collapsing on top of us. If he's naked, I'm gonna need it to collapse.

Griff rolls his eyes and splashes me. I didn't think I'd ever use the word *playful* to describe Griff Booker, but that's exactly how he looks now, grinning crookedly at me. "Boxer briefs."

My face does something weird, and I dive under the water to hide it.

We swim to the outside of the dome and climb up the hot sandstone. It grows slick from the water dripping off our skin, but I fly up the rock, climbing as quickly as possible so I don't accidentally glance at Griff in wet boxers. Even looking at his face makes my cheeks grow warm in the humid air. At the top, we inch our toes to the edge and look down into the slate-colored water. I glance up at the sky, not really surprised to see how quickly it's changed in the time since we pulled into the grotto. It's thick with ominous gray clouds, and the air is wet and sticky in my lungs.

"Ready?" Griff asks. I nod. "On three. One, two—" He grabs my hand on three and we leap from the edge.

We free-fall, both of us screaming at the top of our lungs. My mouth is open as I plunge into the cold water; the shock of it almost knocks me breathless, but then Griff's hand has slipped out of mine and I'm pushing up, up, up.

I gasp for air as I break the surface, every nerve in my body tingling.

"Again?" Griff asks.

I eye the sky. Lake Powell monsoons rarely announce themselves; our late-afternoon storms almost always strike without warning. In the span of thirty minutes, the sky can change from clear and sunny to a dark deluge of water, then back to sunny again.

I look in Griff's dark eyes and I can't tear myself away from this moment. "Again."

We're laughing and gasping and counting all our lucky stars as we race back to the marina, a pair of bank robbers who just made off with the money.

A clap of thunder tears the sky open as we pull up to the dock, a cold, stinging downpour attempting to pound us back into the earth. I throw everything I can in a storage compartment. Griff grabs his guitar with one hand; with the other, he reaches for me. We lace our fingers together and jump onto the dock, running and laughing and shrieking with pure summertime joy.

"I can't believe we made it," I gasp as he pulls open the door of the gift shop. We duck inside for shelter, and I'm still in blind shock that we made it off the lake before the sky split in two and lightning threatened everything on the lake.

Griff keeps one hand around mine, but with his free hand he spins the rack of name key chains next to us, his eyes scanning.

"If there's no Gemma, there's no Griff," I say.

"I'm not looking for Griff," he says with a grin. I don't get to find out what he is looking for because he turns his back on the key chains.

A puddle of water collects beneath our feet as we shiver in the cold artificial air. Another crack of thunder rolls across the sky, vibrating through my head all the way down to my toes. A flash of lightning electrifies the earth, lighting one half of Griff's face, making him look dark and dangerous.

"We dodged a bullet," he says, and I can't tear my eyes from the trails of water that run from the ends of his hair, down his face, and over his lips.

"We really did," I say, vaguely aware that we could have been trapped in a narrow channel on the lake, our boat capsizing, us barbecued like chicken on a backyard grill.

But I can't bring myself to care. I'd live the afternoon a hundred times over, just for the way he's looking at me now.

Chapter 21

Griff becomes relentless. He has a plan for us every night, some of them on my list, some of them not. I've never had more fun in my life, but the ticking clock of Beau waking up hangs like a cloud over everything. It's not lost on me how quickly my new life could evaporate.

"I've got an idea," Griff says with a wolfish smile. We're sitting together on the end of the dock after work. This how it always starts. *I've got an idea—let's crash a beach party. I've got an idea—let's play Yahtzee with a group of senior citizens at the retirement home. I've got an idea—come to the restaurant and let the servers sing you a birthday song in front of everyone.*

"Lay it on me," I say, realizing not for the first time that excitement is outweighing my nerves.

"The Bowl," he says with forceful enthusiasm.

The Bowl is part bowling alley, part dive bar, and basically the only nightlife we have in Page. "Bowling's not on the list."

"Who's bowling?" Violet asks, strolling toward us.

"We are. You're not invited," Griff says to Violet, though his eyes never leave my face. "Are you in?" he asks me.

"I'm coming," Violet declares. "I desperately need some fun."

"We're not fun," Griff shoots back.

"Hey, Cannon, you want to go to The Bowl tonight?" she yells across the water. He gives her a thumbs-up. "My daughter's at my mom's tonight," Violet says, "and I haven't been out in forever. What time are we leaving?"

Griff rolls his eyes. Strangely enough, he looks less excited by the idea of Cannon joining us than I am. "Nine," he says, jaw tight.

"It's a date!" She snaps her bubble gum and leaves.

Griff and I look at each other. "It's not a date," he says quickly.

"Obviously."

A loaded silence hangs in the air.

"I almost forgot! I got you something!" He reaches into his pocket and pulls out a souvenir key chain from the gift shop. It's a license plate that says GEMMA. I gasp in surprise before realizing that originally it said EMMA, but he meticulously added the G in black marker. My heart does something weird in my chest that makes it hard to breathe.

"You were listening to my story that day at the gift shop with Sofía?" I can't believe he remembered.

He shrugs. "You took me on your boat, I got you a key chain."

"No!" I sputter, flustered by his attention and thoughtfulness. "The boat trip was repayment for helping me with my list. Every time I repay you for helping me, you do something in return and throw off the balance."

He shrugs. "What's wrong with that?"

"You're keeping me forever in your debt. It's not fair."

"It's a gift, then. No repayment needed."

I roll my eyes, but as I do, my fingers curl around the key chain.

I don't want him to take it back like he threatened to do with the Marge name tag. This gift has earned a permanent place next to my one-eyed monster fuzz.

"Wait—did you steal this after the storm?"

"No comment." He checks the time on his phone. "We've still got a few hours until bowling. What do you want to do until then? Anything else we can cross off your list in the meantime?"

I pull the worn paper out of my pocket and hand it to him. I've already called my local representatives and left a voice mail in favor of stricter gun laws (which made me want to barf, thanks) and struck up a conversation with a stranger. (Something I will not do again; the old man filling his truck at the gas station seemed to think I was hitting on him. Griff had to put his arm around my neck and pretend to be my boyfriend to make the man leave me alone.)

"We're almost done."

"Are you sure?" He scans the paper. "You crossed off 'befriend Griff'?" He smirks. "Are you sure, though? Have you asked him?"

"Ugh. You're annoying today," I say.

"I'll remember that next time I'm tempted to steal you a present. Hey, here's one." He points to the last item on my list. "We'll throw a Fourth of July party."

"That's only a few days away. There's not enough time."

"Sure there is. It's easy. All we have to do is tell people to show up."

"No way. It's too much pressure. People expect to have fun on Independence Day. They expect to kiss under the fireworks!"

"They can still do that."

"They also expect to sing 'The Star-Spangled Banner' and eat potato salad and have three-legged races."

"What century do you think we're in?"

"Go away." I put my hands on his chest and push him toward the water. He digs his heels in and captures my hands under his, pinning them against him. His heart thumps hard under my palms. I resist the urge to curl my fingers into his shirt.

"If I go in, you go in with me," he warns.

I glare. "My phone's in my pocket."

He puts his hand in my back pocket, takes out my phone, and gently tosses it on the deck. The contact only lasts a second, but it completely derails my train of thought. I swallow and force my mind back to the issue at hand. "I'm not ready to throw a party."

"Yes, you are. We'll do it on your houseboat."

"And if I drown?"

"Literally? Because I don't know CPR and Beau would have died on my watch."

"You know what I mean."

"I'll pull you out," he says seriously. Then he throws me a cocky smile and steps backward off the dock. We fall in a tangle of limbs and splash into the water. Fish scatter around our legs and I fight to untangle myself from Griff and push him away. I come up gasping for air. He flips his hair out of his eyes with a laugh and pushes himself up on the dock. He reaches for my phone.

"What are you doing?"

"Texting Sofía and telling her to invite everyone to your party."

He pushes send on the text and glances back at me. "I'll pick you up tonight before nine."

I groan and sink back under the water.

Four hours later, Griff and I are the third and fourth wheels on the most awkward date of all time. Violet and Cannon are all over each other. My mind short-circuits every time he slaps her butt as she bends over to pick up a ball from the chute.

I shrink lower into a sticky leather couch as Cannon pulls Violet tight against his side and dips his head to her neck. I block my face with both my hands and look at Griff with wide, desperate eyes.

"Is he whispering to her, or sucking on her neck?"

"What do you think?"

"I'm going to pretend it's the former." I glance at them again through my fingers. "Nope. I just saw tongue."

"Why do you think I didn't want them to come?" Griff mumbles.

So *that's* why he opposed them joining us. An unexpected pang of disappointment hits right between the ribs. I had thought maybe Griff wanted to be alone with me. It's something I've thought a lot lately, ever since the storm on the lake. I can't allow the thought to go further without getting caught in a swirl of panic, but sometimes I wonder what's going on in his head. And if he's really giving up his entire summer just to help me conquer my anxiety.

"Come up for air and bowl. It's your turn," Griff barks. They untangle themselves and Violet stands and bowls a spare. Then it's my turn. The backs of my thighs make a sucking sound as they unstick from the leather couch.

I bowl a mediocre frame and spin, letting my slick shoes take me all the way around. When I look up, Griff glances quickly away. Let it be known that the worst part of bowling is the knowledge that people are watching the long walk up to the alley and the longer walk back to the couch. I don't care how confident you are, that moment is painful, and I feel the heat of Griff's intermittent gaze over every inch of me as I approach the coach. "Your turn."

Violet moans softly on the couch across from us and climbs into Cannon's lap. I clap a hand to my mouth and look at Griff. His expression is pained, a mirror image to the horror I'm feeling.

He clears his throat. "This isn't what I imagined."

"What did you imagine? Or better yet—why are we here? What does this have to do with my list?"

"Can't we hang out without it being about your list?"

I don't know how to answer that. I don't know if it is normal for a girl to hang out with her boyfriend's brother. Then again, nothing about this situation is normal. Beau's in a coma, I still don't know what secret of his I'm protecting, and the tension between Griff and me is so strong I jump to my feet just to get away from it.

"You want fries?"

His face falls, a flash of disappointment burning in his dark eyes. "No thanks."

I'm standing in line for fries, sliding the smooth toes of my rented shoes back and forth across the floor, when the generic pop music playing over the loudspeakers comes to an abrupt halt. A loud screech of microphone feedback radiates from a tiny stage in the corner of the building. Under the dim lights, a teenage girl with waist-length hair and a belly button ring stands with the microphone and a piece of paper in her hand.

"Please welcome tonight's performer, Griff Booker." She gives three unenthusiastic claps. My stomach bottoms out as Griff walks onto the stage, which is so small it hardly qualifies. He picks up a guitar case that was leaning against the wall.

"It's your turn." The boy behind me in line nudges me in the shoulder blade. I trip over my feet up to the counter.

"Um, what?" I can't take my eyes off Griff. He's sitting on a stool in front of the mic stand, tuning his guitar.

"Miss. Would you like to order?" the balding man at the counter asks in a bored voice.

"No." I leave without ordering my distraction fries and make a beeline for the stage. A few folding chairs have been set up front and center, and they're all empty.

Ah, vicarious embarrassment, my old friend.

Griff raises his eyes, easily finding mine. He flashes me a quick smile, and I have no choice but to sit.

Nervous anticipation brews in my gut as he fiddles with his guitar. I don't know if he's ever played in public before, and I'm viciously annoyed at everyone in this establishment for ignoring him, for acting as if bowling—*bowling*, of all things—is more exciting and important than this moment. Music is Griff's home; he's as comfortable with a guitar in his hand as I am on the lake; he deserves a gig better than this one.

"I'm Griff Booker, and I'm gonna sing a few songs for you tonight," he says into the microphone. There's a shakiness around the edges of his words, betraying his nerves. My stomach clenches painfully.

He launches into a Jason Isbell cover first, a song I recognize immediately. "Tupelo." It strikes me as an odd choice for an open mic night because it's not one of Isbell's most popular songs. If Griff wanted to get the attention of the crowd, he should have picked something else. But as soon as he puts his lips to the microphone and starts singing, I realize it doesn't matter.

He's mesmerizing, his voice low and soulful. But it's his face that surprises me most. He's transformed. Every single day that he spends making small talk with strangers at the pump or slinging pizza for his dad sucks a little bit of the life from him as he works hard to distance himself from his past. I always suspected he was wearing a mask, but I've never realized how much he was hiding until now.

It's almost hard to watch him; he's painfully earnest, his face more vulnerable than I've ever seen. Every expression, every shadow betrays him as he sings a sad song about leaving. Understanding strikes me square in the chest.

It's not a question of whether he'll leave again. The firm set of his jaw and the shadows in his eyes make it clear that he will. And when he sings that "there ain't no one from here that will follow me there," I realize that's what he wants.

To leave and not be followed.

Griff finishes his song and a scattered, half-hearted applause limps through the building. He pushes his hair off his forehead and smiles like he's playing Madison Square Garden. He's never been so beautiful.

"Thanks for listening. I've got time for one more song, and I'm going to be joined by a friend of mine."

I turn, confused. But Violet and Cannon are still mauling each other on the couch. As far as I know, Griff doesn't have any friends. It's got to be the reason he spends all his free time with me. He leans close to the microphone and fixes me with a stare that cuts through me like a laser. *Oh. Oh no.*

"My friend is working on conquering her fears—"

I'm going to kill him.

"Give a warm welcome to your hometown girl, Gemma Wells."

Chapter 22

Crickets.

The Bowl patrons do *not* give me a warm welcome. The cold silence in the building matches the icy feeling dripping down my spine. Griff fixes me with a piercing gaze. I shake my head.

He moves the microphone to the side and leans toward me. "C'mon, Gem. You've got this."

I pinch the skin on my inner forearm. "Is this a nightmare? It feels like a nightmare."

His face falls. "You said you wanted to sing in front of a crowd. What's wrong?"

"Not all daydreams are meant to come true!"

"Isn't putting yourself in embarrassing situations the whole point of this?"

"When I have time to mentally prepare."

"Life doesn't always let you prepare for scary things. Sometimes you just have to suck it up and sing."

Gritting my teeth, I stand. Griff pulls up a chair next to him in front of the microphone and has the audacity to smile at me. I glare back as I sink into the chair. We're sharing the microphone, so we're sitting close. Too close, really. The detergent-and-spice scent of him almost knocks me sideways.

"You pick the song," He smiles crookedly, playing a few chords. "I can bluff my way through any Isbell. What's your favorite?"

Across the bowling alley, Violet comes up for air. Cannon nuzzles her neck, but she swats him away, her eyes on me. She waves with both hands and give me two thumbs-up. I almost vomit. More than a couple of people are watching us now, their expressions ranging from boredom to mild curiosity.

"Gemma?" Griff nudges me. I missed whatever he said last.

"I can't do it."

"If you can drink milkshakes in a pirate costume, you can do this."

He's wrong, though. I can't. Maybe my list and this whole stupid mission to conquer my social anxiety are a joke.

The legs of my chair scrape against the floor as I stand; we're attracting a few curious glances now, and my cheeks burn hot as my insides writhe uncomfortably. I hate Griff now more than ever; I'm furious at him for putting me in this position. I try to run, but my foot catches on my chair and drags it with me. I slam into the microphone stand and crash off the stage. Ringing silence follows as I jump back up on my feet.

Cannon's smirk is the only thing I can see as I make the walk of shame back to our lane. "You're a walking disaster," he says.

"Don't be an asshole," I snap.

His jaw goes slack. "Relax. It was a joke."

I hate being told to relax. It's not like I *want* to be a tightly wound ball of anxiety. "You're a jerk to me. What gives?" I swing my messenger bag over my shoulder. He shrugs, but now I'm angry and I've got nothing to lose; I press harder. "Tell me."

"You're weird! You don't really fit in at work, that's all. It's hard to be around you."

My chest tightens. I fight to keep steady breaths.

"What did you say?" Griff demands. I jump, surprised by his sudden presence.

"Ignore him, he's drunk," Violet says. "We pregamed a little."

Cannon laughs. "All I said was your girl is weird. She fell face-first off the stage! Who does that? She's so awkward I'm surprised she leaves her house."

Griff swings, his fist connecting with the side of Cannon's face with a sickening thud. Violet screams, drawing every eye in The Bowl directly at us. It's too much. This whole night has been too much. I take one last look at Griff cradling his hand, and then I run out the double doors at the front of The Bowl into the still, stifling air.

I sit on the curb and drop my head into my hands. Griff is seconds behind me.

He hesitates before sitting. Blood runs down the knuckles of his right hand, new cuts appearing where the old ones have just barely healed.

"His opinion is garbage. Drunk or sober," Griff says.

"I know." *Still hurts, though.* "You need to stop punching things."

"I never punched anything in Cleveland."

"When will you stop blaming this town for your crappy decisions?"

"I'm blaming the person this town turns me into. In Ohio, I worked so hard to control my temper. Every single day I made a conscious effort to be a better person, and then I show up here and I turn back into that angry kid I used to be. My brother's in a coma and I still get the urge to one-up him, to beat him in a never-ending competition. I don't sleep. I pick fights with my dad. I bloody my damn knuckles. I'm trying to be better, Gem, but it's like ever since I got here, there's a boot on my chest and I can't breathe."

"Well—Cannon deserved it a little," I admit.

"He one hundred percent deserved it." Griff flexes his hand, watching the scabs crack open. I want to curl my fingers around his hand, but I don't. I want to kick the boot off his chest, but I don't know how.

"I'm sorry no one paid attention to your show."

"Are you kidding? That was the best show I've ever done!"

I suppress my smile; I'm not in the mood to be cheered up.

"No, seriously. That's the biggest crowd I've ever had," he says.

"It was just me."

"Nah. The guy behind the counter was totally into it."

"How could you tell?"

"His face almost made an expression."

There he goes again, making me laugh without my consent. This is not the right time for happiness. This is the time for wallowing and regret, for angst and crying. All I want is to crawl under my covers and replay this horrible night on an endless loop until the sun rises. Either that or visit Beau in the hospital.

"We'll take open mic night off the list," Griff says.

"It wasn't on the list," I snap, the weight of my body too much to hold up. I'm ready for this day to be over.

"Even better," Griff says. "No harm, no foul."

"Big harm, big foul!" I counter. "And if you don't understand that, then I don't know why I'm letting you help me. You don't understand me at all."

Why did I ever think he did? Because he looks sad when he plays the guitar and doesn't get along with his dad?

"Do you want me to cancel the party?" he finally asks. His tone is indecipherable. For all I can tell, he's talking about canceling a doctor's appointment, not the Fourth of July blowout that is supposed to mark my completed transformation. I've been telling myself that after the party I'll be the kind of girl who can be social without getting sick, but now it feels hopeless.

"I don't know." I want to finish my list, prove to myself that I don't have to spend the rest of my life as an anxious mess. But I've wasted so much of my time lately with Griff that I haven't made enough time for his brother. My stomach sinks when I realize how little I've thought about Beau. Not that I haven't worried about him or wished for him to wake up. I do both of those things every day. But I don't daydream anymore.

I glance sideways at Griff in time to see his jaw clench. "It's a simple question. Do you want to throw the party? Yes or no."

"I don't want to talk about it."

He gawks at me. "You can't run away from every slightly hard conversation."

"Sure I can." I start to stand, but he reaches out and clasps his fingers around my elbow, stopping me in my tracks. I'll never understand why some people dive headfirst into awkward conversations.

"Throw the party or don't, I don't care, but I need to know whether I have plans that night." His fingers are still on my elbow and I'm distracted by every single point of contact between his skin and mine.

I pull my arm out of his grasp. "I'll be at my houseboat at eight o'clock. If other people want to hang out there too, I won't *not* let them."

The corner of his mouth twitches. "Fine. What time should we meet up?"

"I'm visiting Beau after the dock closes and then I have to go to the store to pick up food, but I'll be back by seven."

"Are you sure you'll have time?"

"I can't not go. I was supposed to visit him today, but instead I'm here, humiliating myself at a public bowling alley." Tears blur my vision as I stare at my rented shoes.

"Last I checked, the hospital is closed to visitors at this hour," Griff says in a steely voice.

"You haven't been to see him in weeks, so you'll excuse me if I don't listen to your opinion on visiting Beau."

"What good does it do to sit in his room when he doesn't know we're there?"

"You don't know that."

He rubs a hand over his face, sighing. Streetlights illuminate his bloody knuckles. "Sometimes it feels like you'd rather hide out in Beau's hospital room than hang out with me in the real world."

"I—I don't know what you want me to say to that."

"Don't worry about what I want to hear. What do you want to say?"

"Beau's going to wake up in *four* days. I can't just ignore him to spend all my time with you."

"That's not what I meant. I just thought it might be more useful to work on your list than sit next to a kid in a coma, but what do I know?"

"He's not just a 'kid in a coma'! He's your brother! And my boyfriend!"

Violet pushes the door open; her eyes dart between us. "You want a ride home, Gemma?"

"With Cannon? No thanks."

"Sorry about him. He was out of line." She ducks her head. "I'll return your shoes." I untie them and hand them to her while Griff stews beside me.

"When I asked you to sing with me tonight, I thought I was being helpful." The strain in his voice breaks my heart a little. I look up, startled to see how close he's standing.

I cross my arms. "Beau wouldn't have done that." It's a bit of a stretch, pretending like I know what Beau would do, but I feel it in my bones. Beau would never push me to do something uncomfortable. The fact is, being in the hospital with Beau still feels easier than my time with Griff, who expects bowling alley open mic nights and houseboat parties and uncomfortable vulnerability. He expects, and he deserves, eye contact and honest conversation. I'm starting to think it's more than I can give.

There's a reason Beau Booker is my dream guy. There must be. Otherwise, why have I gotten myself into such a mess?

Griff steps back, looking stunned. "You're right," he says as his face falls. "He's always been the better brother."

"That's not what I meant."

"It's exactly what you meant." He stops pacing and crosses his arms over his chest, challenging me to argue with him, but I can't.

I bow my head miserably. "Take me home, Griff."

Chapter 23

The Fourth of July comes faster than I'm prepared for. Every day that brings us closer to Beau waking up passes in a blink. If I survive tonight's party, there will only be a couple of days left until I have to face him for the first time. But that's *if* I survive the party. I make it back to the houseboat by seven fifteen, overloaded grocery bags hanging from both arms.

"Is Griff here?" I ask Dad as I set an entire paycheck's worth of snacks on our small table.

"Who?"

"Beau's brother. He's helping me with the party tonight. Have you seen him?"

"Negative." Dad helps me unpack chips and crackers and packaged cookies. When he reaches the last bag, he pulls out two spiky green vegetables and inspects them critically. "What are these?"

"Artichokes."

"*Why* are these?"

"I thought we needed something healthy to balance out all the sugar." I stare at the twin artichokes; they look more like a medieval weapon than a casual appetizer. "I panicked. I have no idea how to do this."

"Chin up—you'll be fine."

"What if I'm not? What if no one shows up? What if they do show up and have a terrible time? What if everyone hates my taste in music? What if everyone hates *me*?"

A knock sounds on our glass door, and my existential dread evaporates. It's about time Griff showed up. I turn, surprised to see Sofía standing on our deck, her arms around a large speaker.

"I'm about to drop this on my feet!" she calls.

"One second!" I turn back to Dad, panic seizing my chest. "I take it back. I call it off."

He hides the artichokes in the nearest cupboard and slams the door. "Go get 'em, kid. I'll slip out the back and see you in the morning. Don't do anything stupid." He gives me a fist bump and then takes my shoulders and physically turns me toward the door.

Sofía and I set up food and music on the top deck. Now that the sun has all but disappeared behind the horizon, the temperature is tolerable and our slip in the marina has a view of the clubhouse and the fireworks show scheduled for tonight. After we finish with setup, we head downstairs. I glance critically at my reflection while Sofía applies her makeup in the bathroom mirror.

"How do you live like this?" she asks, leaning over the small sink to get a closer look at her reflection. "There's no counter space."

"I don't wear much makeup," I say, stepping into the already crowded bathroom.

"That's true," she muses as she wings her eyeliner with a practiced flick of her wrist. I feel a sharp stab of envy. Between growing up without a mom and spending so much time on the lake, makeup is not on my list of skills.

"Will you do mine?"

Her perfect eyebrows ratchet up in surprise. "I thought you were purposely going for a too-cool-for-makeup, natural look."

"I've never been too cool for anything in my life."

She laughs and instructs me to close my eyes. "You know what this means, don't you?" she says as she brushes powder across my cheeks.

"What?"

"We've shared makeup. We're officially friends. No going back now," she says, and my heart pangs with preemptive regret. I mentally add "friendship with Sofía" to the pile of things I stand to lose when Beau wakes up in three days. "Done. Open your eyes."

"Wow." I blink, shocked at my reflection. The winged liner and rosy cheeks match hers, but she's also given me bubble-gum-pink lips that are so bright they're impossible to ignore. "Is it too much?"

"Not a chance. You should let me do this before they wake Beau up. Will you be at the hospital when it happens?"

I nod. Mrs. Booker said I could wait with them while Beau's medical team brings him out of sedation, which is a relief because it means I'll be able to talk to him before he says anything about me.

"Are you nervous?"

"Um—"

She waves her hands in front of her face. "I'm an idiot. Forget I said that. The party will be the perfect distraction, and in three days, your super-hot boyfriend is going to wake up and kiss your face off."

"I hope so," I say, which makes Sofía laugh. "Should I change?" I glance at my cutoffs and T-shirt. It's another oversized one, with a stretched-out neckline and a tourist vibe. LAKE POWELL is written across the front in retro font, with thick yellow and orange underline. I tug on the hem of my shirt. Nina would never let me out in public like this.

"Like I said: You look too cool for the rest of us. Effortless." She pulls my shoulders back until I'm standing straight. "A little confidence goes a long way." She checks the time. "It's eight o'clock. We should get out there."

"Already?" I check my phone for what feels like the hundredth time, but my notifications are painfully empty. I wish Griff were here already.

"You really miss him, don't you?" Sofía asks.

It's not a lie when I answer, "I really do."

Thirty minutes later, the top deck of the boat is crowded with people awaiting fireworks. Sofía, Kodi, Deja, Shandiin, and a few other girls from the gift shop. Violet, *not* Cannon, and some of the fuel team members from other docks. Ian Radnor and a bunch of guys from school. They're all milling around as music blasts across the water, smiling and laughing and *not* looking like they'd rather jump overboard than spend another social second in my presence. Progress!

Me: **The party started.**

"Have you seen Griff?" I ask as I move through the crowd. Heads shake no. "Have you seen Griff?" I ask the next group I see as I move through the party, always on my way somewhere else. I flash back to the beach party that started this all, and my impatience morphs into worry. I glance at my phone, wondering if something bad happened to him.

Me: **Where are you?**

As I hover around the periphery of my own party, it's impossible not to compare the person I am now against the girl I was at the beginning of the summer. At that first party, all I wanted was someone, *anyone* to pull me into the group and make me feel like I belonged.

Me: **At least tell me you're okay.**

Now I don't want just *anyone*. The disappointed ache I feel in my chest isn't the generic pain of not being invited to the party. It's the pointed, specific ache of being excluded when I didn't expect it. No one is more surprised than I am how quickly Griff's become my best friend in Page, and now that he's not here, I realize how much I miss him when he's not around. Not just to help me through my anxiety, but because I'd rather stand on the fringe of the crowd and laugh with him than be the glowing, magnetic center of attention.

My phone finally buzzes in my pocket.

Griff: **Almost there.**

I scan the marina again and a shadow on the dock catches my attention. I bolt down the ladder, sprinting toward Griff. I throw my arms around his neck and pull him into a hug. "I was worried something happened to you."

He quickly squeezes me in return and then drops his arms. "Sorry to scare you."

I step back and survey him. Both the dark circles and the

facial hair have returned with a vengeance. "What happened?"

"Nothing."

"You're almost two hours late and you look like crap."

He hesitates. "You don't."

"Gee, thanks." I roll my eyes, newly aware of my bubble-gum-pink lips. "I thought you stood me up."

"Interesting choice of words."

"Come on. Let's go to the party." He grimaces, and, worried he's going to bail, I lace my fingers through his and tow him across the dock and up to the party.

"I'll see you later," Griff says as he moves into the crowd, slipping away before I have time to object. For the next thirty minutes I pretend not to stare at him, and he pretends not to stare at me, our gazes darting away from each other like frightened fish. I can't help myself, but I'd be lying if I said it's a new feeling. It's not just tonight—not just the way his scruffy face looks in the dark or how his biceps are straining against his T-shirt. I find myself wanting to look at him *all the time*.

An almost-painful heat blossoms in my stomach every time he glances my way, catching my eye from the end of the fuel dock or winking at me as I cross another item off my list. My favorite time to look at him is when he's distracted or busy with something else and I'm free to study his features, the way I did for so many years with his brother. The thing about Beau Booker and his Instagram dimples is that he always looks exactly how you'd expect him to. Except for that last day on the beach, nothing about Beau ever surprised me. Maybe that sounds boring, but I took comfort in his familiarity. Every morning I walked into school, my stomach in knots, and there was Beau with his messy curls and big smile, his expression open like he was waiting for life to delight him.

Griff Booker is not like that. His face is all shadows and angles, wry smirks and smoky eyes. Beau's eyes are open, friendly, and easy to read. Griff's are a canyon of emotion, especially when he has a guitar in his hand.

Unfortunately, he's wearing my least favorite expression right now. Across the top deck of the houseboat, he's leaning against the guardrail, chatting with Sofía and Shandiin, his face a mask of boredom and indifference. I'd rather see him get angry than pretend he doesn't have feelings.

He catches my attention across the crowd and rolls his eyes, confirming my suspicion. Sofía says something and waits for Griff's response, but I can tell from the set of his jaw that he's done with this conversation. Bored with his refusal to charm them, Sofía and Shandiin shrug at each other and go in search of other entertainment.

I remember the first true conversation Griff and I ever had. *I'm not in the habit of charming anyone.* Goose bumps erupt across my neck at the memory of the steady timbre of his voice as he made me that promise.

I don't need your approval is what he meant. He doesn't care who likes him and can't be bothered to pretend that he does. But that lack of concern or effort is every bit as alluring as Beau's boisterous laugh and constant mugging for attention, which means Griff is charming in his own way. Judging by the longing glances and secret smiles thrown his way even now, I'm not the only person who feels this way. He's just as antisocial as I am, but he's made it work for him. He's not out here with a list in his pocket and a lifetime of social trauma. At the risk of sounding like Bennett when he doesn't win a game—*it's not fair*.

Griff frees himself from conversation and stalks over to me, his face grumpy and brooding.

"Why aren't you talking to anyone?" he asks. In lieu of socializing, I've been distractedly wandering between groups of people, one eye on Griff, and always pretending I'm on my way to someone else.

"Why aren't you?"

"I just had a whole-ass conversation with your friends."

"Glaring and nodding doesn't count as talking," I point out.

"I'm not the one trying to change myself."

"Yeah, let's talk about that," I say, brimming with an annoyance that I didn't feel five minutes ago. "Why aren't you trying any harder to be funny or interesting or likable or—"

"Because I'm not a performing monkey, Gemma. And neither are you. You don't owe shit to anyone here."

"That's not what you said when you were teaching me how to get tips."

"If three minutes of polite small talk means the difference between earning money to leave town and staying here forever, you better believe I'm gonna play nice. But at a party? I'll tell a joke if I feel like telling a joke, but I'm not going to put on a show for these people."

"Right," I say, flustered. He has a point, but he's also missing the point. "Unlike me, you can stand here and glare at every person without being labeled a freak or a bitch. It's a total double standard. If I did what you're doing, people would hate me."

"Who cares what they think?"

"I care!"

"That's the difference between us," he says. "I honestly don't give a single shit whether anyone on this deck likes me or not."

Ouch. That hurts way more than I'm comfortable with.

"That's easy to say when everyone already does."

"I'm not Beau."

"No. But that doesn't mean every straight girl on the boat wouldn't throw herself overboard for the chance to be charmed by Griff Booker."

He raises a dark, questioning eyebrow. "Every girl?"

My throat dries. "The single ones, anyway."

"So—not you?" His voice rumbles through me and I can't bear to look at him.

I turn my back on the party and lean my forearms against the guardrail. The marina is packed tonight, hundreds of boats floating in the dark water. They shine like fireflies in the dark, small pinpoints of light hovering in the dark. Griff leans his elbows against the rail, facing the opposite direction.

"Trust me, I wish I were like you. I wish I didn't spend every waking moment of my life worried about what other people think of me." The admission is too personal, so I cap it off with a shrug, attempting for cool detachment and missing by a country mile. "Nina says no one else thinks about me that much."

"Who's Nina?"

"My best friend." I grow conscious of the heat of Griff's arm inches away from mine. "Sort of," I amend, twisting myself around, unable to keep still in his presence. My foot taps against the deck. I'm a fidgety mess.

"She's right. Most people think about themselves most of the time." He points to Ian Radnor. "See that guy? He's not thinking about me, or you, or anyone else here. He's thinking about the shiny Pokémon card he's trying to win on eBay. It'll cost him an entire summer's worth of allowance, but once he holds the card in his hand for the first time, every weed pulled and yard mowed and old-lady toenail clipped will have been worth it."

I laugh, and Griff moves closer, nudging me. "And see that girl? She's thinking about the two chocolate cookies she had after lunch, and instead of enjoying herself at this party, she's going to spend the whole time miserable about something she ate and worried that she looks fat."

"Wow, that took a dark turn," I say.

"I have a dark mind," Griff says.

I roll my eyes. "And the guy in the blue shirt accidentally put his tighty-whitey underwear on backward and is dealing with a serious wedgie situation." We go back and forth like this for a long time, inventing increasingly absurd backstories and problems for everyone on this boat.

"We just demonstrated that your sort-of-best-friend, Nina, is right."

"Yeah, but she said people think specifically less about me than anyone else because I'm invisible at school."

Griff's brow wrinkles in disgust. "No offense, but Nina sounds like a jerk."

I freeze, wondering if I should hate him for saying that. But honestly, it's a relief to hear someone express the thought that's been nagging me for a while. Nina's never treated me all that well, and this summer has only made it more obvious. I've texted her multiple times since our last phone conversation and she's left every text on read. "She kind of is."

A loud crack sounds in the distance and a burst of red, white, and blue fireworks lights the sky. We watch in silence for a few minutes. Sweat drips down my neck and the small of my back. I'm a human sprinkler system tonight. "Fireworks aren't as romantic as I imagined they'd be," I muse, disgusted by the Slip 'N Slide forming under my clothes.

Griff shifts, turning so he's leaning against the rail, staring at my profile instead of the fireworks. "You thought this would be romantic?"

I don't know if he means "this" as in the fireworks, or "this" as in us. My neck flushes. I imagined this moment so many times, but it was always Beau by my side. Beau as my boyfriend. Weird how nothing is at all like I thought it would be.

"It's never this sweaty in the movies," I say. Griff's face is lit up by another blast of fireworks, and he's smugly grinning at me. I cringe, mortified. "I'm trying to say that it's hot out here."

We're too far from the fireworks to hear the star-spangled soundtrack, but throbbing music blares from Sofía's speaker. I'm suddenly envious of the girls brave enough to dance under the fireworks.

He shifts so that he's leaning into me instead of the rail. "You have that expression again," he whispers in my ear.

"What expression?" I turn, surprised to find his face so close to mine. I can smell peppermint on his breath.

"Sparkle eyes. You want something, but you won't let yourself have it." He follows my gaze to the dancers. "Do you want to dance with me?"

"I don't know how."

"I'll show you." His hands slide to my hips and he pulls me toward him. He moves to the beat, his hands guiding me to move with him.

It's a disaster. Everything about my body feels wrong. I'm all elbows and hips and I don't know what to do with my arms. Sofía spots us and nudges Shandiin so she'll look too. My face heats and I pull away. Griff lets me go easily. "I can't," I say.

"Sorry. I shouldn't have assumed you wanted to."

"I do want to. But there are too many people watching."

He looks at me for a long moment, during which my heart thunders as loud at the fireworks. "Follow me." He leads me down the ladder to the first deck, where we can still hear the music, though it's slightly muted. He slides open the glass door leading into the boat and closes it firmly behind us. He checks that the other door is also closed.

"What are you doing?"

"Private dance party," he says. He pulls out his phone and scrolls through the music.

"No Isbell," I tease.

He rolls his eyes and presses play on a Calvin Harris song. "I have one or two surprises in me."

More than one or two, I think as the dance track blares through the small room. "It's still embarrassing if you can see me."

"I have a plan for that." He opens and shut drawers in the tiny kitchen until he finds a pair of scissors. He picks up a discarded gauzy swim cover-up that was left on the couch and cuts into it, tearing off two long strips of fabric.

"Someone's gonna be furious."

He grins wolfishly. "I don't care." He tosses me one of the strips and keeps one for himself, tying it around his eyes like a blindfold. "Now I can't see you," he explains. "You're free to do the same, or not."

My stomach flips in nervous anticipation as I double the thin fabric around my eyes until I can't see. I stand there stupidly for a few seconds, the throb of the music working its way into my body. Griff's hand finds mine. "Is this okay?" he asks.

Part of me wishes I could see his expression, but the other part of me feels emboldened by the fact that I can't. Slowly, I guide his hand to my hip. He follows suit with the other one. And for a beat, we stand there unmoving, his hands on my hips, my hands on his hands, and both of us surrounded by darkness. "Just move," he says.

"How?" I laugh nervously.

"Do whatever feels good."

Again, my throat goes dry.

Awkwardly, I try it. My body follows his as we dance, jump, and spin, our sweaty bodies bumping into each other, his breath on my neck, his smile against my ear. It's weird at first, but then I stop caring and I just let myself dance, all my senses narrowing to the music and to Griff.

We dance like this for one, two, three songs, and I've never felt so free in my entire life. Unstoppable. Happy. My arms are slung around Griff's neck, pulling him as close as possible to me. Our hips sway to the music, my breath growing heavier with every passing second.

"Gemma?" Griff whispers the question in my ear, his breath sending electric shocks down my spine. He nudges my chin with a finger, tilting my face up, and slides his other hand up my back and into the hair at the nape of my neck. His breath is whisper-light against my lips, and I've never wanted anything more than I want to push myself onto my toes and kiss him hard.

I'm stopped by a buzzing against my thigh. It takes me a peppermint-scented breath to realize it's his phone in his pocket, pressed against me.

"Ignore it," he whispers, his lips so close I could explode.

I almost do. I would, but then my phone is buzzing in my pocket. It stops, and his starts again; he breaks away, growling in frustration. We both pull our blindfolds off, breaking the spell. I self-consciously smooth my hands over my hair, once again unsure what to do with any of my limbs. "I'll silence it," he says, glancing at the screen. His expression falters and my stomach bottoms out.

Something is wrong.

He answers the call. "Mom?" He listens, then looks up at me with wide eyes. "Beau's awake."

Chapter 24

"He's awake!" Griff looks stunned as he runs a hand through his hair. "I can't believe he's finally awake. I know they said it would happen eventually, but—" He shakes his head as his shocked expression is slowly replaced with a grin. When Griff looks up at me from under his lashes, I hardly recognize him. For once, his face isn't clouded with dark circles and half shadows. He grins openly, looking happier than I've ever seen him.

"How? They said it wouldn't be for a few more days."

"I don't know and I don't care. He's awake."

"I can't believe it," I whisper, feeling dizzy. I've been waiting for this news since the helicopter lifted Beau from the beach, but I never expected my relief to be so tangled with worry and fear and confusing feelings for Griff. I smother those thoughts and force myself to focus on the good. After weeks of gnawing uncertainty— *Beau is awake.*

Griff tips his head back and laughs, and then he squeezes me into a bear hug and swings me in a circle, knocking my equilibrium so off center that when he sets me down and takes my face in his hands, it doesn't occur to me that we're about to fall off a cliff together. "I don't think I realized how scared I was until this moment." His eyes shine with unshed, happy tears. He touches his forehead to mine and exhales, his hands sliding down to grip my shoulders.

I inhale the scent of peppermint and discarded fear. "What did your mom say? Is he okay?"

"I think so." Griff takes a deep breath and closes his eyes. We stand in perfect breathless silence, the warm air around us shimmering with summertime promise. My heart thunders in my throat. I have sparklers in my blood. As much as I clung to Mrs. Booker's insistence that Beau would be fine, a part of me always worried I'd never see his perfect dimples or hear his booming laugh again.

Griff shifts. My stomach clenches with anticipation. He presses his lips to my forehead, and I stop breathing. His lips on my skin sends a shock through my veins. We stay like that for a breath, and then he releases my shoulders like he's been burned. We spring apart, his eyes mirroring the panic in my chest.

"*Shit.*" He looks at me like I'm dangerous. "No no no no no. I can't believe that I almost—"

"I can't believe that *I* almost—" I bite my lip. The moment I've been waiting for all summer is finally here, and I nearly wrecked everything.

Griff rakes a hand through his hair and paces the houseboat, his eyes frantic. "I'm the world's worst brother." He stares out the window over the kitchen sink. Inky black water stretches to eternity.

"We have to go to the hospital," I say. Even now, Beau could be blowing up my entire life. If I can't convince him to cover for me (and hopefully fall in love with me in the process), I'll lose my new friends, I'll have to quit my job, and the Bookers will never invite me to dinner again. I'll be the new Lizzie Spalding: a blight on the small town of Page, Arizona.

Griff blinks, looking too dazed to function.

"I'll get everyone out of here and meet you on the dock." I run up the ladder and find Sofía in the crowd. "You have to get everyone out of here!" I shout over the thumping music. "Beau's awake and Griff and I need to get to the hospital ASAP."

"Beau's awake?" Ian shouts, and every head turns my way. The sudden attention makes my ears buzz, but it doesn't ruin me like it would have a few weeks ago. People shout and cheer, and at least one person starts to cry. Everyone's favorite golden boy is back. And unless I get to the hospital immediately and do major damage control, by this time tomorrow every single one of them will know I'm a social-climbing, desperate fraud.

Sofía grabs my arm. "Hey, are you okay?"

I blink, confused by the question. I should be overjoyed. I *was*, until the tragic truth of my reality caught up with me. "Why?"

"I saw you and Griff. He was kind of—leaning into you." Sofía demonstrates by bringing her body close to mine, studying me with an intense look for three long seconds before she leans away and shrugs. "Then you two disappeared."

"I—" My brain short-circuits as I scramble to come up with some plausible explanation for what Sofía saw.

"I'll only ask you this once—do you like Griff?"

"What?! No!"

Sofía lowers her voice to a whisper. "Some people think you're trying to switch brothers, which is kind of low, considering Beau's been unconscious for the last month."

"Is this because of 'The Incident' on the cliff?"

"That's when the rumor started, but I see the way you look at each other when you think the other one isn't looking."

My chest seizes, and the only thing I want to know is how Griff looks at me. "It's not true. I'm in love with Beau."

Sofía's eyes search mine for a moment before her face softens. "Good."

"Gemma! Let's go!" Griff barks from belowdecks.

"Text me after you see Beau!" She squeezes me in a quick hug and then nudges me to Griff. He's waiting for me on the deck, impatience radiating off him in waves. I follow him to his car and climb in the passenger seat.

My legs bounce the whole ride to the hospital, and I feel the strangest sense of déjà vu for that evening in May when I made this trip with Ian. But instead of worrying for Beau's life, I'm rehearsing my plan in my head.

Step one: Look gorgeous when Beau sees me.

I pull down the sun visor and flip open the mirror. Remnants of my winged eyeliner are smudged across my cheeks. I lick my fingers and scrub. It only makes things worse.

Griff scoffs.

"He's seeing me for the first time in weeks!"

"Carry on," he drawls.

Step two: Let Beau see me at ease with his friends and family.

I didn't plan to arrive at the hospital with Griff, but it can't hurt my case.

Step three: Make sure Beau knows I saved his life.

It's important the boy has the facts!

Step four: Ask to speak to him alone and tell him the truth.

Most of the truth, anyway.

Step five: Be so witty and interesting and NOT anxious that he's mesmerized by me and wants to be my boyfriend for real.

Okay, step five might be pushing it. And I still don't know if I'm capable of getting through step four without throwing up or passing out. But it's my only option. My deadline is here. It's time to see if my checklist changed anything.

I sneak a glance at Griff. His face is tight and unreadable. "Griff." I take a fortifying breath, preparing myself for the awkward task of thanking him for helping me. If my plan goes south, I'll never get another chance. My stomach protests that thought violently. "I—um—we should talk—"

"It's fine. I understand."

"What do you mean?"

"Gem." His voice cracks. His knuckles whiten on the steering wheel. "Can we talk about this later?"

Gem. The nickname makes me want to cry. I've never had one before.

I sit on my hands and clench my jaw until the air-conditioning turns icy and goose bumps erupt across my forearms. I rub my hands across my skin to warm up.

"There's a sweatshirt in the back," Griff says. I reach back and pull a thick black hoodie off the floor. I immediately recognize it as the one draped over me the night I fell asleep at the restaurant. I dropped it in the lost and found before I left that night, but Griff must have taken it out because it was his all along. I pull it on. The inside is worn and soft against my skin. I sink deep into the seat and pull the fabric to my nose, inhaling the smoky, spicy scent that has come to define my summer. Ten years from now I won't be able to separate this smell from the way Griff's hair falls over his forehead or the pluck of his fingers against guitar strings. A swell of emotion in my throat nearly chokes me.

My body revolts as we pull into the dark parking lot.

My knees tremble. *Don't get out of the car.*

My stomach riots. *Don't walk through that door.*

My heart is in my throat. *Don't follow Griff down this hallway.*

I ignore every self-preservation signal as my flip-flops slap against cold tile. A blast of icy air blows across my face and I'm glad to have the added layer of Griff's hoodie to keep me warm.

"You can't wear that, by the way." His eyes cut sideways as we approach Beau's room.

"It's cold in here."

"Don't care. Give it back." He holds his hand out.

I swat it away. "You gave it to me!"

"Not permanently. I let you borrow it—and now I want it back."

"Seriously?"

"We'll look suspicious if you wear it."

"It's a generic black hoodie."

"He'll know."

"*How?*" I glance down at myself. The jacket hangs mid-thigh, almost completely covering my shorts, but I don't understand why Griff thinks Beau will immediately make the leap from "she's wearing an oversized hoodie" to "she's cheating on me with my brother." "He has other things to worry about!"

"Give it to me!"

"I don't want to!" Keeping this hoodie feels vitally important.

The door opens and Winnie stares at us. "Are you coming in or not?"

I swallow and glance sideways at Griff. He looks as reluctant as I am to enter the room. He goes first, and I take a deep breath and follow. Every part of me is trembling. This is the moment I've been waiting for—the chance to talk to Beau before he can burn my life to the ground—but my plans have never felt so paper thin. My time is up. I spent the last few weeks trying to turn myself into the kind of girl who's capable of having a relationship, and now my fate is in Beau's hands.

Beau's bed is flanked by his parents: Mom on one side, Dad on the other. They lean over him, blocking my view. But when Mrs. Booker sees Griff and me, she springs to her feet. Happy tears course down her cheeks as she pulls her eldest son into a hug. She whispers something into his ear and then moves back to allow Griff to see his brother.

"How do you feel?" Griff asks.

"Better than you look," Beau says. "Are you trying to grow a beard? 'Cause it's looking a little patchy." He reaches his hand toward Griff's chin.

Griff smacks Beau's hand away with an eye roll. "Have you looked in the mirror, Joe Dirt?"

"Never forget I started shaving before you did."

"How could I, when you bring it up every other sentence?" Griff says dryly.

A touch on my elbow makes me jump. It's Winnie again. My

heart beats so fast I expect it to explode any minute. "I apologize in advance if I pass out on top of you," I whisper. I would crush her tiny bones.

"What?"

"Never mind. Is Beau okay?"

"Yeah, but we're not sure what he remembers."

"What do you mean?" I ask sharply.

"He's confused about how much time has passed and . . ." She hesitates, frowning at me. "The doctor warned us he might have forgotten certain people or memories."

With a tentative step forward, I tuck a wayward strand of hair behind my ear, and the hoodie slips off my shoulder. The phantom heat of Griff's hands lingers on my sticky skin. Nausea rises in my stomach.

"Hey, can I have a mirror?" Beau asks.

Griff mimes checking a watch. "It took you five whole minutes to ask. Have they checked for brain damage?"

"Enough!" Mrs. Booker says. "Beau—look who's here." She looks pointedly at me.

"Gemma." Beau's easy smile is unchanged, his dimples as dazzling as ever. And as relieved as I am that he's okay, I'm too sick to appreciate them. My stomach feels like it's filled with rocks. If I jumped off a cliff right now, I'd never come back up.

Beau pushes himself up into a sitting position and folds one arm behind his head. He looks at me squarely. "So, I hear you're my girlfriend."

Chapter 25

I freeze, unable to breathe. "What do you remember?" *Does he know who he is? What year it is? That he took a picture on the beach and asked me to pretend we were close?* My plan is already off the rails. This conversation was supposed to take place in private. I can't think properly with Griff glowering over us.

I've never been so aware of silence as I wait for Beau to speak. His eyes bore into mine. Every aspect of my flimsy plan evaporates from my brain as my breathing turns jagged.

"Of course he remembers you," Mrs. Booker soothes. She covers my hands with hers. They're so warm and soft that I want to cry. "He must! You remember her, don't you, Beau?" When he doesn't respond, her voice falters. "She saved your life. Beau? Tell her you remember."

Beau's eyes flick to Griff, and they make brief, loaded eye contact. Curiosity burns bright and hot in my belly.

"Can we have a minute alone?" I blurt when I finally find my voice.

Griff's face goes carefully blank as his family shuffles into the hospital corridor. He gives Beau and me one fleeting glance before closing the door behind him. I sink into the chair next to my fake boyfriend and wipe my sweaty palms on Griff's hoodie.

"Finally." Beau sighs. "I can't think with them in here."

"Let me explain—" I say at the same time Beau says, "Tell me what happened." He picks up the large pink plastic cup next to his bed and slurps through the straw.

My heart stutters. "You really don't remember?"

"That night on the beach is fuzzy."

My heart sinks. If he doesn't remember asking me to pretend that we're close, my job gets a whole lot harder. "Ian flooded the engine of his boat. And while you were helping him hook it to the trailer and get it out of the water, you slipped and hit your head on the propeller."

"And then?" he prompts.

I shrug. "And then you went to the hospital."

"*After* you pulled me out of the water and gave me CPR."

"Correct." I play with the zipper on Griff's hoodie, but Beau's eyes narrow at my fingertips as I draw the zipper up and down. I force myself to stop fidgeting.

"Everyone says you're my hero," he says.

I may not be brave enough to say anything worthwhile out loud, but at least step three of my plan is working. I pull the zipper to my neck with shaking fingers.

"Is that Griff's?" he asks.

Crap. Griff was right. "He let me borrow it. Hospitals are so cold."

"When did he come back to town?"

"As soon as you got hurt."

Beau considers this for several seconds before saying, "You came here together tonight." It's not a question.

"He's been nice to me. Surprisingly nice."

His eyes narrow again. "What's surprising about it?"

"I've heard the rumors about him," I say, but I wish he'd change the subject. I'm not here to talk about Griff; I'm here to find out if I've changed myself enough to make Beau like me.

"Which rumors?"

"All of them. Drugs, booze, theft. Punching you in the face."

Beau sighs and rubs his eyes. "We've had our problems."

"For what it's worth, the only reason he's been nice to me this summer is because he thinks it's what you'd want."

"Because you're my girlfriend." Beau smiles easily, and the complicated knot in my stomach begins to unravel. My entire summer has been leading to this moment, and I cannot believe I'm going to get away with this.

"We don't have to use that word," I say. Just because I don't want him to know the truth doesn't mean I'm going to gaslight him into dating me. "Or any word. It's okay that you don't remember me. We can just give ourselves a clean slate. Start over."

"Gemma." Beau catches my hand in his. My palms are wetter than Niagara Falls. "Do you want to be my girlfriend?"

"C'mon." I laugh. This is the most absurd situation of my life. It's way too close to a daydream to be true. "Don't make me say it." He raises an eyebrow. Unbelievable. He's going to make me say it. "Don't be an idiot, Beau Booker. At least half the school wants to date you—probably more."

"Even you?"

Especially me. My stomach is full of caged butterflies, making me feel a little sick. "I've had worse propositions."

"Have you?"

"No," I admit. But I haven't had better ones either. Griff's face flashes in my mind and I feel the heat of his lips on my forehead. I dismiss the thought. It's irrelevant for a hundred reasons. I would never live down being the girl who ditched her comatose boyfriend for his brother. I wouldn't survive that type of gossip.

Beau, on the other hand, might be a possibility. Charming Beau Booker and his Instagram dimples wants to be my boyfriend. I frown, suddenly concerned about the severity of his head injury. "Don't date me just because I saved your life."

"That seems like as good a reason as any."

"Beau Booker, do you have a traumatic brain injury?"

"Why do you call me that?"

"It's your name."

"But the way you say the full thing. *Beau Booker.* It sounds like I'm a celebrity or something."

"Wait until you see the PRAY FOR BEAU BOOKER signs hanging all over town."

"No kidding? That's awesome."

I shudder. We have vastly different definitions of awesome.

"It doesn't sound like something a girlfriend would say," he explains.

I groan. I'm trying to let him off the hook, but he won't swim away. Maybe it's a chivalry thing; he doesn't want to dump the girl who saved his life. "I don't have to be."

His brows draw together. "Do you want to break up?"

I sigh. During all those one-sided coma conversations, I

convinced myself that Beau was easy to talk to. Now that he can talk back, it doesn't feel so easy. "Do you?"

"Do *you?*"

We're still for several seconds, the tension in the air pressing on my chest as we stare at each other in the most bizarre standoff of all time. But then he bursts out laughing, and I can't help but join him.

"This is weird," he says.

"So weird." I pick at my fingernails to avoid his eyes.

"Mom said a reporter has been calling. She wants to film an interview with us?"

"It's just for a local website, but I've been dodging her calls."

"Let's do it." Beau throws me one of his careless, dazzling grins, and I'm a little breathless. After everything has gone my way, it feels wrong to deny him this request.

The door opens and an unfamiliar nurse pokes his head in the room. "You." He points to me. "Time to go. Visiting hours are long over and he needs to rest."

I don't want to leave. Too much between Beau and me feels unsettled, and none of it makes any sense. I walked into this room expecting him to torch my social life. Instead, he asked me to be his girlfriend *for real.*

I'm in a daze as I walk into the hall. Mrs. Booker pesters the nurse into letting everyone say good night to Beau before leaving, but Griff stays with me. "You were right," I say numbly as we head toward the elevator.

"About what?"

"He recognized your jacket."

I unzip it, but Griff waves me off. "The damage is done. Keep it as a parting gift."

I don't know what to say to that. I don't want to "part" with Griff.

"What's the verdict? Does he remember you?"

"No."

Griff steps into the elevator and stretches his arm across the door, waiting for me to join him. "That sucks," he says.

"It's not a big deal." The last thing I need is more unwarranted sympathy.

"That's a lot of memories, though. First dates, first kisses—" Griff clears his throat as I flash back to his lips on my forehead. How is it possible that was only an hour ago? I felt so close to him in that moment, and now there's a Beau-sized chasm between us. "Your whole history gone, just like that." We make painful eye contact for a fraction of a second too long before looking away. "I'd be disappointed if I forgot—" He cuts himself off, hesitating. "My girlfriend."

Jealousy stings like a sunburn. "Since when do you have a girlfriend?"

He smiles so wryly it's barely a smile. "Hypothetically speaking. I believe we've already had this conversation."

Right. I'm gonna need a few minutes for my heart rate to return to normal. "Well." *Well. Say something. Anything.* "If you forgot someone, you wouldn't know you forgot them, which means disappointed is not something you could be." The words come out in a confusing jumble, but Griff seems to understand my point.

"I'd know enough," he says. "All memories have a bit of

heartbreak in them. But the ones that make you feel alive? The first dates and first kisses—" He shakes his head. "Those are the ones you hold on to." He makes eye contact that pierces right through me. "And I'd know. Just by looking at y—*her*—I'd know that she's important." His face is illuminated in the soft glow of light from the elevator walls, the silhouette of his messy hair as it falls over his forehead.

The breath rushes out of me. If he were talking about me, that'd be the nicest thing anyone ever said. It would require a response that I don't know how to give.

Fortunately for my anxiety, he's speaking hypothetically.

"You're not nearly as scary as you pretend to be," I say as the exit doors slide open and we leave sterile hospital corridors behind.

"I don't pretend to be scary."

"You wear a lot of black."

He rolls his eyes. "So?"

"You play sad music, and you frown too much."

My attempt at playful teasing lands like an anchor. Griff scowls. "I know, I know. I'm the opposite of Beau."

"I didn't mean—"

"Sure you did," he says blandly. He opens the passenger door and waits for me to climb in. "And trust me, I get it. There's a reason all the girls choose Beau."

The detached expression in his eyes breaks my heart a little bit. I've seen hints of it before, shadows that threaten to expose the parts of his past he's trying so desperately to hide, but the raw pain has never been so clear on his face. I don't want to be the one to make it worse.

"You're the only one comparing."

"Oh yeah?" he asks wryly.

"I'm serious! The competition doesn't have to exist anymore. It's not like girls are 'choosing Beau' because—" I stop myself, suddenly worried I've gone down the wrong path.

"Say it," he dares me. When I don't, he fills in the blank. "No one is choosing Beau over me because I never even entered the equation."

I swallow. When he says *no one*, is he talking about me?

I don't know whether to protest or allow him to believe the worst about himself. It sounds terrible, but there's truth to what he's saying—at least for me. I can't consider having feelings for Griff now that I finally have a chance with Beau. "Don't listen to me. My opinion is irrelevant."

Griff's eyes never leave the road, but there's no mistaking the regret that is threaded through his next words. "If only that were true."

Chapter 26

I've spun a hundred fantasies about my first date with Beau Booker. There'd be cotton-candy sunset boat rides and milk-shakes at R.D.'s—one cup, two straws! There'd be prom nights, football games, and under-the-bleacher make-out sessions. There *wouldn't* be reporters or news cameras. But not even Karly's presence can crush the impatient butterflies in my stomach as I get ready to see Beau a few days later. She wasted no time cashing in on that TV interview I promised, and I spent the last three days practicing my answers to all the questions she's bound to ask and batting my eyelashes in the mirror. (The eyelashes are for Beau, not Karly. This will be the first time he's seeing me outside the fluorescent mood killer that was his hospital room.)

Operation Make Beau Love Me is officially under way.

His regaining consciousness has slashed my time in the hospital by more than half. It's not that I don't want to spend time with him; it's just that I don't know how. I learned quickly that he's easier to talk to when he's in a coma. But today I'm crossing all my fingers and toes that if we can make it through this interview unscathed, something will spark between us. Or spark for him, anyway. He's been sparking for me since I was twelve. If he's not interested, I'll break up with him. It'll be devastating, but I'm not going to force this boy to date me forever just because I happened to know CPR.

When I hung up the phone with Karly, I scheduled a makeup appointment at Sofía's Salon. Aka: her bedroom. She promised me winged liner, thick brows, and a coral lip that'd make Beau faint. (Her words, not mine.) When I pull up to her house half an hour before the interview, I'm surprised to see Kodi's car parked in the driveway. And when Sofía's mom answers the door, she looks surprised to see me.

"Jenna, right?" she asks.

"Gemma. Is Sofía here?"

"Is she expecting you?" Ms. Lopez frowns.

"Yeah." My stomach twists.

"Sofía's in her room, but she's had a tough week. I don't know if she'll be in the mood for hanging out."

"Is she okay? Which way is her room?"

She points down the hall. "First door on the right."

I knock. "Sofía? It's Gemma. Can I come in?" A crash comes from inside her room. I open the door. Sofía is leaning over the edge of her bed, mopping up her carpet with a discarded pair of leggings while she laughs so hard tears stream down her face. Kodi and Shandiin are all piled onto her bed in their pajamas, also doubled over with laughter.

Sofía's laughter dies as she looks at me. Her eyes widen. "What are you doing here?"

I pause with my hand on the doorknob. "You're supposed to help me with my makeup for the interview."

She drops the soggy leggings on the floor. "I forgot."

"Oh. Okay . . ." I stare at them numbly, reliving every time Nina and her other friends would hang out without inviting me.

"I can do it now!" She slides off her bed and glances around her messy room. "Um, sit here." She swipes a pile of clothes off the beanbag chair in the corner of the room and rummages through a pile of stuff on top of her dresser. "I have this shade of lipstick that would look perfect on you, but I don't remember where I put it." She drops to her hands and knees and swipes a hand under her bed. Kodi and Shandiin avert their eyes.

"I'll leave."

"You don't have to." There's no conviction in her words.

"No, it's fine."

"Sorry. It's, um, it's been a bad week."

"Are you sick?" I ask, my cheeks turning red. It's a stupid, useless question. Her room wouldn't be filled with friends if she were sick.

Eyes on the floor, Sofía shakes her head. "It's hard to explain."

I trip over my own feet as I back out of the room.

Sofía's mom watches me from the end of the hall. "Maybe try again tomorrow."

I nod, mortified, but I refuse to cry over another person who doesn't like me as much as I like them. I've wasted all my years crying tears over girls like Nina who only consider me when there are no other options. I won't do it anymore. I furiously blink away the tears as I drive to Booker Brothers'. I didn't think it was possible, but my determination to nail the interview and impress Beau has doubled since this morning.

I can't spend another year so crushingly alone. Not when I know what it's like to jump off a cliff with someone who makes me feel wanted.

"Gemma! Hey!" Beau's face lights up as I enter the empty dining room. The restaurant doesn't open for another hour, and Karly loved the idea of filming here. He opens his arms for a hug and I only balk for a breath before quickly and stiffly accepting the hug.

"I wanted to be there when you came home yesterday, but I couldn't get out of work," I say.

"I left on Tuesday, actually. The doctors said I'm a miracle case. Quickest recovery they've ever seen, not that I'm surprised. But I know you've been really busy."

"I have!" I nod. "So busy. So super busy. It's like 'Ahh! When did I get so popular?'"

Beau stares at me blankly and I cringe. *Why am I like this?*

This is why I've been avoiding him. I haven't wanted to wreck my chances by being in the same room with him. From afar, I'm that mysterious girl who saved his life. Up close, I'm the living embodiment of an awkward pause.

He scratches his cheek. "Are you nervous for the interview?"

"Nope! I'm easy breezy!" (Operation Make Beau Love Me: time of death, 9:55 a.m.)

"Okay . . ."

"Are you nervous? What if they ask you something you don't remember?"

"I'm not worried."

"Gemma! You look beautiful!" Mrs. Booker calls from the kitchen. She's wearing a dress and a full face of makeup and her hair is curled around her shoulders.

"You look great too, Mrs. Booker," I say. She fluffs her hair self-consciously.

"She's very excited to be on camera, in case you couldn't tell," Beau whispers.

"They're here!" Mrs. Booker points out the window and rushes outside to greet Karly and her cameraman. While they unload their equipment, Beau's mom rushes back inside and moves trays of appetizers and pizzas out of the kitchen to a big table in the dining room.

"Gemma! Beau!" Karly smiles viciously when she comes inside. "Wow. You're gorgeous," she tells Beau. Her eyes cut to me. "You lucked out with this one."

"Yes, ma'am."

"Okay, so just relax and do your best to answer me in complete sentences. And the more we play up the romance between you two, the more likely this will get picked up by a larger station!" Karly rubs both of our shoulders with her hands and ushers us into a corner booth. "Don't be afraid to get close!"

Beau closes the gap between us and casually slings his arm around my shoulder. "You ready?" he whispers.

"Where do I put my hands?" I ask Karly in a strained voice.

"Whatever feels natural."

I put them up on the table, but that feels terrible, so I put them on my lap, but then I'm worried that looks strange. "Nothing feels natural."

"We're recording," the cameraman announces. "Ready whenever you are."

Karly is sitting behind the camera. "Beau, why don't you tell us what you remember about the accident. I've heard you have some memory problems."

The front bell chimes and I swivel instinctively toward the sound. In walks a scowling Griff Booker, ushering in thunder and clouds with him. My gaze follows him as he strides toward us. My heart leaps into my throat when it looks like he's going to crash the interview, but he stops just behind the cameraman and leans against a pillar. He crosses his arms over his chest and just . . . stays there. My heart picks up speed as I clutch the edge of the booth. I bite my lip and glance up at Griff under my lashes only to find him staring directly at me. I can't breathe.

"Gemma?"

"What?" I tear my eyes off Griff and look at Karly. I can feel the heat creeping up my chest and I pray for it to stop.

"Tell us how you were feeling when you saw Beau fall."

"Awful. And terrified." I glance back at Griff. His flat expression doesn't budge. "He, um, I mean, I know how quickly drowning can happen and I, uh . . ." My eyes dart back to Griff. Is he planning to watch the whole interview? I wipe my sweaty palms on my thighs.

"What were you thinking when you ran into the water?"

"Um." I shift in my seat, trying to get more comfortable. Griff's gaze is a physical weight. "It's hot in here," I gasp. "Can we, um, turn the air down?"

"In a few minutes. Gemma, can you tell us about your thoughts as you pulled Beau out of the water?"

I practiced these answers until I was sick of my own voice. I rehearsed exactly what to say, but it all feels wrong now. How am I supposed to cosplay a happy relationship with Beau while Griff is staring me down? My body reacts to his gaze in a way it never has with Beau; when he looks at me, I can feel his breath on my lips and his hands on my hips. "Sorry. Yeah. I didn't want him to die—obviously."

"Is this hard for you to talk about?"

I fidget in my seat as impatience creeps into Karly's eyes. I'm crashing and burning. "Can we take a break?"

"Just a few more questions. Tell us about your and Beau's first date. And don't be afraid to look at him."

I glance at Beau. He takes my sweaty hand under the table and pulls it into the camera's view. He squeezes it reassuringly and gazes at me adoringly. It's enough to pull my focus away from Griff and back to my objective. I recite my memorized talking points about Sonic and *Avengers: Endgame*. I even flutter my eyelashes a few times.

"Beau, what is it about Gemma that makes her the one for you?"

I hold my breath. "Well, she saved my life, for one." He laughs. "Other than that, I don't know." He glances at me. "She's pretty hot."

My face bursts into flames. Beau Booker called me hot. On

camera. In front of his brother. It doesn't feel as incredible as I imagined it would.

Karly fires a long string of questions at us while I silently die inside. Beau does a fantastic job taking the heat off me by keeping Karly's attention on him. Pretty soon, he's answering even the questions directed at me, and he seems to be loving it.

"Let's take a break and bring out Mom to sit with them," Karly says after an unbearable length of time.

Mrs. Booker stands in the kitchen doorway and waves frantically for Beau to come over. As he walks to her, I slip out of the booth, grab Griff's wrist, and drag him to the other side of the restaurant.

"What are you doing here?"

He falls into a chair and kicks his legs up onto the table. "I'm your moral support."

"You have to leave."

He slides a Parmesan cheese shaker back and forth across the table. "Why?"

I grab the shaker and glare at him. "Are you *trying* to mess with me?"

"I'm just watching. Why are you so worked up over it?" he asks. We lock eyes and stare until the tension is so thick my chest feels like an overfilled balloon.

Beau jogs toward us, sliding in the last few feet on the soles of his flip-flops. "We've got a problem. The walk-in freezer died. Mom's covered in melted ice cream. She won't come out for the interview."

"You two ready?" Karly calls to us.

"My mom can't come. She's taking care of a small emergency."

"You." Karly points to Griff. "You're the brother, correct?"

"I'm leaving."

"Sit. We need more footage," she orders.

"No."

"C'mon. For old times' sake?" Beau asks.

A muscle in Griff's jaw jumps. Unbelievably, he says, "Fine."

She surveys the three of us. "This is good. Two attractive brothers are better than one. Gemma in the middle."

Beau slides into the booth first, followed by me, then Griff. Griff pushes his hair off his forehead and his spicy scent hits me square in the chest. I close my eyes. *Please be over soon.*

Karly focuses on Griff. "Where were you when you heard the news about Beau?"

"In Ohio."

"Can you state that as a full sentence and elaborate?"

"No."

I smother a laugh while Karly rolls her eyes. For the next five minutes she tries to get something good out of Griff, but he sticks to one-word answers as he lounges lazily in the booth. He's got a foot up on his knee and his toe keeps bumping into me under the table. My heart stops every time.

"Is there anything you *would* like to say?" Karly finally asks.

I expect another curt answer, but Griff doesn't say anything for a long time. Finally, he looks over my head at Beau. "Don't screw this up."

Karly doesn't seem to know what to do with that, so she turns her attention back to Beau. "What are your plans for the rest of the summer? Do you think you'll go back to the lake?"

"Oh yeah. My family's camping on Lone Rock Beach next week. We go every year. Those trips are some of my favorite memories."

"What is it like to remember some things and not others?" Karly asks.

Beau frowns. "It's hard to explain."

"What else do you remember?" I ask, looking at him for the first time since we all sat down.

He shrugs. "Lots of stuff. The score of last year's Super Bowl game. How to tie my shoes. The password to unlock my phone."

"But not Gemma?" Griff asks, his voice hard as steel. I stomp on his foot under the table.

The room is silent. Everyone stares at Beau. I've never been more aware of the camera and its blinking red light than I am at this moment.

"I'm lucky. How many guys get to fall for the same girl twice?" Beau gives the camera a dazzling smile and I wilt with relief.

"You're brave to venture back to Lone Rock. Are you going to bring your guardian angel with you?" Karly jokes from behind the camera. Beau picks up my hand and kisses it.

"I'll bring Gemma anywhere she wants to go." He puts his arm around me and pulls me into his side. "What d'you say, Gemma? You want to come sleep in the sand with my family?"

My stomach squirms uncomfortably, and I can't untangle whether it's because of the camera or Griff or Beau himself. Whatever the reason, my heart sinks. Beau is offering me everything I'm imagined, but instead of feeling happy, my chest is hollow. *Am I destined to be alone and unhappy for the rest of my life?*

The thought makes me feel a little panicky. I just need to try harder.

I mimic his bright, camera-ready smile. "I'll follow you anywhere."

"Let's end it there!" Karly announces. "Good job, you two." Before the words are even out of her mouth, Griff vaults himself over the table and rushes to the kitchen. I slide down several inches in the bench as my muscles go slack with relief. It's over. We did it. I did it. I officially survived Beau waking up and the interview with Karly.

I take my first easy breath since Beau fell. Unbelievably, I'm going to get away with this.

"Did you mean it? You'll really come with us?" Beau asks, seemingly shocked by my acceptance. I can't blame him. *I'm* shocked by my acceptance. But I'm also giddy with relief. Nothing feels impossible.

"Why not?" I shrug. "Yes! I'll camp with you!"

"And my family," he warns as he slides out of the booth and comes back with a large plate of pizza for himself.

An alarm goes off in the back of my brain. A dark, brooding alarm. "Everyone in your family?"

"It's always been all seven of us, except last year when Griff left."

"Do you remember why he left?"

"No. Not really." He picks up a slice of pizza and shoves half of it into his mouth. An awkward silence falls over us as he chews. My eyes stray to the kitchen.

"Do you think Griff will come this year?" I ask as Beau chews.

I won't survive another second of silence. And by silence, I mean his decibel-shattering chewing. Listening to people chew food makes my skin crawl.

"Hey!" Beau shouts to Griff, who is trying to sneak out the front door. Head down, Griff raises his hand in one of those waves that's five percent acknowledgment and ninety-five percent dismissal. Beau rolls his eyes. "Are you camping with us this year?"

Griff stops in his tracks and finally deigns to look up.

Look at me. I hold my breath, silently hoping that Griff's eyesight shifts to the right. *Please look at me.* After weeks of spending all my time with him, of sharing secrets and listening to the strum of his guitar and doing scary things with his knee touching mine, I feel like I might explode if another second passes and he doesn't even *look* at me.

Griff's gaze finally flicks to me, and his eyes are a storm of emotion. I hold my breath under his scrutiny, wishing he'd *stop* looking at me. Blood rushes to my ears as my face heats miserably.

Griff spins his keys around his finger and looks back at Beau. "Not a chance in hell." He strides outside, leaving me to stew in my sweaty anxiety.

Beau rolls his eyes again. "I know he's nice to you, but he sucks."

"Yeah," I mumble.

"You're still excited, right?" Beau asks, licking pizza grease off his fingers. "I don't invite just anyone to the Booker Family Camping Trip, you know." He puffs his chest out and it's kind of . . . cringey. Even still, Beau is offering me an invitation so good I never dared to dream it. It's exactly what I've always wanted.

"I'll be there with bells on."

"What does that mean?"

I sigh. Daydream Beau never chewed too loud and he always understood my references. "I'm excited," I say. And then I screw on my biggest, fakest smile and ignore the aching bruise in my chest.

Chapter 27

If it were strictly up to me, I wouldn't be caught dead at Lone Rock Beach in mid-July. This entire stretch of sand turns into my own personal hell at the height of tourist season. The peaceful empty sand from May has given way to a mini civilization. Instead of one big beach party, the shoreline is littered with dozens of them, each one seemingly bigger and louder than the one before it. I don't know what I hate more: the droning generators, which run into all hours of the night, the drunken 2:00 a.m. fights, or the lack of reserved camping spots. The shoreline is packed by the time we arrive on Thursday afternoon, so we wedge a small tent between a massive RV to the left and an entire fleet of massive RVs to the right.

It doesn't help that this place now triggers all sorts of weird memories for me, or that the weather will be blistering hot this weekend and the sand will transform into lava. Add a dose of late-afternoon wind, which is constant in July and August, and suddenly that lava sand is everywhere: in your food, your tent, your swimsuit. It's caught in your eyelashes and wedged between your teeth.

"Can you help put up the shade?" Beau appears from nowhere and I jump at the sound of his voice. I smile up at him. *He's the* reason I'm here. With the interview safely behind us, I can spend all my energy manifesting the relationship of my dreams. And hopefully, this weekend will shed light on whether any of his interview responses were true. I've replayed them in my head so many times: He said I was hot, that he was lucky to fall for me twice, and that he'll take me anywhere. I can't imagine the last two are true. He doesn't know me well enough to think either of those things. But if he sees me spending an entire long weekend bonding with his family and I'm able to hide my anxiety, anything is possible.

"Of course." I stand and wipe the sand off my butt as Beau calls Winnie and Bennett to help us with the shade structure. He shows us how to assemble the poles and attach them to create the structure for a large tarp. The shade it provides will be the only thing to keep us alive as the temperature inches toward 112 degrees today. It's nice to have something to do with my hands; if I've learned anything this summer, it's that distraction is a key factor in keeping my anxiety under control.

The anxiety that is currently preoccupied with the itty-bitty tent standing near the back of our camp. I really should have asked about the sleeping arrangements, or insisted Dad ask about them. He didn't, of course, because broaching such an awkward topic would have rendered him speechless for days. Possibly years.

"Is that tent some sort of Mary Poppins contraption?"

"Huh?" Beau sorts through a pile of shade poles.

"Is there more room on the inside than it would appear from the outside?"

He looks up, baffled. "What?"

I sigh. "Where are we sleeping?"

"Under the stars! Mom and Dad get the tent." He fits one support pole into another, his biceps flexing in the early morning sunshine. His shirt came off the second we stepped foot on the beach, and a few months ago, the sight would have made me dizzy. He still radiates the same Beau Booker charisma that initially drew me to him, but something is different. He's as attractive as ever, but my stomach doesn't zip when I look at him.

Try harder.

"Are you going to stay in Page after you graduate?"

He rests his hand on the pole above his head. "I haven't given it much thought."

"How is that possible?"

"I was in a coma for a month."

"What about the seventeen years before that?"

He shrugs. "I'm going to inherit the restaurant, so yeah, I imagine I'll end up here."

It's not the declaration of hometown love I was hoping for, but it's more than I've ever gotten from Griff.

"I'm staying too," I say. I bite my lip and flutter my eyelashes.

"Do you have sand in your eye?"

I sigh and drop the sad attempt at flirting. Back in his bedroom, I thought I'd be able to transfer my acquired social skills from Griff to Beau, but that doesn't seem to be possible. Out of the corner of my eye, Noah crawls across the warm sand until he's crouching next to my feet. "Boo!" he yells, springing up. It scares away a flock of overfed ravens already scavenging our campsite for food.

"Ahhh!" I pretend to be surprised and he dissolves into a fit of giggles. Beau watches this with a thoughtful expression, and I wonder if it's weird that I've obviously spent so much time with his family, or if it's simply confirmation that we've been happily dating for a long time.

"I scared you." Noah grins a gap-toothed, Cheeto-dusted smile.

"Just like last time," I confirm as a smiling Beau catches my eye across the rapidly heating sand. If only it were as easy to talk to him as it is the rest of his family. His easy, dimpled grin reminds me that he should be the one I want.

But I can't stop thinking about Griff.

My blood warms every time I think of Beau's brother, my emotions caught somewhere between heartache and anger, with unrelenting pangs of homesickness.

Heartache, because I miss him.

Anger, because he won't speak to me.

Homesickness, for reasons I can't fathom. He is not my home. The sparkling blue lake at my feet is home. *My soul is filled with ancient sandstone walls and winding canyon paths. My heart belongs to the water.*

It's a mantra I adopted when I was little, repeating it to myself whenever I got lonely or started to feel like my life here wasn't enough. I wrapped those words around myself like a security blanket, and I've come to rely on them.

No friends? Who needs them? I have 186 miles of heaven.

Little family? That's fine; I have more than 1,900 miles of perfect shoreline.

Soul-crushing social anxiety? No worries. I have Lake Powell: a place that always loves me back.

We finish assembling the shade and I wander to the shoreline and dig my toes into the wet sand, allowing cold water to rush over my feet. Of the storm of emotions in me, it's the homesickness that worries me the most; if I don't feel at home here, then what chance do I stand anywhere else?

I'm trying, though. It's why I made my list and why I'm on this beach. I take a deep breath and turn, shaking away all thoughts of Griff. Beau is knee-deep in a hole he's digging with the little boys. "Hey!" I shout.

Beau looks up. "What's up?"

I nod to my boat, already anchored offshore and tied to a stake in the sand. "Who wants to go tubing?"

"I do! I do!" Noah and Bennett shout, dropping their small shovels.

Beau smiles and walks toward me, his face full of mischief. "So, we're finally going to get that tubing trip?"

"Prepare yourself," I warn. "I'm ruthless."

"Just don't knock me out and I can handle it."

I drive the boat while the kids ride behind it on a giant inner tube. Despite his repeated requests, I refuse to let Beau ride—not when his brain is still healing. But I do bounce Noah, Bennett, and Winnie all over the lake like it's my job, and they laugh like it's the best day of their lives.

A couple of hours into our joyride, everyone's hungry. I point the boat back toward our campsite, only to see a giant cloud of sand rushing down the beach. The wind has picked up out here too, and the water is busy and choppy, making it hard to steer.

"I'm starving!" Noah moans. "And my fingers are stuck like this!" He holds up his cramped hand, his fingers molded into a clawlike shape from gripping the tube so tightly.

"Should I go easier on you next time?" I ask.

"No!" all the kids shout in unison.

I'm feeling ridiculously happy as I navigate the boat up to our beach. If Beau and I can make it work, it could be like this all the time. If it doesn't work out, I'll miss his family almost as much as I'll miss him. *(Maybe more?)* Beau jumps out and holds the boat still while the kids swim in, and then he helps me tie it off on the anchor line.

"Have fun?"

"Not as much fun as you." He stands chest-deep in the water and holds out his hands, offering to help me down. I glance at myself; I'm still wearing shorts, and they're about to get soaking wet. I also have my phone and flip-flops in hand. He sees my hesitation and turns, offering to let me sit on his shoulders. "Hop on."

"Don't you dare drop me," I warn as I carefully lower myself onto his shoulders. He walks through the water and the shallower it gets, the more precarious it feels to sit up this high. "Careful!" I grab his shoulder with my free hand, squeezing tightly.

"What—you don't want me to do this?" He lunges forward and I scream as he pretends to lose his hold on me.

"I hate you!" I laugh as I swat him on the shoulder, my heart hammering double time.

He laughs loudly and walks up onto the sand, taking me with him all the way to an empty beach chair. A car door slams behind the tent, and I look up. Griff is standing outside his car, watching us.

Chapter 28

"Let me down!" I insist, conscious of every point of contact between Beau and me.

The abrupt awareness makes me realize how little I noticed it before now. Beau bends forward so I can hop off his shoulders, but I slip and tumble headfirst toward the ground. He catches me in a bear hug, saving me from crashing into the sand.

Griff witnesses the whole miserable mess. His hands have been where Beau's are now, and I burn scarlet at the thought. I leap away from Beau and do a quick wardrobe check, making sure my swimsuit hasn't slipped. I glance at Griff again, and he's still staring, jaw sharper than I've ever seen it. Guilt lashes through me like a whip.

"What are you doing here?" I ask.

Griff folds his arms over his chest. "I'm not allowed to be here?" he snaps.

"She didn't say that." Beau drapes his arm around my shoulders. "I know you're mad at me—"

"You *do* remember. I've been wondering."

So have I. Part of me hoped that the drama between the brothers would have slipped through the sporadic holes in Beau's memory. I guess I can't be lucky twice.

"Don't take it out on Gemma."

Griff scoffs. "You're one to talk."

"Back off. This isn't about her."

"Where have I heard that before?" Griff raises an eyebrow and Beau tightens his hold on me. I shrug out from under his arm and reach for a hat that is hanging off the corner of a beach chair. I pull it over my wind-whipped hair, hoping to hide the visible emotion blooming on my cheeks. I feel like I've been dropped into the middle of a standoff and given zero context. I glance back and forth between the fake boyfriend that I'm still lying to and his brother—the one who makes my blood hum. The tension in their respective stances goes deeper than whatever almost happened between Griff and me on the houseboat. They're clearly digging up old graves.

Beau reaches out and laces his fingers through mine. It's the closest he's ever come to physical intimacy, and I hate it. It makes me feel guilty and weird. Everything about my hand in his feels wrong.

"I'm glad you came. It wouldn't be the same without you," Beau says. Griff's eyes flash with leashed frustration.

He looks at me for a long moment and I swear we're both holding our breath. When he exhales, all the fight drains from his eyes. He clears his throat and runs a hand through his hair, eyes returning to Beau. "Someone has to be here to make sure you don't pee in camp."

"Ew! What?" I gasp.

Beau laughs. "Shut up, man."

"I'm just sayin'. I'll make sure you don't get lost on your way to the bathroom tonight," Griff says.

"Explain yourselves. Now."

"Beau was half asleep and peed on my sleeping bag in the middle of the night," Griff says.

"Gross!" I yell.

"*One time!*"

"That you remember." Griff laughs. "For all your damaged brain knows, you did it every night."

"Really? You're gonna gaslight the kid with the traumatic brain injury?"

They both crack up with laughter. "Brain injury or no, I can still kick your ass in horseshoes," Beau boasts. He does that chest-puffing thing again. "Let's go! Right now!"

Griff rolls his eyes. "Don't tell me you're still keeping score."

"Griff!" Winnie shrieks at the sight of her eldest brother as she comes out of the water. "Gemma flipped me off the tube, like, ten times! I went in headfirst! Will you play horseshoes with me? Will you build a drip castle? Will you bury me in the sand?"

Griff crouches until he's eye level with his sister. "I'll do all those things, I promise. But it looks like dinner's going to be ready soon. Can we eat first?"

"All right," she pouts. "Will you sit by me at dinner?"

"Deal." He holds his hand out and she gives him knuckles. It makes my stomach flip.

"I'm not sleeping anywhere near you tonight," I warn Beau ten minutes later as I scoop hot chili into a bowl.

"It was *one time!*" He groans again.

"That's one too many times."

The wind picks up as we eat, blowing hot sand sideways into

our shade tent. A fine layer builds on my skin, and no matter how much hunching we do to protect the food, there's no help for it. We're eating sand chili. It's so ridiculous that I glance at Griff every three seconds, trying to catch his eye so we can commiserate together, but this is not like when we used to dodge glances all day at work. He seems perfectly content to never look at me again.

Once upon a time, that might have been okay with me too. But not anymore. He already hates me, so I don't have anything to lose by confronting him. When Beau slips away to use the bathroom and Mrs. Booker sends the littles down to the water with a stack of dishes to rinse in the lake, I lean across the empty table. Griff pushes back like he's going to stand, but I grab his forearm.

"What are you doing here?" I whisper.

"This is *my* family!"

"You said you weren't coming."

"Yeah, well. Winnie guilted me into it. She played the you've-been-a-crappy-absentee-brother card." His tone is self-deprecating, but I can hear the hurt under his words.

"Oh."

"Yeah. Apparently, I blew our family up when I left, and she was hit by the shrapnel. She still hasn't recovered."

"I'm sorry."

"Not your fault," he says tightly.

"I wouldn't have come if I'd known you'd be here."

He grimaces. "I've already proved I'm a crappy brother. I don't need to wreck your relationship on top of everything."

"Have you told him that?" I ask. He rolls his eyes. "I'm serious. Have you apologized for punching him?"

"It's not that simple."

I'm so frustrated I could scream. "What happened between you two? Just tell me!"

He goes completely still. "I can't."

"Why not?"

"Because I don't want you to hate me!"

We stare at each other across the table for a tense moment.

"Griff!" Winnie calls from down the beach.

Griff stands. "I have a drip castle to make."

I watch him walk down the beach, and I cannot comprehend how different my life is since the last time I sat on this beach, gazing at a Booker brother. Winnie and Griff sit in the wet sand and let it drip between their fingers, piling up into tilting Seussian structures. Winnie tries to get me to join them, but I can't bring myself to leave my safe spot under the shade, away from Beau and Griff and the family I don't deserve. After some time, Mrs. Booker pulls up a chair next to me. She sits with a heavy sigh. "I'm exhausted. But this view"—she motions to all five of her children playing in the sand and water—"makes it all worth it. I wasn't sure I'd ever see Beau and Griff together like this again."

Griff and Beau are throwing a football back and forth, carefully dodging the dozens of holes that litter the shoreline. Noah and Bennett make quick work with those small shovels, and I make a mental note not to walk across the sand once it's dark. The last thing this trip needs is a broken ankle.

"Are the kids showering tonight?" Mr. Booker calls from down the beach, where's he joined the game of catch. The sun is almost completely gone behind the horizon.

"There's showers here?" I sit up straighter, looking around. Besides the porta-potty-style toilets placed every few hundred yards, I haven't seen any other amenities. I run my hand through my wind-whipped, sandblasted hair. I could really go for a shower.

"You're looking at it," Mrs. Booker says, pointing to the lake. She gathers a basket of shampoo and body wash, a tub to hold them in, and a stack of clean towels, and lines her three youngest children up in the dark and chilly water to scrub the sunscreen and sand off their bodies.

Griff and Beau grab their own bottles and swim until the water reaches their shoulders. "You coming?" Beau calls. I walk to the edge of the water and dip my toes in. Now that the sun has gone, the normally cool water feels glacial.

"I don't think so."

A few yards away from him, Griff scrubs his hair, his back facing me.

"It feels amazing!" Beau says. "And all our swimsuits stay on. Promise." I can see his dimples all the way from the shore. I wait for the zip in my stomach, the race of my heart, the tremble in my knees. It doesn't come.

All I can think about is the shampoo lather running down Griff's neck and shoulders.

"Maybe tomorrow," I say, the words rasping in my dry throat.

Tomorrow doesn't come soon enough. After the shower, the Bookers started pulling out cots and lining them up under the shade canopy. My heart climbed to my throat as I waited to see where they would put me, my skin itching with the discomfort of doing nothing. They've been doing these camping trips for nearly two decades, everything a well-oiled machine. I feel like I'm in the way most of the time, or else standing uselessly, waiting for someone to tell me what to do. As much as I love the Bookers, I don't love this feeling.

One of the best parts about my life on the lake is how much it feels like mine. Dad's been letting me drive the boat, pick our location, and plan our days for so long that anything else feels like a violation. Being here is like experiencing the fun-house-mirror version of Lake Powell; it's a distorted version of home.

The little kids go to sleep first, in a line of cots under the shade tent. Mr. Booker also goes to bed early, but Beau, Griff, and I play hearts with Mrs. Booker for the next hour, none of us saying anything that isn't a direct comment on the game. As soon as she gathers up the cards for the night, Griff yawns loudly and announces he's going to sleep. Our three cots are under the stars, and he takes the one on the right. Beau then claims the one on the left, and I'm stuck in the middle. I slip into my sleeping bag with my heart in my throat and pray I make it through the night without Beau peeing anywhere near me.

It isn't long before Beau is snoring. But I stay awake for hours, staring at the diamond-bright stars and listening to the shifting and creaking of Griff's cot, sure that he's awake too, hyperaware of his every movement.

"Are you awake?" I finally whisper.

"Can't sleep," Griff responds. I glance over at him, his face illuminated in starlight. He has both hands behind his head, his gaze fixed on the endless night sky.

"I'm sorry I screwed everything up." It's easier to say things like this in the dark.

Griff's hand drops to his side. It hangs over the edge of the cot, and the nearness of him almost undoes me. Our cots are only a foot apart, and now his hand is less than six inches from my sleeping bag.

It's just a hand. It's just a hand. It's just a hand.

But if that were true, my lungs wouldn't feel so tight in my chest. Every part of me wants to lace my fingers with his and stay like that until sunrise.

"You and Beau are different than I thought you'd be," Griff finally says. To my left, Beau breathes the deep, even breaths of someone fast asleep.

Here it comes. He finally knows the truth. I want to cry with relief. "What does that mean?"

Griff is quiet for a long time. Finally, he turns onto his side and stares at me from under his lashes. One arm is still tucked under his head like a pillow, and the other hand is still an invitation. We both glance at it. "It means I'm going to do something stupid."

I hold my breath, but he doesn't move. Instead, he closes his eyes and falls asleep, his hand palm up, waiting for me to decide what I want.

My eyes open when the first sliver of pinkish sunlight appears on the rocky horizon. I sit up slowly, pushing the sleeping bag off my legs, and slide off the end of my cot. I try to maneuver carefully out from under the canopy, but the sky is still inky black, lit only by a scattering of stars. I trip over a stake in the ground and gasp, holding my big toe and screaming internally as I try not to wake anyone up.

No luck. A rustle and squeak alerts me to the fact that someone else is awake. I ignore it and hobble to the water, getting my feet wet before realizing I'm still in my pajamas. Yesterday's swimsuit is hanging over a beach chair. I grab it and step carefully into the water.

"Hey!" Griff's voice sends a shiver down my spine. "What are you doing?"

"What does it look like?" I whisper.

"Can I come?"

I glance back at camp. Noah stirs in his bed and I hold my breath, as if he can hear me from twenty feet away. He rolls over and settles back to sleep.

Griff's words from last night come back to me in a flash of awareness. *I'm going to do something stupid.*

So am I. "Fine. Be quick and fast."

"Can I get my swimsuit?"

"No!"

"Geez. Okay, okay." Griff holds the line for me while I start the boat, then shoves the nose out to the lake while he swims around back to climb on board. He pulls himself up, soaking wet in the clothes he slept in. I throw a towel at him and turn around, my cheeks burning in the golden morning light.

We settle into silence as the boat slices through the glassy water. I bypass Wahweap Marina and the Castle cut and take us to Antelope Canyon. We cruise in the misty morning light, and while I'd usually be lost in my own world, I'm too preoccupied by the boy sitting next to me to enjoy it like I usually would. I glance at him and his face shows the same apprehension I feel.

He makes a slicing motion across his neck, asking me to cut the engine. His hair is messy from sleep, his face less guarded than I've seen it in days. The hazy early light softens his hard edge. Or maybe that's just the way he's looking at me, his eyes liquid dark, pupils wide. He gazes at me for a long moment, his expression somehow intense and soft at the same time. I pull the throttle into neutral.

"What's up?" I ask, my fight-or-flight instinct kicking into high gear.

"I think we should talk."

I blow out a shaky breath and glance out at the calm water around us. "About what?"

"What almost happened between us on the houseboat."

I slouch in my chair, eyes still on the water. "Nothing happened, so—"

"*Gemma.*"

One word from him halts my spineless protests in their tracks. My name sounds safe in his mouth, and it's a melody I never knew enough to want. Until now. It makes my blood burn. I'm bouncing with unspent, anxious energy; with feelings I don't know how to channel. I've long since overcome my normal anxiety in Griff's presence (mostly, anyway), but this feeling is something newer and bigger. *Worse.* Griff locks his hands behind his head, grimacing as if he hates the words he's about to say. "I think it might help to talk about our feel—"

"Nope!" I jump to my feet and glance around for something to do with my hands. The searing in my chest is unbearable. If this is what it's like to fall for someone, I don't want it. I can't handle it. It's too messy, too hard, too scary. The stakes are too damn high, and I'm beginning to think every item on my list was a joke in the face of this stolen morning with Griff.

Bring on the pirate costumes and impromptu midnight shows. Give me back my safe fantasies about Fourth of July parties with Beau, the boy who has never asked anything of me other than an Instagram picture. Those are social interactions I can handle. This is not.

Still in my cotton pajama shorts and tank top, I put one foot on the edge of the boat and jump overboard. The water doesn't feel as cold as it does during the heat of the day because the contrast to the air temperature isn't as stark, but it does snap every nerve in my body into the present, washing away some of the anxiety simmering in the pit of my stomach.

When I break the surface, Griff is laughing. "Seriously?" he asks.

I bite my lip, unsure whether to laugh or cry.

"I'm not laughing at you—" He tries to maintain a straight face as he wipes a tear from his eye.

"Yes, you are," I say, the words carrying easily across the gently rippling water. "But it's okay. I jumped off a boat." I shrug, smiling through the self-consciousness nipping at my toes.

"You literally threw yourself off the edge of a boat—"

"—in my pajamas."

"—in your *stupidly cute* pajamas," he corrects me, "just to avoid talking to me. If there was ever any proof that I'm not my brother, there it is." He lifts his arms out to the sides and lets them drop heavily. "The mere thought of talking about our feelings—"

"Say that word again and I'm not getting back in the boat," I warn.

He rolls his eyes. "The thought of talking to me sent you running—sorry, *swimming*—in the other direction. I'd like to say I'm surprised, but . . ." He shrugs, taking the steering wheel and turning the drifting boat around. "You'd rather swim literal miles to shore than talk about your feelings."

"You knew that about me!" He shouldn't be surprised; he knows exactly what this summer has been about.

"I thought—" He stops himself.

"You thought what?"

He closes his eyes. "I thought I could be your exception."

"That's not how anxiety works. I don't get exceptions!"

"You realize this isn't easy for me either, right?" he says. I tread water, watching him with a surprisingly steady gaze. "The last thing I wanted to do when I came back to town was fall for my brother's girl. If y'all are in the middle of some epic love story, I don't want to get in the way. That's not what I see when I watch the two of you, and it's not what I feel when we're together, but maybe I've misread every sign since the night we met. And I know we're sleeping on the same freaking beach where your relationship started, and I can't compete with whatever history he forgot—"

"Stop!" I hold my hands up as something clicks into place in my brain.

"I have to say this."

"No! Stop." Yesterday on the beach, what was it that Beau said? *We'll finally get that tubing trip.* He claims to remember nothing from the night of the beach party, but he remembers *that?* "What did Beau tell you about Lone Rock Beach?"

Griff groans. "Can't a guy throw his hat in the ring without being interrupted?"

"I'm serious. What did he say?"

"That this is where you two got together." His brows draw together as he scans my face.

I can't believe I didn't realize it before. Beau remembers everything. He knows our relationship is a sham, and he's going along with it anyway.

I swim to the boat. "We have to get back."

"Because you need to talk to my brother," he says flatly.

"Yep."

Griff steps onto the back deck and holds out a hand, helping me out of the water. He wraps a dry towel around my shoulders, rubbing his hands once on my shoulders to help me dry off. I brush the strands of wet hair off my face, wishing I could stay in this moment forever while simultaneously knowing that Beau and I have some serious issues to work through first. "We have to go," I say again.

Griff nods once and stands to the side. "Message received. I won't mention it again."

I feel a nudge against my rib cage, urging me to argue with him, but I can't worry about that until after I've dealt with Beau.

Chapter 29

"So what else did you forget?" Adrenaline carries me out of the boat and splashing to shore. It helps me ignore my pounding heart and sweaty palms and the feeling like I'm about to puke. For the first time in my life, my body has chosen fight instead of flight or freeze.

Beau is stretched out on a beach chair, a bowl in his lap. "What are you talking about?" he asks around a mouthful of cereal. He takes in my damp pajamas, his eyebrows rising sky high. Under the canopy behind him, three little bodies snooze peacefully. The tent door is still zipped. I'm grateful that it's early because it means that Beau and I can hash this out alone, without the prying eyes and ears of his family. I glance back at my boat, where Griff is still in the pilot's seat. He drove us back to camp, and in his defense, he drove fast. I think it had more to do with his desire to get away from me than anything else.

"Kayaks. Now."

"Sure. When I'm done—"

"*Now.*"

A visibly shaken Beau Booker drains his bowl of cereal in one gulp and then we each choose a bright orange kayak and drag it off the sand into the water. We paddle away from camp—far enough that I'm positive Griff can't hear us.

"Want to race?" Beau pulls out in front of me, but I nudge the back of his boat with my paddle until he turns to looks at me.

"Name one thing—other than our 'relationship'—that your head injury caused you to forget?"

He stares at me with wide, panic-filled eyes. Fire runs through my veins.

"I'll wait."

"Gemma—" He holds his hands up while still maintaining a grip on the paddle.

"I *knew* it!" I shout.

"Please listen—"

"I can't believe it." I put my face in my hands, the fire in my belly sputtering out way too quickly. The flames are replaced with shame, curling and smoking through every inch of my blood. "Did you think this was all a joke? Has everyone been laughing behind my back? You must think I'm a total idiot—"

"No! Gemma, that's not what happened."

I groan and turn away, unable to look at him. I *cannot* remember the last time I felt so humiliated.

"Gemma! Stop! Relax. Let me explain."

"Don't tell me to relax," I snap.

"Please look at me," he begs. The note of panic in his voice softens my fire.

"No." I'll listen, but I don't have to look at him. We stop paddling and the wind carries us farther away from the beach, out toward Lone Rock. I hate kayaking and the way the wind has all the control. Getting back to the beach is going to be a slog, fighting the wind and the waves. Plus, it's too slow. What am I supposed to do if this conversation turns south and I need to run?

"When I woke up from my coma, I was so disoriented. It felt like the worst hangover I've ever had multiplied by twenty."

"Cool story, bro." It's not mature, but neither am I.

He laughs. "My head was pounding. I had no idea what happened. As Mom and Dad explained, bits and pieces rushed back. I quickly remembered everything up until I went to help Ian with his boat. That part of my memory is still gone, by the way. Then they told me that my girlfriend, Gemma, saved my life, and I put the pieces together. I remembered taking a picture of us and asking you to pretend we were close. I assumed that after you rescued me, you were mistaken for my girlfriend and you went with it. Was I right?"

I nod.

"I'm grateful, don't get me wrong, but why would you do that for me?"

Self-consciousness flickers to life in my belly. I don't know if it's possible to explain this without revealing my own selfish motivations, or how lonely I've been.

"It felt like getting swept up in a current; one misunderstanding led to another, which led to the whole town thinking we're together. Your mom said you've been disappearing a lot, and when she saw me, I fit perfectly into this narrative in her head about you and a secret girlfriend. She seemed so relieved that you weren't getting into trouble or on drugs—"

"That's not what she was worried about," Beau mutters.

Flustered, I'm not sure how to continue. "Yeah, well—she was relieved. And I didn't know how to break her heart and tell her that I was just some girl. Lying seemed like an easy way to bring her some happiness. Between your mom's comments and the fact that you asked me to pretend that we're close . . . I thought you might *want me* to pretend to be your girlfriend."

He reaches out and grabs the side of my boat. Our kayaks clank together. "I did!" Even now, his smile is so easy. I wish I had whatever quality makes him float through life without a single concern. "That's why I didn't correct anyone at the hospital!"

"Why, though? I don't understand."

"It's complicated."

"I've got time."

He leans toward me. "I'll tell you what. If we can keep up this charade of ours—I'll tell you the truth."

I startle so much that I nearly tip my kayak. "You want me to keep pretending to be your girlfriend?" I can't fathom what he's gaining from this scenario.

"Just for a couple of weeks. I need time to make things right with someone, and having a girlfriend will make that a lot easier."

"Then find a girlfriend. A real one." The words taste a whole lot less sour than they would have last month because it wouldn't bother me if he did. The realization is a jolt to my system, forcing me to acknowledge the truth I've been avoiding since Beau woke up: I don't like him nearly as much as I liked the fantasy of him.

"I can't. I need to explain the last year of my life, and you're the one I have history with. Ours is the relationship I need people to believe."

"What do I get out of this arrangement?" I'm half joking; it's obvious that my life has wildly changed for the better since people started thinking I'm Beau's girlfriend.

But when Beau says, "What do you want?" I freeze.

"Nothing," I say quickly. "It was a joke."

"No, you're right. I'm benefiting from this—you should too. Name your price. Free pizza? Guaranteed party invites for the year? A spot at my lunch table? A date to senior prom?"

I stop breathing.

Belonging.

That's what I hear in his offer, and it's so tempting it makes my chest hurt. It's all I've ever wanted.

Until I met Griff.

He makes me feel like I belong, and he doesn't ask for anything in return. When I'm with him, I don't care about prom dates or lunch tables or party invitations. I think giving those things up would be worth it—if it meant I got to be with Griff.

I try to imagine a scenario in which I come clean for lying to him all summer.

I'd stand in front of him, and . . . I'd choke. My fingertips would go numb. My breath would turn shallow. I'd vomit or pass out or swim across the lake just to avoid him. Talking about my *feelings* would make me spontaneously combust. My cheeks heat at the mere thought. Surviving that conversation would take a miracle.

I mentally skip that hurdle and fast-forward to a point in the future in which I've miraculously explained my lie in a way that doesn't make me look like an awkward, lying weirdo.

And then! *Then!* He'd still have to forgive me! He'd still have to want me!

The necessary miracles are really piling up. As a socially awkward girl with a dead mom, no friends, and zero evidence that my company is worth the trouble, I don't have much faith in divine intervention.

When I play it out in my head, the answer is clear. Griff won't forgive me. Sofía doesn't need me. Nina's not a friend worth having. Beau is all I have left, and if I take him up on his offer, I can secure some sense of belonging.

"Lunch," I say finally.

To his credit, he's waited patiently for my response. "Done. Pretend to be my girlfriend until the end of summer and you have a permanent invite to my lunch table. Do we have a deal?"

"Deal." We shake on it, and I ignore the nagging dread in my belly. "Now tell me what's going on."

He leans back on his forearms and sighs heavily. "Long story short, I dated someone I shouldn't have. We kept the relationship a secret. It started badly and ended badly, and people were getting suspicious—"

"*Beau Booker!*" I smack him in the arm with my paddle. "You used me to break up with someone else?"

"There's more to it than that!" He raises his arms to protect himself against further attacks. "The truth will upset my family. I just want us to be okay again."

I halt my attack. The Booker family has been under so much stress over the last few weeks and I agree with Beau—they deserve a break from the drama. I lower my weapon with a sigh. "Who is she? Or he?"

"She's not important."

That earns him another smack. "That's a terrible thing to say, Beau Booker!"

"I'm Beau Booker again?" He raises an eyebrow, looking only mildly abashed.

"Yes."

"Because I'm a celebrity?" He smiles hopefully.

"No! Because you lied to me and you lied to this girl!" I reach toward his boat and grab the side with both hands.

"You wouldn't dare," he says.

"You don't know me at all." I flip the kayak over and dump him in the lake.

Twenty minutes later we make it back to shore, where he makes a show of pulling my boat onto the beach for me. He grabs one kayak in each hand and hauls them up on the sand. And as we walk into camp, he slings a sweaty arm around my shoulder and pulls me closer. I tell myself not to look for Griff as we approach camp, but my need to find him in any situation is compulsive. I scan the beach, and he's nowhere to be seen.

"Where's Griff?" I blurt.

No one seems to know. Noah and Bennett are climbing through a sand tunnel that the boys built, and Winnie is braiding a friendship bracelet that's taped to the end of the picnic table. "This one's for you, Gemma!" She holds up her foot, showing off the matching braided rope around her ankle. She looks up at us and her eyes widen when she sees Beau's arm around my shoulder. "Oooh! Have you two been kissing?"

"Knock it off, Win," Beau says playfully.

"That means yes!" she declares.

"Maybe, maybe not." He pulls me tighter against his side and plants a kiss in my hair. I stiffen, shocked by the contact.

"Congratulations, *little bro*." Griff wades in from the water, his voice heavy with sarcasm. I can't bring myself to look at him.

"For what?" Beau asks. His arm stiffens around me.

"For being the exception to every freaking rule." Griff claps his brother hard on the shoulder, and maybe I'm imagining it, but his words feel like a callback to our earlier conversation. I force my eyes up to meet his, and the pain there crushes me.

He picks up a shirt and pulls it over his soaking-wet chest. "I'm leaving," he says to everyone and no one and especially to me.

In my fantasy, I tell him not to go.

But here in the real world, I wilt under his accusing gaze, unable to utter anything at all.

Gemma Rae Wells 2.0 was only ever a fantasy. I wish Griff could be my exception, but I can't gamble my future on a version of myself that doesn't exist.

Chapter 30

One week later, the water is the color of cold steel. Of sharp propellers and guitar strings. The only rainbow at my feet today is the braided rope knotted around my ankle, gifted to me by a little girl who doesn't know I'm a mess and a liar. The wind drives in wave after foamy wave, each one biting my toes with a frigid snap. It's been a week since my ill-fated camping trip with the Bookers, and I've been in a crappy mood since Griff stormed off the beach. He's sitting on the far dock now, avoiding me the way he has been all week.

"It's supposed to rain all weekend," Sofía says as she slips off her sandals and sits next to me on the end of the fuel dock, dipping her feet into the chill with mine.

"We need it," I say, my eyes drifting to the Castle Rock cut. Even that stopgap measure will be ineffective if we keep losing water at this rate.

"I've heard the water is dropping three inches every day. We've lost forty feet in the last year."

I've heard the same thing. When I dwell on it too much, my chest feels like it's too small for my lungs. If the lake goes dry, what does that mean for me? If my heart doesn't belong here, where will it go?

The sky above us matches the angry water. *Cold. Gray. Stormy.* The waves turn over, bringing frothy whitecaps to the surface, warning boaters to stay away. The sky looks like it could break open any second, and as a result I've only had two customers all day.

"What are you doing here?" I ask. We haven't spoken since I barged into her room uninvited.

"I'm sorry I forgot about our plans. I know it must look like we were all hanging out without you, but that's not exactly what happened."

"Okay." I'm too tired and embarrassed to fight with her about this.

"Don't you want to know what happened?"

I shrug.

"I have depression," she says.

I'm shocked into silence for ten long seconds. "What does that mean?" Maybe that's a stupid thing to ask, but it's hard for me to compute that gorgeous, popular, TikTok-perfect Sofía has depression.

"Sometimes I'm sad for no reason. Sometimes it feels worse than sadness and I don't want to get out of bed or talk to my friends. That's what happened to me toward the end of last week. When I'm in a depressive spiral, my brain tells me nothing matters and that no one wants to hear from me."

"That's not true."

"Logically, I know that. But it's hard to feel it in the moment. I didn't ask Kodi and Shandiin to come, but they showed up because they knew I needed it. That's what you walked in on."

I remember all the offhand comments Sofía has made this summer about not wanting me to get sad and stay in bed all day. I ask her about them, and she admits she was trying to protect me from getting depressed like her.

"I was projecting, but I don't regret it because now we're friends." She links her arm through mine and rests her head on my shoulder.

"I have anxiety," I say. "I think I do, anyway. It's called social anxiety disorder, and it's the reason I tend to panic and get weird in social situations."

"I knew it!"

"You did?"

"Well, no. I had no idea. But I knew there was something about you that was like me."

We hug, and in that moment, my fake-dating agreement with Beau is completely worth it because I know she'll never find out the truth about my lie, and we can stay friends for as long as she's here.

"Do you think you'll stay in Page after you graduate?" I ask.

Sofía pulls the elastic out of her braid and combs her hair through the waves. "I hope not. I want to go to school in the Valley." Everyone talks about Phoenix like it has something we don't, like there's not enough sunshine in this *patch of dirt*. My stomach twists bitterly.

"Aren't you leaving?" she asks.

"I don't know." I shrug, tired of asking and answering this question. I've yet to get the response I'm looking for, and with each passing day, the idea of staying here feels like trying to outrun a storm.

"Are you and Beau coming to the end-of-summer party next weekend? Please say yes. I'll help you if you feel anxious."

"Parties aren't as bad as they used to be, especially when I have time to mentally prepare myself. Where is it?"

"Ian's house."

"Why isn't it on the beach?"

She laughs. "Because of the rain? Because every beach is crowded with tourists? Because making out with sand in your swimsuit gets uncomfortable after the second or third or hundredth time? You'll still come, right?" When I hesitate, she nudges my shoulder with hers. "If you don't come, I'll think you like the lake more than me." I bite my lip, and she laughs. "Fine. I already know I come in second place to the lake. Or third, after Beau. But you can spare one night to party with your friends—right?"

"Would we still be friends if Beau and I weren't dating?"

"Why?" She kicks her legs back and forth, splashing us both with icy water. "Are you going to break up with him?"

"Hypothetically. Would we still be friends?" I grip the edge of the dock until my knuckles turn white.

"Duh. No boy comes between us, okay?" She holds out her pinkie and motions for me to link mine with hers. It feels silly, but I do it anyway. And once we've sealed our friendship, it doesn't feel so silly anymore.

"So, you and Beau are a yes. What about Griff?" She turns her head. "Where is he, anyway?"

I nod to the far dock, where he's sitting with his earbuds in, his back resting against the fuel pump. We don't talk anymore, and every avoided glance and unsaid word hurt worse than any embarrassing conversation I've ever had.

"Do you want me to invite him?" Sofía asks.

"I'll do it," I say impulsively. I've been searching for any reason to talk to Griff for the last week but haven't come up with anything better than "It's hot out here, huh?" His eyebrow rose all the way to his hairline when I tried that line, and then he had the gall to pretend not to hear me. Well, he won't be able to ignore me now. I stand and slip my sandals on. Sofía and I hug goodbye and I march to Griff's dock.

I stand above him and kick his shoe. He looks up. I mime taking out his earbuds. He ignores me, so I lean over and do it for him. He grumbles a protest but doesn't move to stop me from slipping them into my pocket.

We stare at each other for several seconds, and I realize I should have planned this better.

"May I help you?" he asks evenly.

"There's a party at Ian's house on Saturday. Do you want to come?"

"Did you break up with my brother?"

"No."

"Then I respectfully decline your invitation." He turns his attention back to his phone.

"I'm not asking you as a date."

Eyes still fixed on his phone, he says, "I know. Which is why I respectfully decline your invitation."

"I've never been to a party without you." My voice wavers and I clear my throat. *Get it together, Gemma.* "And this one isn't at the lake. I can't jump overboard if it gets stressful."

Griff sighs and slips his phone back into his pocket. His gaze finally finds mine, and I'm heartbroken to see how cold and distant his eyes are. It's like the summer never happened, and we're back in the hospital on day one. "This time you have Beau to hold your hand. You don't need me anymore. Your list is done and you're a total pro when it comes to the party scene. You just have to stay calm and trust yourself." I swear his eyes betray a warmth behind his otherwise detached words, but it's gone in a blink, leaving me to wonder if it was just hopeful imagination. All I see in front of me now are his squared shoulders and icy expression.

He steps quickly toward me and leans down, lowering his voice so I strain to hear him over the whistling wind. "I can't go to the party. You know that, right?"

My face falls, but I know he's right. It's not fair to ask him to babysit me in social situations. I clench my jaw and wrap my arms around my stomach, turning so he won't see the tears.

"If I go, I'll want to kiss you," he says. I spin back toward him, breathless at his admission. The wind whips my hair around my face, and he tucks a wild strand behind my ear. His fingers brush so lightly against my skin it might be my imagination. "And that wouldn't be fair to me. Or you. Or my brother. Besides, I bet you could name a hundred reasons why you and me would be a disaster."

One—He'll never forgive me for the lies I've told.

Two—I wouldn't survive the gossip that comes with being the girl who "switched brothers."

Three—I'm not brave enough for a real relationship.

Four—

"You're doing it right now, aren't you?"

I wince. "I wish I wasn't."

"I know. But all those thoughts in your head are the reasons I can't be where you are. Later tonight, when you're worried about it, replaying this conversation in your head, that's what I want you to remember. And when you get to the party, and I'm not there, it's not because I hate you, or because you did something weird or awkward or wrong." He stoops, meeting me at eye level. "Will you remember that when I'm gone?"

I nod, not trusting myself to speak. He moves past me, his fingers grazing against mine. His whisper-light touch shocks every part of me, and it's not until I'm alone under a stormy sky that I register his last words.

When I'm gone.

I add that to the list of reasons we'd never work. I've known it for weeks; I see it every time I look at him.

Five—Griff is leaving.

Chapter 31

When Beau Booker arrives on my doorstep on the last Friday of summer vacation, he looks like a daydream. He whistles when he sees me, and I hold my breath waiting to feel something. My stomach can't even muster a baby butterfly. It's incredible how wrong I was. Beau and I have the chemistry of toothpaste and orange juice.

Sometimes I wonder if I picked Beau, if I allowed myself to fall for him and never look back, because I knew he wouldn't surprise me. I could live safely in my daydreams, without having to work for small talk or eye contact or vulnerability. He was an impossible dream who would never pick me, and that suited my anxiety just fine.

"You ready for our last night as a couple?" Beau asks as we climb into his car. After two weeks of bonfire nights and lake hangouts, we've come to the end of our contract. Once upon a time, this night would have been the source of hours of daydreams and half a dozen anxiety attacks. I would have wanted to go but bailed at the last minute, choosing instead to burrow my head under a blanket while doom scrolling through social media.

It's a testament to my progress that I don't bail on Beau. I'm not the same girl who panicked on a beach back in May. And while I'm proud to not be sidelined by overwhelming anxiety, a small part of me wishes I could appreciate the thrill of attending a party on Beau Booker's arm. In honor of the girl I used to be, I tried to psych myself up to have a good time. I flicked my eyeliner the way Sofía taught me and fantasized a perfect night for myself. But in every imaginary scenario I opened my front door on bated breath . . . and *Griff* stood on my porch. Not Beau. Never Beau. Griff, with his tight T-shirts and rough guitar calluses, is the new lie I tell myself.

The late-summer air is warm, and as we step into Ian's house, I slip my fingers out of Beau's and wipe the sweat off on my shorts. "Sorry, I sweat a lot," I say.

He nods. "I noticed."

He noticed. I die a little inside. I'm not in love with him anymore—not that I ever truly was—but no girl wants to be told she's sweaty.

The house is crowded, the music loud, the smell skunky. Beau surveys the house. There's a pool table in the front room, surrounded by people holding cues but not really playing. From the front hall we also have a view of the beer pong game happening in the kitchen. Beau lasers in on the competition, his gaze growing sharp.

"Oh, it's on." He cracks his knuckles and makes a beeline for the table.

"Gemma! You made it!" Ian throws his arms around me and pulls me into a hug. It's easy enough to hug him back. "Wanna play pool?"

"No thanks."

"Next time," he promises over his shoulder as he maneuvers out of the room. I finish making the rounds, just for something to do. The party has everything I imagined it would: Furniture pushed to the walls? Check. A large group of girls dancing in the center of the room? Yes. Skunky puffs of smoke billowing in from the backyard? That too. It's the party I've been thinking about for the last three years . . . and it kind of sucks. Everything about it is anticlimactic, and I can't even fantasize a scenario that would make this experience more fun than boating with Griff or binge-ing *The Island* reruns with Sofía.

I move through the crowd like water, slipping through groups virtually unnoticed. I'm not "cured" of my social anxiety (if that's even possible), but the fact that I can be here without panicking is evidence that I'm improved. Unbelievably, my list helped. I search every room and do a full spin around the exterior of the house, but Sofía isn't here yet. I'm about to pull out my phone and text her when a hand lands on my waist and spins me. I yelp in surprise when I come face-to-face with Beau.

I startle. "Are you drunk?"

"Nah. I won. I always win."

"Then what's with the death grip?"

He loosens his arms around my waist. "Sorry. My ex is here."

"Oh?" I crane my neck, looking for this mysterious girl. My curiosity is dialed to ten. Beau and I have been attending social functions for weeks and this girl has yet to make an appearance. "Where is she?"

"Don't be obvious." He lifts his hand and smooths a strand of hair off my forehead. I freeze, waiting for it to be over. He

279

chuckles. "Sorry again. She's looking over here. I thought about kissing you but didn't figure you'd appreciate it."

"No," I agree.

"Ouch." He puts a hand to his heart.

"I mean—it'd be okay if it helped sell your story—"

His lips are on mine, hard and wet. I don't breathe, and it's over in three seconds. He pulls back and I'm too stunned to move. Out of the corner of my eye, I register movement over Beau's shoulder. Before I look, a horrible awareness prickles my skin, and I know Griff is here before I confirm the fact with my eyes. Horrified, I glance at him from under my lashes. He's standing in the open doorway, illuminated in yellow porch light, watching Beau and me with a gutted expression.

Instinctively, I pull Beau's arms off me and step toward Griff when a girl with a bouncy brown ponytail accosts him. She pulls him into a tight hug. When he wraps his arms around her, the painful squeeze of my heart is the final nail in my coffin. I can't drown in my river of denial anymore.

"Who's that girl with Griff?"

"That's my ex, Drew," Beau says flatly. The name triggers something familiar, but I'm too relieved to examine it.

"Have they always been close?" I ask. Beau winces, rubbing the back of his neck with his hand. "What's that look for?"

Beau sighs heavily. "Drew was Griff's girlfriend first."

It doesn't make sense, until in one paradigm-shifting second— it does. A rush of nausea washes over me as the whole party tilts like an Etch A Sketch, erasing everything I thought I knew about Griff Booker.

Drew releases Griff from the hug, but her hand is on his arm as they chat. I try not to stare . . . but who am I kidding. A tsunami couldn't tear my eyes away.

"How long were they broken up before you two started dating?"

Beau sighs, and that rush of breath tells me everything I didn't want to know. The greeting-card line from D bulldozes me.

I'm sorry for the beginning and the end, but never for the middle.

"You saw the card from Drew in the hospital, didn't you?"

"Yeah. I hid it before you two arrived, but I was scared Griff had already seen it. It's why I didn't tell you the truth and let everyone believe we were together."

"She cheated on him with you." I wait for a denial that doesn't come. "That's why he punched you. That's why you two don't talk, why he can't stand to be in the same room as you. You 'stole' Griff's girl."

It's a clumsy term; I don't believe someone can "steal" a person who doesn't want to go, but it doesn't change the fact that Beau violated every "bro code" in existence. He betrayed his brother by taking his girlfriend, and then—*Griff took me.*

The realization knocks the wind out of me. I remember the first day I met Griff; he said he was in town to set things right. I naively assumed he wanted to repair his relationship with his family, but now a sinister awareness crawls down my spine. I close my eyes and picture the hard and angry boy I met in the hospital.

I don't want to believe he'd use me to get revenge on his brother, but he made it perfectly clear he had "personal reasons" for helping me. Nothing else makes sense.

I grab Beau's shoulder, feeling unsteady on my feet. I mentally list the facts, praying they don't add up the way I think they do.

One—Griff has known from the very beginning that I was dating his brother and yet he *insisted* on helping me with my list.

Two—That night at The Bowl, Griff told me that he still feels the need to beat Beau in their endless competition.

Three—He never told me about Drew, even when I specifically asked him about Beau's exes.

Understanding is a blow to my most vulnerable places. I should have been suspicious of Griff's quick and easy friendship, but instead I tricked myself into believing he understood me in a way no one else did. This whole summer has been a hoax, and I'm the biggest idiot in the world.

"We didn't plan it," Beau insists. "It started when Drew was in the car accident with Griff."

Another flashback. This time, of Griff telling me that he "hurt someone he cared about." I didn't even consider there was a passenger in the car.

"They were both lucky to walk away without injuries, but she was freaked out and confused. Griff refused to talk about what happened, but she was in the restaurant a lot, and we started talking . . ." Beau continues to explain his actions, his voice growing more defensive with each word, but I tune him out as my blood rushes to my ears. He's not the Booker brother who owes me an explanation.

I leave Beau sputtering through his self-defense and weave in and around groups as I march toward Griff. My hands shake and my heart gallops wildly, but I don't consider stopping, or turning around, or swallowing my words. Not for a second.

"We need to talk." I grab Griff's wrist and pull him out the door, slamming it behind us. The sky is cloudy dark, an incoming storm weighing the air with sticky humidity that has driven everyone inside. We're alone in the gravel yard, facing off like I saw Beau and Griff do not so long ago.

"That was your ex-girlfriend." I'm relieved to find that hurt and anger have chased all trepidation from my voice. I sound every inch as fuming as the fire running through my blood.

Griff's jawline hardens. "And?"

"You didn't think to tell me about her?"

"Again, you don't get to be jealous when you're here making out with my brother."

"*You* don't get to be jealous of Beau when you used me this whole summer to get revenge on him!"

Confusion flicks across his face. "What are you talking about?"

"You and Beau have been in one big competition for years, constantly keeping score and trying to one-up each other, right? He 'stole' Drew and then you came back to town and tried to take his girlfriend. Tell me I'm wrong."

He crosses his arms and fixes me with a cold, hard gaze. The brief softness I saw earlier is gone, and he has no intention of letting me see it again. "You're wrong."

"I don't believe you."

"You don't have to believe me. As long as you're with him, it doesn't matter what you think of me." Heartbreak and anger simmer off him in choking waves, and finally I snap. I'm too hurt and tired to lie to him for another second.

"I'm not with Beau! It was fake! I lied after his accident—our relationship was never real. I'm just some pathetic, lonely girl who saw a chance and took it. Beau and I have never dated," I shout, my chest heaving.

Griff freezes, his jaw clenched. I step toward him, and he takes three steps back, his arm out. "You lied to me?"

Shame turns my angry fire to ash. I nod, absolutely mortified.

"And you still chose him?"

"What?"

Griff laughs bitterly. "Shit." He runs both his hands through his hair. "You chose a fake relationship with him over a real one with me."

My body protests, making my insides feel twisted and *wrong*. "It's not like that."

"Stop lying! Be honest for once in your life. Why the hell are you kissing him if it's 'fake'? What do you get out of that other than a convenient excuse not to be with me?"

A spot at Beau's lunch table. It's too awful to say out loud. Griff will think I passed on him for a chance to be popular. He still doesn't understand that he and I will never work. That I'm not cut out for real relationships because my anxiety screws up everything. That since I'm going to lose him anyway, either to my lie or his penchant for leaving, I seized my opportunity to secure a sense of belonging.

"I'm waiting."

Tears build in my eyes and I blink into the dark sky to get rid of them. *Talk,* I plead with myself. But the truth is, I don't know how to explain the decisions I've made and the tangle of emotions coursing through my body. I open my mouth and every valid excuse is gone. I'm so frozen and panicked that I doubt I could tell him my own name.

"Geez, Gemma. *Say something.*" Griff's voice breaks and it breaks me. I cover my eyes with my hands as the tears fall. I've never felt so damaged.

"He promised me a spot at his lunch table." I barely choke out the words, and to my horror, they sound even worse out loud than they did in my head.

Griff stalks toward me with heavy strides. It takes every ounce of strength in my body to meet his eyes. "Thank you for confirming everything I've known my entire life. No one will ever, under any circumstance, choose me." His eyes are the bleakest I've ever seen them, and I hate myself for hurting him again. Griff isn't safe with me. "Seriously," he says more quietly. "Thank you. This is exactly the push I needed to get out of this miserable town and never look back. I'm leaving tonight."

Regret and disappointment surge through me. "Of course you are," I say to his retreating back. His footsteps stop, but he doesn't turn. "Don't kid yourself. You were always going to leave."

Griff hesitates for half a second or an eternity. He looks over his shoulder and his eyes widen at something in the distance. He levels me with a worried expression. "Good luck."

I scrub the tears from my cheeks and turn back to the house. My stomach drops. The door is wide open, a dozen kids from school staring directly at me.

Chapter 32

For the span of a heartbeat, I wonder if the people on Ian's small porch heard the fight between Griff and me. And then in one, horrible, comprehending second, I register the expressions. Some shocked, some gleeful. Several cell phones are up, recording everything. And of course, because this is always the way my life works, Beau and Drew are standing front and center.

My hands sweat, my heart hammers, my cheeks flush under the cover of night. The Gemma Wells trifecta. I'm never making it out of here alive.

"Gemma!" Sofía's heels click up the cracked sidewalk. "Sorry I'm late. My mom—" She falters, close enough to see my face. "What happened? What's wrong?" She throws her arm around me and leads us toward the house. Her heels wobble over the rocks and we falter.

"Hang on." She bends to take off her shoes. "I don't know why I wear these. I always end up taking them off." She looks up and notices for the first time the *panic* of teens is staring at us. "What's going on?" She turns to me for answers, but I can't take my eyes off Drew, who is about to blow up my entire life.

Drew turns slowly to Beau. The porch light illuminates her face, and I see the hurt in her eyes. "You're not dating her?"

"No." Beau stuffs his hands in his pockets and looks at me, shrugging nonchalantly, as if to say, *We tried.*

"And you two weren't ever dating? Not even before the accident?"

Beau has a shit-eating grin. "Guilty as charged."

"I don't understand. She claimed to be your girlfriend"—Drew frowns at me before turning back to Beau—"and everyone just believed her?"

I stop breathing. *Please lie. Please lie. Please lie.*

"That's the gist of it."

"I knew she wanted to get in Griff's pants," someone says. Laughter bounces through the party.

"I knew she could never get Beau. He's way out of her league."

"Right?! That's what I've been saying all summer!"

Laughter drowns out the rest of the comments, but it's not enough to block the hurt in Sofía's words. "You lied to me? To all of us? All summer?"

My mind blanks.

I have a reasonable explanation; I know I do.

I'm not crazy; I know I'm not.

(I hope I'm not.)

My head spins with the need to get the right words out. I can't risk saying the wrong thing, not now, when I've already lost Griff and Beau, and everyone else in school will know I'm a freak by Monday morning.

But there's nothing there. No words, right or wrong.

I can't articulate how it happened, or why I did it, or why we kept it going after Beau woke up. "Sofía—" I start; it's a sentence without an end. I swallow again, wrapping my arms around my stomach as my tears spill like a waterfall. "Sofía—" I try again.

She steps back. "What kind of person lies about dating someone with a brain injury? I can't believe I fell for it." Her expression is devastated, and I know exactly how she's feeling. She's reframing her entire summer armed with new information, and she doesn't know what to trust.

"I don't—I—I—" My heart thunders a warning beat in my chest, so I do the only thing that makes sense.

I run.

My shoes sink into soft asphalt the whole way home. When I turn to my street, I stumble, falling to my knees, barely catching myself with my palms. I hold them up, and they're filled with loose gravel. I gasp for breath, leaning forward until my head touches the road, sobbing salt water onto black tar. I gulp for air, waiting for someone, anyone to pick me up and carry me inside.

But once again I'm alone. Just like I was that first day on the beach. But this hurts worse because I know what I'm missing.

The sky breaks open and fresh water mixes with my hot tears.

The storm doesn't pass as quickly as I'd expect, and it's still raining when I pick myself up and walk the rest of the way home. I open the door, prepared to fall into bed alone, but Dad stands at the sight of me wet and bloody, and I fall into his arms instead.

Dad didn't ask questions. I sobbed myself half to sleep on his shoulder, dripping rainwater all over our ancient carpet, and when I finished, he told me to take a hot shower and get some sleep.

I didn't expect to be able to fall asleep. Not with my classmates' laughter ringing in my ears and the weight of Sofía's arm still heavy on my shoulders. But when I closed my eyes, all I saw was Griff's face and that split second of hurt before he left.

Even boiling over with regret, though, I still fell asleep, and when Dad flipped my light on before sunrise and asked if I wanted blueberry muffins, I rolled over and told him to go away.

He did, but only for an hour. When he comes back the second time, the pinkish-gold thread of dawn has given way to an orange sunrise, and he doesn't take no for an answer. He gives me five minutes to be in the car, and his voice is so quiet that I don't argue.

Thirty minutes later we're on the water, but instead of asking me where I want to go or letting me steer, Dad veers to the right, taking us the long way down Antelope Canyon. We go slow enough that it's easy to hear when he clears his throat the first time. And the second time. When he does it the third, I finally take the hint.

"Dad."

"Yeah?"

"Do you need a lozenge or something?"

He tilts his head in question. I loudly and repeatedly clear my throat until he smiles softly. "I wish your mom were here. I always wish that, but especially right now."

"Why now?"

He sighs. "I'm not good with words."

"You wanna send a meme?" I smile at my joke.

He doesn't. "You scared me last night."

Oh. My stomach tugs uncomfortably. I look at my toes, bare-foot against the carpet. I press them hard into the carpet. "It wasn't a big deal."

"You came home soaking wet, crying your eyes out, and bleed-ing. Did someone hurt you? I know you've been spending time with those Booker boys."

"No, nothing like that."

"Good." The relief in his voice is obvious. "What happened?"

"I had a bad night and I fell on the way home, but I'm fine. Honestly. No worries."

"The first time you ever squeaked 'no worries,' you were three years old. You sounded so precocious, and your mom and I laughed and laughed. But now I worry about how much you say it because something tells me you have a lot of worries bottled up in there." He reaches over and taps my forehead with his finger.

"It's not a big deal." I shrug uncomfortably.

"I wish that were true, but I'm afraid my reluctance to talk about feelings has rubbed off on you."

"I don't mind being like you."

He frowns. "Before this summer, I worried about you all the time. You weren't doing any of the things I thought a kid your age should do."

"Like what?"

"Hang out with friends. Go to parties. Enjoy life without a rain cloud of doom hanging over you."

"That's not your fault." I duck my head as my cheeks heat. Even my dad thinks I'm a loser? *Fan-freaking-tastic.*

"I worry you got it from me. I don't do any of those things either—" He cuts himself off, his face pained. He takes a breath and tries again. "I haven't showed you how to make friends or have a relationship. I worry I haven't taught you anything you need."

"But you've taught me everything! How to drive a boat and navigate through a storm and fix an engine and avoid shallow water." I could go on forever. He's given me a home.

"It's not enough."

"It's everything. This lake is all I need."

He looks so sad now, and I don't know why. "I don't want you to be lonely."

"But *you're* not lonely."

He hangs his head. "I am, though." He takes my hand in his and squeezes tightly. "I love you, Gemma. Our mornings on the lake are the best part of my life. But I want you to have more than this town, more than me. I want you to have everything."

"Dad." My throat burns with unshed tears. I throw my arms around him and the tears quickly fall, his and mine. "I love you too."

We hold tight to each other for longer than I can ever remember, and when I finally pull away, he seems to regret letting me go. "Do you want to tell me what happened last night?"

"I just embarrassed myself at a party. No wo—" I cut myself off, realizing he's right. I do use that phrase a lot. It's become the facade I hide behind when I'm filled with nothing *but* worry.

He cringes. "Sounds rough." I can tell he means it. He maybe even understands.

"Dad." I sit up as nervous energy zips through me. "I think I have social anxiety."

He digests this information and then nods slowly. "I wouldn't be surprised if I did too, kid."

"I want to go to therapy," I blurt. His forehead wrinkles. "I read that it could help," I say, and press my toes down again to keep from bouncing them.

He wants to say no. It's his gut instinct, and a lifetime of growing up under his roof prepares me for his answer. So when he says, "Okay. We can talk about that," I'm shocked. I burst into tears again and he wraps me in his arms, smoothing my hair with his hand.

"What's wrong now?" He transitions his hand to pat my shoulder. I'm not going to lie, it's a little awkward. But in a nice way.

"I thought you'd say no."

He puts his hand on my shoulders and pulls back so he can look at me. "I'll be honest with you, kid. I don't know if we can afford it." He hesitates before adding, "Selling the business would help."

"You can't."

"I'd do anything for you."

"Then keep the business. You love it, and I want to love it too. I've just been too scared to try something new—especially because that something involved a small space and a lot of strangers."

His eyes tear up again. "You've got it, kid."

"Thanks, Dad."

After we've both mopped ourselves up, he lets me take the wheel and we cruise until the sun is high and hot. The last of yesterday's clouds have burned away, leaving a bright, clear day. Dad checks the clock on the dash and tells me to head back to the marina. "Do you have a tour today?"

"I canceled it," he says. When I start to protest, he won't hear it. "You needed me today."

The closer we get to the marina, the higher my stress level climbs. As far as I know, Griff could already be gone. I've tried not to think about it all morning, but the painful thought has danced around the edge of my subconscious. I pull into our slip and he grabs the stern line to tie us off. "Do you have plans for the rest of the day?"

I shake my head, the admission weighing me down. Other than school, I'll be shocked if I ever have plans again. *Ugh, school.* Those crowded hallways are always painful, but for a few weeks I pictured myself eating lunch with Beau and Sofía, maybe even pairing up with Shandiin to be her lab partner. Ian Radnor might have nodded to me in the hallway.

For the first time in thirteen years of public school, I anticipated a sense of belonging. My chest aches at the thought of the football games and school dances I will never, ever attend. It's painful to think about, but I let my mind linger on the sorrow because thinking about Griff is impossible. When I finally admit to myself that I lost him, I don't know how I'll recover.

Dad squares his shoulders and squints into the distance. "What about with those boys? Do you want to tell me what happened there?"

I groan, covering my face with my hands. "I screwed up."

He inspects my face closely. "With which one?"

"Griff. But he's gone now, so we don't need to talk about him."

He hesitates before tugging on his collar. Poor Dad. I avert my eyes because I can't bear the discomfort in his. "Fair enough. Although—" He waits patiently for me to look at him. "If you ever do want to talk to me, I would like to listen."

"Noted." I help him finish tying off the boat, hoping that we never again broach this subject. I love that he wants to be more involved in my life, but I draw the line at my romantic problems.

"Actually—" Dad makes a show of checking the time on his phone. "I'm getting a call about a boat that needs to be fixed." He stares at his phone with the weirdest expression.

"Are you going to answer it?"

"It's a text. I'm going to go into the shop if that's okay with you."

"No worries. And I mean it this time."

He nods. "I just remembered, I was going to go to Rock Creek Canyon today and take new pictures for the website. We haven't updated it in forever."

"No kidding." Dad hasn't updated his website since I was in elementary school.

"Will you go?"

"Sure." I shrug. At least out on the lake I can pretend my life hasn't fallen apart. "Does it matter where? Last Chance Bay is really pretty right—"

"It has to be Rock Creek Canyon," he says quickly.

"Okay. Let me just grab some food and then I'll go."

"It's supposed to rain. You should go now. There's a bag of Cheez-Its in the back compartment."

"Fine." I untie the rope we just secured. "What camera should—"

"Your phone is fine." He gives me knuckles before shoving my boat away from the dock. "Good luck!"

My stomach flips with foreboding as I float away from the marina.

Chapter 33

"Dad!" I call across the water. He waves obliviously and watches until I float beyond the no-wake buoys. My dad's an odd guy, but that was the strangest interaction we've ever had. Not that I'm complaining about an excuse to spend an afternoon on the water, but after an already weird morning with him, he went and made it weirder by sending me out to sea with nothing but a cell phone camera and a stale bag of Cheez-Its.

He was right about the rain, though. By the time I reach the mouth of Rock Creek Canyon, clouds are quickly piling on the horizon. They add a gloomy and foreboding ambience to the photographs that will scare customers instead of attracting them. I start on the right side of the canyon and snap dozens of pictures of the rocky outcroppings and small beaches. A couple of houseboats are nestled into the craggy coves, but otherwise the water is empty.

At the back of the canyon, a line of low cliffs juts out from a narrow stretch of shoreline that was likely underwater at the beginning of the summer. A Jet Ski sits beached in the sand, and awareness jolts my bloodstream. I've never seen that watercraft in my life, but suddenly, I know he's here. My eyes comb the beach, and sure enough, there he is: sitting in the sand with his arms resting on his knees.

Griff.

My boat brings in waves that lap over his toes. He looks up and I almost drop my phone overboard as his eyes pierce right through me. I'm a live wire. I anchor my boat away from the cliffs and any potential hazards, and without overanalyzing anything about this moment, I dive into the water and swim to shore.

The dripping-wet walk to him is a little awkward, but all I care about is the fact that he's here. I thought the worst thing to ever happen to me would be total social humiliation, but now that I've lived through it, I realize I was wrong. It would be worse if he left.

"You made it," he says. "I wasn't sure if you'd beat the rain."

I want to say a million things, so I start with the easiest. "You called my dad?" I cannot imagine how *that* conversation went.

"Last night," he confirms. The sand around him is all carved up, like he spent the morning anxiously tearing it apart. Or maybe he's sketching whatever melody is currently living in his brain. But I can't look at anything other than him. For the first time since our argument last night, I feel like I can breathe. "I was thinking about what you said about how I've been ready to leave since I pulled into town, and I realized you were right." He stands and wipes sand off his shorts while eyeing the sky critically. "Want to climb? We don't have much time." He nods to the cliffs and doesn't wait for my answer before setting off.

I jog to keep up with him, wet sand squishing up between my toes. "Does that mean you're not leaving?" I ask as the sand transitions to stone under our bare feet. The supernatural electricity in my blood is back, and this time I quickly recognize the feeling of hope.

"I don't know yet."

He stops abruptly at the top of the cliff. I bump into his back and he turns to face me. He looks dangerously like the boy I met at the start of the summer. The tired insomniac who went too many days between shaves.

"I'm sorry I lied to you." The words tumble out in a rush.

"I forgive you," he says just as quickly. We smile tentatively at each other, and I want to run my hands against the stubble on his jaw. But he doesn't move, so I don't either.

The wind picks up, whipping through my clothes and wild hair. Below us, inky water churns up frothy, foreboding white-caps. "What are we doing up here?" I ask. The sky grows darker every minute we stand on this cliffside, but I can't worry about that—not when the violent beat of my heart makes my knees feel like they're going to collapse.

"There are some things I need to say. First, I was never using you to get revenge on Beau, and I hate that you thought that." Regret pierces Griff's eyes. "All I wanted was to make things better with him. I hoped that being nice to you was the way to his forgiveness. Helping with your list was supposed to be a peace offering—at first."

"What changed?" I hold my breath, hardly daring to hope for an answer that makes me trust him.

"You weren't scared of me." His eyes spark with restrained happiness. "You didn't write me off because of my reputation. You understood why Isbell's lyrics live in my bloodstream."

Hearing so many compliments at once is overwhelming. I swallow my discomfort and make a joke. "I sound pretty great."

His lopsided grin finally makes an appearance. "You have no idea. Seventeen years in this small town and I've never met anyone who surprises me the way you do. The way you live and breathe this place is the coolest thing to see. And your bravery blows me away, Gem. The way you fight for a new life is inspiring. I want to be better because of you. By the time I realized what was happening, I was in way too deep. I hated myself for it, but I couldn't keep away from you." He's wearing his honest eyes, the same expression he has when he plays the guitar. The force of those eyes on me is more than I can handle.

"I'm not that girl," I confess. I step back, overwhelmed by this fictional version of myself. Pain flashes across his brow and I feel it over every inch of me. All I do is hurt him and I almost choke on my regret. "I lied to you for so long."

"I told you once that whatever you've done, I've done worse. I still believe that. I'm not proud of my past. I know what it's like to feel stuck and scared and lonely. *And* I know that Beau asked you to pretend to be in a relationship with him so no one would find out he's been seeing Drew for the last year."

"Are you and Beau going to be okay?" I ask.

"We're idiots with a lot of regrets. But we both came into this summer hoping to fix our relationship, and that's all that matters when it comes to family."

"Are you telling me that this whole summer could have been avoided if the two of you had put away your egos and apologized to each other like you wanted to do all along?"

A ghost of a smile flicks across Griff's lips. "Do you really wish this whole summer hadn't happened?" He grins, and my brain goes a little bit fuzzy. I could probably kiss him right now, and he'd let me. But he still hasn't answered the most pressing question of all.

"If things are better with your family, why are you thinking about leaving?"

He drags a hand through his hair. "Page has never been my town."

I've known that for a long time, but hearing it is still a total gut punch. "Then why would you stay?"

"Funny you should ask that, because that's exactly why we're here. You once told me you do your best thinking out here. Well . . . it's time to think about what you want."

Breath rushes out of me. *You. I want you.* The words are so close I could cry.

Griff's gaze strays over my shoulder. He takes a deep breath and then cuts his eyes to mine, raw determination evident in the set of his jaw. "Give me a reason to stay."

I swallow, buying time. "I've given you a dozen reasons to stay." I try to laugh. Griff pins me in place with his liquid dark eyes, and the sincerity in them makes the laughter die in my throat. I know what he wants; I'm not an idiot. This is the part of the fantasy where I admit all the mushy-gushy feelings fluttering nervously in my chest. I want to be brave enough to do that, but what if I'm not?

I avert my eyes and pivot toward the lake, but Griff holds my shoulders and roots me in place, refusing to let me look away from him. "Not the lake. Not my family. Not this town. None of those reasons are good enough."

I swallow, my heart thundering like the building storm. "I don't know what else to say."

"Yeah, you do. You survived seeing me naked—" He flashes a wicked grin. "You're braver than you give yourself credit for." He spins me away from him, toward the beach.

My heart short-circuits. From up here, I see what I couldn't before; down on the small beach, a message is carved into the sand in giant SOS letters.

TELL ME TO STAY.

"I'm falling for you." Griff's low voice scatters goose bumps across my skin. "I want to be with you, and I've tried to tell you every way I can think of," he says. "I've said it in song lyrics and gift shop presents, and now, by writing a message in the one place you can't ignore." His hands fall from my shoulders and he walks backward toward the edge of the cliff. "I'm leaving tonight. Unless you can think of a reason I shouldn't."

He turns and jumps off the cliff just as the sky opens.

Chapter 34

Rain pounds into me as I stare at Griff's message. TELL ME TO STAY. Within seconds, the edges of the words blur as the storm unleashes a deluge of water. A frantic instinct seizes me. I reach for my phone to take a picture; I need something, anything to keep as proof that this is really happening. But my phone is on the boat, a hundred yards away and likely submerged in a puddle of water. I stare at the words, desperate to memorize the swoop of the *S* and the hard lines of his *E*s. If Griff leaves tonight, all I'll have of him is a hoodie, this beach, and the memory of his hands on my skin.

It's not enough.

"Griff!" I scream as he reaches the beach. He doesn't hear me over the rain, and I'm gripped by the sudden, overwhelming panic. I can't let him leave town. Not like this. He swings one leg over the Jet Ski and glances up at me. He only holds my gaze for a few seconds, but it's enough. I don't hesitate before I jump.

I plunge into the water and then push myself up . . . into more water. I gulp for air and inhale a mouthful of rainwater.

"Give me your hand!"

I push my hair out of my eyes. Griff's brought his Jet Ski out to meet me. His hand is outstretched, and when I place my palm in his, he pulls me out of the water and onto the back of his water-craft. I wrap my arms around his torso and shiver as he drives us back to the beach.

The rain softens, the drops turning fat and soft. I wipe the water out of my eyes as I stumble off the Jet Ski, and when I look up at Griff, he's watching me carefully. His chest heaves once. Twice. "Does this mean—"

I tackle him, slamming into him so hard that he stumbles back a few steps before finding his footing. I wrap my arms around his shoulders, and he takes my face in his hands, pausing to look at me just long enough for me to grin. *Yes.* He presses his mouth to mine, kissing me hard. The rain tastes sweet against his lips and I could drown myself in the taste of him. He brushes wet hair back from my face, his hands steady where mine are shaky.

An ache blossoms in my gut and I need to get closer. I try to step toward him, but my feet are stuck. I break away and look down. The rain and the water lapping against the shore have sunk our feet down into the soft sand. We're buried.

I laugh and glance up at him. Round water droplets stick to his eyelashes and I want to kiss them away. "It's looks like we're stuck."

His answering grin is wolfish. "I can think of a few ways to fill the time," he whispers before pressing his lips to mine again. I melt into him with a sigh, determined to make the most out of every second we have.

By the time the rain has slowed to a mist, we're lying on the hard-packed sand. My head is on his chest, my leg draped over his. His fingers lazily trail a line of fire along my arm.

He kisses the top of my head and then says, "I want you to know that I'm all in." The hoarse rumble of his voice vibrates against my cheek. I don't know what to say to that, so I tip my head up and kiss his stubbly chin. The scratch of his new beard has left the skin around my mouth swollen and tender; it's the most pleasant pain of my life.

Griff glances at me, his eyebrows contracted in a troubled line. I close my eyes and listen as his steady heartbeat picks up speed. Neither of us says anything for a long time. Too long. "So . . ." He draws the word out, waiting for me to add something, but my own heart is now thump-thumping, and I hold my breath, nervous for whatever he's about to say next. "I'm still waiting, you know." He forces a fake laugh. I hate the sound of it.

"For what?"

He points down the beach, and I can almost see the ghost of the outline of his message. "Are you going to ask me to stay?" he says casually.

"It's not my decision to make," I say lightly. We're both treading so carefully, trying to act like this conversation isn't balanced on the edge of a knife.

"But you do *want* me to stay, right?"

When I don't answer immediately, his hand freezes. I push myself up into a sitting position. I cross my arms over my chest, feeling unbearably vulnerable.

"I kissed you, didn't I?"

"That's not an answer."

Yes it is! I want to scream. *That should be enough.* Obviously I want him to stay, but I don't want to be the only reason he does. I can't handle that kind of pressure. The list of things that could go wrong writes itself.

One—What if I ask him to stay and he's miserable?

Two—What if he misses the coffeehouse open mic nights he had in the Midwest?

Three—What if being my boyfriend isn't enough to make him happy here, or I don't know how to be a girlfriend, or I make him feel second best to Beau?

Of every mistake I've made this summer, making Griff feel inferior to Beau is the worst one. It might be the worst thing I've ever done.

I dig my fingernails into the sand and look out at the water. I jumped off a cliff and kissed him until we collapsed. I'm trying, and I don't understand why he can't see that. "I want you to do whatever *you* want to do. Don't stay on my account. I can't promise you anything."

"Look at me," he says softly. I drag my eyes up to his. The way he's staring at me is too much; it makes my chest feel tight. "I don't need promises. I just want some indication that you're in this."

Flames burst across my skin. None of my Griff fantasies have included this can't-speak-can't-breathe-can't-even-look-at-him pressure sitting directly on my heart. It's overwhelming, how terrified I am.

I'm choking, just like I always knew I would.

"Gemma—" Griff's voice breaks, and my heart shatters alongside it. Someday soon he's going to realize I'm not worth the trouble because not even falling in love with him is enough to fix my anxiety.

"You're better off without me," I whisper. His face falls, disappointment written all over it. I'll never know why he had so much misplaced faith in me.

"It'll take a couple of hours to get my stuff packed, but I'll leave tonight if you want to say goodbye," he says quietly.

I watch as he roars out of the cove, wishing I could be the girl he thinks I am. Griff thinks I'm brave, but I've never been that. I can jump off a forty-foot cliff and fly off a tube at twenty-five miles per hour, but none of that counts for anything because it never scared me. If we're talking pulse-pounding fear, that's what grips me when I think about telling Griff I'm falling in love with him. That I'm worth changing his life for.

I sit on the beach for too long, ignoring the hollow ache in my chest and the growl in my empty stomach. When my hunger gets to be too much, I swim out to my boat in search of Cheez-Its. They're soggy and inedible. I toss them aside and pick up my phone, but that's ruined too. It won't even turn on. *Awesome.* I tow in the anchor and turn the key in the ignition. The engine sputters and dies. I try it again, but the same thing happens. On my third try, I realize the fuel tank is empty.

With a bone-deep sigh, I pull an oar from the waterlogged storage space on the side of the boat and begin to row. With thirty miles to Wahweap, Griff will be long gone by the time I reach shore.

Two hours later, the muscles in my shoulders and arms are screaming in pain. My arms are shaking so badly I've dropped the paddle in the water three times already and I've only passed one mile marker. At this rate, I'll be rowing all night.

When my arms get too sore and I need a break, I search through every cubby and storage compartment in the boat, looking for a pen and paper. I'm clearly going to lose Griff, but maybe I can save a different relationship. The instruction manual that came with the boat has yellow, time-worn pages and a blank back cover. It'll have to do. I tear it off and find a glittery purple gel pen at the very bottom of the cubby. It must have been here for at least five years, but incredibly, the ink still works.

Whenever I need a rest from rowing, I add another line or two to the letter. It's not easy to pour myself and my anxieties into the words, but whenever my fingers start to tremble from fear instead of exhaustion, I tell myself to be as brave as Griff thinks I am.

The oar slips from my shaky grasp again and I bend to reach for it. When I stand up straight, a boat is floating on the opposite side of the channel. It's the first one I've seen in hours. I drop the oar at my feet and scramble for our orange alert flag. I stand on my seat and wave it in the air. "Help!" I call. "Help me!"

I scream and wave the flag frantically as the boat approaches. I refuse to take the chance that it doesn't see me. But as the boat comes closer, I recognize the fancy paint job, and my heart leaps into my throat. It makes no sense for it to be Griff, but I can't stop that hope that zips through me like lightning.

It's not Griff, but it is Beau and Sofía. She kneels at the back of the boat, a tow rope in hand.

"What are you doing here?" I gasp as Beau pulls the boat alongside mine. Sofía throws the end of the rope to me and I loop it around the grab handle at the front of the bow. She attaches her end to the tow bar and then holds out her hand to help me hop aboard.

"Your dad called Griff," Beau explains. "He was worried because he hadn't seen or heard from you, and Griff asked me to come look for you and make sure you're okay. I'll let him know you are." He picks up his phone and sends a text message.

My eyes laser in on his phone. "Is Griff still in town?"

"He was when I left. Anyway, I convinced Ian to let me borrow his boat, and when I ran into Sofía down at the marina—"

"I insisted on coming," she says, folding her arms over her chest. "Just because you're a liar doesn't mean I want you to die or whatever."

My face burns scarlet at the memory of the party last night. I hate what I did to her. "I'm so sorry. I—I have something for you." I pull the folded letter out of my pocket and hand it to her. She looks at her name in purple glitter for so long that I start to sweat. Finally, she unfolds the crinkled page and starts to read.

I'm relieved that she'll get the full story without my tongue-tied anxiety interfering, but halfway through, when her expression is still in a frozen frown, I wonder if this was the wrong approach. There may be nothing in the world more nerve-racking than standing near someone who is reading your heart on the page. "What's that word?" She tilts the paper toward me and points to my illegible penmanship.

"That's a mistake. It's supposed to be 'girl squad,' two words."

She stares at me with a glacial expression.

"I realize now how embarrassing it is that I wrote that, but I'm not making fun of you. I was genuinely excited to have a group of girlfriends for the first time in my life."

It might be my wishful imagination, but I think her eyes soften a little. She continues reading, her eyes moving quickly over the page. She flips it over and reads all the way to the end.

"You lied about Beau because of your social anxiety?" she asks.

My eyes flick to him, but he's mercifully acting as if he can't hear us. "I didn't write that." I was careful not to make excuses. I made the decision to lie. Full stop.

"But your social anxiety is part of the reason you lied, isn't it?"

"I guess so. But I'm trying to take responsibility for my actions."

She rolls her eyes. "And I'm trying to forgive you. I don't really get it, but I *understand*. I've done a ton of stuff I regret when I'm depressed."

"I still can't wrap my brain around that," I admit. "You seem so perfect. You have five thousand TikTok followers!"

She smiles wryly. "And you have a hot boyfriend and a whole '*squad*' of friends."

I groan. "You're never going to let me live that down, are you?"

"Never."

"The boyfriend was fake," I point out.

"I'm just saying, you never know what someone's mental health is like. I'm on medicine, and there are still some days I can't get out of bed or see any hope for my future." Her voice cracks as she says this last part, and I'm struck by the overwhelming urge to hug her. Maybe I'm an octopus girl too.

"Can I hug you?"

"Duh!" She opens her arms and I sink into them as tears spill across my cheeks. "Like I said before, now that we're friends, we can help each other with these things."

I pull away from her in surprise. "We're still friends?"

She smiles. "Only if you tell me about what's really going on between you and Griff."

I groan and sink back into my seat. The tight feeling in my chest is back, and this time it's as familiar to me as home. *Regret.*

"It doesn't matter. He's gone." It's been hours since he left the beach. The sun will be down by the time we get back to Wahweap, and he'll be well on his way back to Cleveland and a life that is free from my anxious drama.

"Actually . . ." Beau hesitates as he rejoins our conversation. He swivels toward us and holds up his phone. "When he found out you hadn't come home, he decided to wait for you."

My heart does a stutter step. "But you sent him proof of life. He has to be gone by now."

"Maybe. Maybe not. Either way, there's still time for you to do something about it."

"I tried and I failed. It wasn't good enough for him. Anxiety doesn't just magically go away because I may or may not have feelings for him."

He rolls his eyes. "Did he ask you not to have anxiety?"

"No," I admit. Griff never wanted me to be anything other than myself. He didn't ask for guarantees.

"He told me about your list," Beau says. I thought this would embarrass me, but shockingly, it doesn't.

"Then you know what an awkward potato I am."

"What I know is that you spent weeks *trying*. Why can't you add one more thing to your list?"

Be honest with Griff.

All he asked for was some indication that I'm willing to try, the way I did all summer for the chance of dating his brother. If I can go to parties and dress like a pirate and embarrass myself in front of strangers, why can't I do that?

Maybe I don't have to be "cured" to deserve a relationship.

"I have to stop him," I say. Sofía squeals in delight and Beau grins as he nudges the throttle forward. The last twenty minutes of the drive are silent, other than the screams coming from Sofía and me as the boat slams over each new wave. She clutches my hand, her eyes shining with excitement.

Beau ignores the no-wake buoys and cruises into the marina at top speed, slowing down seconds before we smash into the dock.

"What if I'm too late? What if he's already gone?"

"I'm calling him," Sofía says as she pulls out her phone. She dials and puts the phone on speaker. It rings once before sending her straight to voice mail.

"I'll call Mom," Beau says. He's only on the line for a few seconds when I know it's bad news. He hangs up and shakes his head. "His car is gone."

"Maybe he's driving around town," Sofía says.

"His room is cleared out. His guitar is gone," Beau says, and the image of their shared room swapped from the way I saw it weeks ago, Griff's side collecting dust, steals the breath from my lungs.

I can't believe I screwed up, *again*. I was too late, *again*. My anxiety won, *again*. I had the opportunity to tell Griff how I felt on that cliffside, and I let it slip like sand through my fingers. My chest constricts painfully. This is the mistake I'll forever replay at 3:00 a.m., the right words on the tip of my tongue.

Despair fills my chest. For as long as I can remember, I've clung to my anxiety like a safety net. *Danger!* my brain screams. *They might not like you.*

Well, so what if they don't? I humiliated myself in front of all my classmates last night, but the important people didn't abandon me. Not Dad or Sofía or even Griff. His beach SOS wasn't for nothing. If any part of my fake summer was real, a deep and steady understanding in my gut tells me it was that message from him. It was real. His feelings for me were real.

I've had a white-knuckled grip on my safe life in this town for so long, and all my anxiety has ever given me in return is heart-wrenching loneliness. After seventeen years of writing stories in my head, of imagining every good and terrible scenario, I cannot accept that the one I'm going to live with is more painful than any of the storybook castles I crumbled in my mind.

"There's only one way out of town," I say.

Sofía immediately understands my meaning. "Go. Run," she says.

I do.

My fingers shake as I try to open Sunday's door and the keys slip from my sweaty hands. When I bend to retrieve them, I accidentally kick them under the truck. I drop to my hands and knees on warm asphalt and crawl. Stray gravel pierces my skin as I squint into the dark, but I quickly spot my horrendous pink key chain. Standing back up, I wipe my sweaty palms across my thighs as I settle into the driver's seat. Sunday groans to life and I inhale a blast of hot, stale air. There's no time to wait for the truck to cool down, so I ease off the clutch, pray my nervous fidgeting remains under control, and pull away from Lake Powell.

I drive southeast on Highway 98, away from my hometown and the lake I love.

Hopefully, with any luck, I'm driving toward Griff.

Chapter 35

Just outside Page, I cross into Navajo Nation. The land, which covers more than seventeen million acres, is the most gorgeous I've ever seen. Red rock and blue sky from here until the end of the world. Dad once took me northeast to see a tribal park called Monument Valley, and I was blown away by the sheer magnitude of the sandstone buttes and mesas I love so much.

Now a long dark road stretches for miles in front of me. Apart from empty stalls that sell handmade jewelry, dreamcatchers, and beef jerky in good weather, there's nothing else in sight. No light except millions of winking stars and nothing to keep me company but the wheezing of my air conditioner. It puts up a valiant fight, coughing out the occasional cool puff of air, but even those become fewer and further between, and before long, musty, warm air is pumped through my cab. I flick it off and crank down the window, too busy scanning the road for Griff's car to care. But although I pass an occasional semitruck, the road is mostly empty.

I wonder if I'll have to follow him all the way to Cleveland, and if Sunday will get me that far. I press on the gas pedal, bring my speed up. But not too much. Not on purpose, anyway.

Halfway through the reservation land, my fuel light flicks on. It was a mistake not to fill up in Page, but I was too high on adrenaline to stop at the Maverik. I sailed right past and into the dark, relying on nothing but hope to get me to Griff.

Thankfully, Sunday can run on fumes, and as I leave Navajo Nation and pull into the first gas station for miles, I'm sure she is. I coast to an empty pump and stumble out of the cab, sweaty and filled with growing dread. I lean against hot metal and mentally calculate how far I can get with the money in my account, how many greasy Jack in the Box tacos I can afford to eat, and how likely I am to cross state lines before Dad sends the police after me.

"Gemma?" Griff's low voice sends electroshocks through my blood. I push myself up and blink away the tears as I stare at him. His car is parked at the pump across from mine, one large gas station taquito in his hand. The soft crooning of Jason Isbell floats through his open window.

Everything inside me goes still. All of it—from the warning bells in my head to the tugging knot of anxiety in my belly—just stops.

We stare at each other under the fluorescent glow of overhead lights. The sharp smell of gasoline brings me back to every day with him this summer, and I'm so relieved to see him my knees could give out. My skin itches with the need to touch him, and it takes everything in me not to race across the lot and throw myself in his arms. The only reason I don't is because he still looks like the same boy I met in Beau's hospital room: wary, sad, unapproachable. Knowing I'm responsible for the shadows under his eyes is crushing.

"What are you doing here?" he asks.

"I owe you one."

His mouth twitches in that way I love. A crack in the armor. "Do tell."

"You gave me the Gemma key chain and I never returned the favor."

"Hmmm." His eyes glint in the moonlight. "So what is it, then?"

My cheeks flame. It suddenly seems monstrously conceited to say "me."

"My monster fuzz!" I grab my keys, and as I'm removing the hideous key chain, the second eye falls to the ground. I leave it there and toss him the fuzz ball.

He catches it and inspects the eyeless pink monster. "I hate this thing."

"Then give it back."

He flashes me a wicked grin. "Never." He drops it and the taquito inside his car.

"I have something to say." I swallow and clench my fists until my fingernails dig into my palms. "Something important."

"A text message might have done the trick."

"My phone is dead. And yours is turned off."

"Then you'll have to say the words." He flashes a cocky grin and leans against his car with his arms and ankles crossed. Now that he knows why I'm here, he's enjoying the hell out of this.

My head spins with fear and possibility and hope and longing. This is the last moment I can construct a perfect fantasy about what it could be like between us. It's time for me to be brave and find out if reality can be better than the daydream.

"I love your smile," I say before I can stop myself.

"Yeah? What else do you love?" He drops the smile and pins me with his dark, smoky eyes.

"You first." My heart hammers in my chest. I can't believe this is really happening.

"No, you first." His words are a dare, and they make my blood burn. I guess it's only fair. He made his feelings obvious on the cliffside, and now it's my turn.

"I want you to stay." My words trigger him into motion. He springs away from his car and stalks toward me, crossing the parking lot in long, quick strides. When he reaches me, I press my hands to his chest, keeping him at arm's length. "But I'm scared you'll regret staying for me."

"Okay. We can talk about that. What else are you scared of?"

Over his shoulder, "Tupelo" plays from his car, reminding me of my least favorite line from the song.

"I'm worried you're like the guy from the song. You want to leave and have no one follow you."

His brow furrows. "He never says that."

"Yes, he does! Listen!"

Griff's chest heaves under my hands. I don't move them. I savor the frantic beat of his heart against my palms as we strain to hear the song lyrics. When Isbell soulfully sings "There ain't no one from here that will follow me there," I'm triumphant.

"I told you."

Griff's eyes search my face. "He doesn't *want* that, and neither do I. I wanted nothing more than for you to follow me here."

Oh. My hands fall from his chest, and he leans into me.

"Anything else you're worried about?" he whispers, his breath sending shivers down my spine.

I swallow. "I'm scared of how much I like you."

His eyes turn liquid dark as his pupils grow. "I can't help you there," he says. "Because I'm scared of the same thing." He turns his head, bringing his lips within a breath of mine. He pauses for one heartbeat, a question in his eyes. In one breathless moment of bravery, I press my lips to his. It's even better than our frantic kiss on the beach because I know it's not a goodbye.

When I pull away, he threads a hand into my hair and brings me back to him, his mouth perfectly firm against mine. I rope my arms around his neck and his free hand lands on my hip. I've always been a water girl, but when I'm with him, I'm made of fire. My skin blazes against his, my blood lighting up in a way it never has before. It's the feeling of wind in my hair, magnified exponentially. For the first time in my life, I feel more alive off the lake than on it.

Griff breaks away, his chest heaving against mine. "I'm falling in love with you, Gem. I'm sorry if that's too much, too fast, but—"

"I'm falling in love with you too," I gasp. "I want you to stay in Page."

He lets his forehead fall until it touches mine. I can feel him grin against my mouth. "Will you still feel that way when I'm a fifth-year senior at Page High?"

"Wait. What?"

"You know I dropped out of school. I missed all my finals to be here."

"Your school won't let you retake them?"

"It wouldn't matter. I was failing almost all my classes, anyway. I skipped school more often than I went. I wasn't exactly thriving in Cleveland like I led you to believe."

"I'm sorry you had such a hard time." My mind scrambles to keep up with this new info. I hate to know how much he's been struggling, but I'm selfishly relieved.

"I was thinking, if it's all right with you, I'd finish my final year of school back in Page."

I bounce off my toes and jump into his arms. This guarantees us a year to figure out our relationship before we have to make any scary adult decisions, and I'm giddy with relief. He laughs and catches me as I wrap my legs around his waist. I lean into him, and he gives me another mind-melting kiss. When I lean back, my lips feel puffy and raw. "I'm going to get scared and try to jump out of the boat sometimes."

"I know," he says. He trails a hand along my spine and my whole body reacts to his touch. I shiver in the hot night air. "I'll be there to jump in with you," he promises.

I tilt my face down to kiss him again. When I close my eyes, I see his beach SOS.

TELL ME TO STAY.

I thought my favorite kind of beach was an empty one, but I was wrong.

I thought my heart belonged to the water, but I was wrong about that too.

My soul will always belong to that blue water and those ancient red rocks, but my heart? I gave that away without even realizing it.

Acknowledgments

I've been trying to write a "Lake Powell book" for five years. It's been a contemporary, a dual POV romance, a mystery, a thriller, and now a rom-com. The plot and the characters have changed so many times it's hard to remember all the versions of Gemma Wells that exist on my hard drive. She's had different names, jobs, families, friends, struggles, love interests, and goals. The only piece of this story that remained consistent over the years is the setting. I wanted to write and publish a book about a girl who lives in one of my favorite places in the world, and I am beyond excited to cross that goal off my author bucket list. The future of Lake Powell is in jeopardy thanks to climate change and the megadrought plaguing the southwestern United States, but it gives me comfort to know that I've done my best to preserve some of its magic in these pages.

I'm so grateful to my editor, Mallory Kass, who said yes to this idea. In January 2020 I was struggling with writer's block. My Lake Powell book had been set aside for more than a year, and I had no clue what to write as a follow-up to *One Way or Another*. My agent, Katelyn Detweiler, set up a phone call for the three of us to discuss ideas. I had almost nothing to pitch, but when I said, "What about a *While You Were Sleeping* retelling?" Mallory was on board. Her enthusiasm gave me the push and spark I needed to fall in love with this story. I knew immediately that I would need to change the setting of the beloved '90s rom-com because the movie is set in a big city at Christmas and I had just written a "big city at Christmas" book. I was ready for something different. Something drenched in sun and sand. Something set at Lake Powell.

It feels a little bit like fate that mere weeks before lockdown I decided to write a book about a lonely girl with social anxiety. I wrote and rewrote this book from March to December 2020, otherwise known as one of the loneliest years of my life. I channeled all my anxiety straight into Gemma's character, and sometimes it was hard to find the "com" in this pandemic-born "rom-com," but writing Gemma and Griff's story is easily the highlight of what turned out to be a messy, terrible, and, yes, lonely year.

So thank you, again, to my genius editor, Mallory Kass, for encouraging me to write this story and for knowing exactly what it needed to come to life, especially when certain subplots weren't working or the stakes were sagging in the middle of Gemma's long, stressful summer. Gemma has higher highs and lower lows thanks to your razor-sharp insight, and the story is better for it! And of course, a huge thank-you to the entire Scholastic sales team, especially Nikki Mutch for her passionate book talks.

I have a million, unending thank-yous for my agent, Katelyn Detweiler, who is one of the most supportive, brilliant, hardworking people I know. I'll never understand how you read so quickly, sell so many books, are an amazing mom to Alfie, and find the time to write and publish your own delightful, charming novels. I'm in awe of you and grateful to be on your team! And thank you to Sam Farkas for championing my books overseas and for bringing my characters and stories to so many places I dream of visiting one day.

Thank you to Ruthanne Snow and Kimberly Gabriel for reading the earliest pages of this story and giving such helpful feedback! Kimberly, I would never have survived publishing a book in 2020 without your friendship and support. Joanna Ruth Meyer, thank you for being one of the first to read and fall in love with Gemma and Griff. Abigail Johnson, I consider myself lucky to know you and am still pinching myself that we got to hold our "2020 Zoom Book Launches" together. Thank you Changing Hands Bookstore for sponsoring the event and working with me to get signed books into the hands of readers.

Thank you to all the amazing book bloggers, YouTubers, teachers, librarians, and readers who have shown enthusiasm and support for my books. Thank you for every review, email, picture, and recommendation. Hearing from you all is the best part of my job!

To Scott, I couldn't do this job without your support. Thank you for always believing in me. And to Owen, Graham, and Emmett. I love you all more than words can say. I hope if you get anything out of watching me write books, it's the courage to chase your dreams.

Every book and character I write has different pieces of myself, my upbringing, and my family, but this book wouldn't exist if it weren't for my dad. I spent my childhood summers at the lake, sleeping in houseboats, and on sunrise boat rides eating blueberry muffins with him. I became a storyteller sitting in the bow of my family's boat, writing elaborate stories in my mind about a version of myself who had exciting, grand adventures. Even now, twenty years later, being on the water lights a spark in my chest that makes me feel like anything is possible.

About the Author

Kara McDowell is the author of *One Way or Another*, *This Might Get Awkward*, and *Just for Clicks*. She lives with her husband and a trio of rowdy boys in Mesa, Arizona, where she divides her time between writing, baking, and wishing for rain. Find her online at karajmcdowell.com, on Twitter at @karajmcdowell, and on Instagram at @karajmcdowellbooks.